Lightning Bug

By the Author

The Cherry Pit (1965)

Lightning Bug (1970)

Some Other Place. The Right Place. (1972)

The Architecture of the Arkansas Ozarks (1975)

Let Us Build Us a City (1986)

The Cockroaches of Stay More (1989)

The Choiring of the Trees (1991)

Ekaterina (1993)

Butterfly Weed (1996)

When Angels Rest (1998)

Thirteen Albatrosses (or, Falling off the Mountain) (2002)

With (2004)

Donald Harington

Lightning Bug

The Toby Press

Paperback edition, 2005

The Toby Press LLC, 2004
POB 8531, New Milford, CT. 06676-8531, USA
& POB 2455, London WIA 5WY, England
www.tobypress.com

ISBN 1 59264 102 4

A CIP catalogue record for this title is
available from the British Library

Typeset in Garamond by Jerusalem Typesetting

Printed and bound in the United States by
Thomson-Shore Inc., Michigan

For William Styron
il miglior fabbro

Cogito, ergo sum.

DESCARTES,
Discourse on Method, IV.

Fear boys with bugs.

SHAKESPEARE,
The Taming of the Shrew, I.

By lust alone we keep the mind alive,
And grieve into the certainty of love.

ROETHKE,
"The Motion."

Movements

Beginning

From a porch swing, evening, July, 1939, Stay More, Ark.

IT BEGINS WITH THIS SOUND:

the screen door pushed outward in a slow swing, the spring on the screen door stretching vibrantly, one sprung tone and fading overtone high-pitched even against the bug-noises and frog-noises, a plangent twang, WRIRRRAANG, which, more than any other sound, more than cowbells or distant truck motors laboring uphill, more, even, than all those overworked katydids, crickets, tree frogs, etc., seems to evoke the heart of summer, of summer evenings, of summer evenings there in that place, seems to make it easy for me to begin this one. WRENCH! WRUNG! WRINGING!

IT BEGINS WITH THESE PEOPLE:

the girl coming out through that twanging screen door, prettied up fit to kill in her finest frillery, swinging her fine hips once to clear the returning screen door being closed by that pranging, wranging spring. Her name is Sonora. The way these folks say it, it sounds like "Snory" so that is what I shall call her. She does not live here; just visiting, for the summer, with the woman who is presumed to be her aunt, who is at

I

least the sister of the woman who is presumed to be her mother, Mandy Twichell, of Little Rock, where Sonora lives and goes to school with the rich city kids. She is a very pretty 17, with red hair even, but I am not yet certain that I like her very much. I guess the reason I don't like her too awfully much is that she is inclined to tease me, if she ever notices me at all. One time when nobody was around, she reached down and chucked me right in my generative organ, and twitted, "My, Dawny, for such a little feller I bet you've got a big one!" Imagine. If she weren't essential to the plot, I would be happy to exclude her entirely from this world.

the woman sitting on the porch, the woman presumed to be Sonora's aunt. Her name is Latha, with the first "a" long, and one would conceive that it might be spoken "Lay-thee," in view of the way Sonora's name comes out as "Snory" but there have been only one or two people who have called her that. She is Latha. Miss Latha Bourne, the postmistress of this place—and the heroine, the demigoddess, of this world. I am not certain yet just how old she is, but she's old enough to be Sonora's aunt, or her mother, for that matter, and she's at least three or four years older than my aunt, who is 35. My aunt thinks that Latha Bourne is "crazy as a quilt," but we shall have to see about that.

the boy sitting in the porch swing, trying to make out Latha Bourne's exquisite face in the pale light coming from kerosene lanterns within the house. He is a tousle-haired little whippersnapper, five going on six, who is not related to either one of these females, although he has in common with Sonora that he is just visiting, spending the summer with his aunt, who lives up the road a ways from Latha's place. He comes down here every evening and sits in that porch swing and watches people, until either somebody runs him off or his aunt calls him home. His name is Donald, but the way they say it, all of them, is "Dawny." He likes to come to Latha's place in the evenings because she is a great teller of ghost stories, but mainly he likes to come to Latha's place because he is in love with her, and will always be, even when he is old. Even when he is old, the thought of her will give him twitchings and itchings [and the only way he will ever exorcise her, the only way she will ever give him any peace, is for him to write a book about her, who is, it should be obvious by this time, *the* Lightning Bug].

IT BEGINS WITH THIS SETTING:

the house of Latha, which is also the combined store-post office of Stay More, a community of some 113 souls in the Ozark mountains of Newton County, south of the county seat, Jasper, and the lovely village of Parthenon, west of the village of Spunkwater, north of Demijohn, Hunton and Swain, east of Sidehill and Eden. [One must not attempt to find it on a recent map; one may find Newton County, and one may find Jasper and Parthenon and Swain, but one shall not find Stay More—not because it is some screwball name that I made up in my own head, but because today it is nothing but a ghost town, almost.] *The origin of the name is obscure. Although the expression is common parlance among the natives of that region, as in, "Don't be rushin off, Dawny. Stay more, and eat with us," it is not certain that this connotation was intended by the founders of the town, Jacob and Noah Ingledew, who came from Warren County, Tennessee, in 1837. Some conjecture that these brothers, with prophetic foresight, realized that the village might eventually become a ghost town, and hence the name was meant not as a mere invitation but as a plea, a beseechment. During the last years of its status as a U.S. Post Office, it was resolutely spelled "Staymore" by the postal authorities, over the protests of the postmistress.*

It straddles two green-watered streams of small, good fishing water, Banty Creek (a variant, "Bonny Creek," appears on some maps), the smaller, which empties, near the center of the village, into the larger, Swains Creek, which empties into the Little Buffalo River to the north. In this year, 1939, a crew of W.P.A. men is constructing a cement bridge for Banty Creek where it crosses the main road. There is no bridge on Swains Creek; to reach the schoolhouse one must drive through water over the hubcaps...or walk across a precarious foot-log. The roads, all of them, are, of course, only dirt and gravel.

The business census back in 1906–07 listed the following: Ingledew's Commissary—Drugs, Groceries, Hotel, Livery and Notary; Jerram's General Store; two other general stores; three blacksmiths; two physicians, Alonzo Swain and J.M. Plowright; two dentists, Sam Forbes and E.H. Ingledew; William Dill, Wagonmaker [one must remember this one]; *Noah Murrison & Son, Sawmill & Gristmill; and the Swains Creek Bank & Trust Company.*

Now in 1939 there is only this: Lawlor Coe, Blacksmith; Latha Bourne, General Store and Post Office; Colvin Swain, Physician; E.H. Ingledew, semi-retired dentist (he pulls but no longer fills); J.M. Plowright, fully retired physician; and what is left of the big Ingledew store, which old Lola Ingledew still runs single-handedly (she lost the other hand in an accident at the sawmill) only for the purpose of providing some slight competition for the store of Latha Bourne, whom she detests with every fiber of her being, or something like that. Last year industry came to Stay More in the form of Oren Duckworth's Cannon Factory, on Swains Creek near the schoolhouse. This opens in June and employs 20 men and women, canning beans during June, and canning tomatoes in July and August; the cans are sent unlabeled to Kansas City where a Big Name Food Processor attaches his own label. The factory does not produce cannon; it is simply known as The Cannon Factory.

The post office is at the head of what would be called Main Street were it not just a dirt road with a few buildings on either side, half of them vacated, especially the bank, a stone edifice whose broken glass window stares the post office in the eye all day long. A traveler passing rapidly south on the main road might miss the post office entirely; it is set back in a kind of hollow a hundred feet up the road that goes to Right Prong and Butterchurn Holler, the same road that my Aunt Murrison lives on. At the foot of the main road is the big old half-empty unpainted Ingledew Store. Lola Ingledew, sitting on the front porch of her store, can squint fiercely and count the number of men on the front porch of Latha's store, a quarter of a mile away.

Latha's store is small; the whole building has only five rooms: the large room with the post office boxes and counter at the front end and the merchandise everywhere else; her sitting room, to the left, her bedroom behind it; the spare bedroom, to the right, where Sonora sleeps; and the small kitchen.

A porch runs the whole length of the front. On it, tonight, we are sitting, I in the swing, Snory in the straight-back rush-seated chair, Latha in the rocker, rocking, some.

IT BEGINS WITH THIS MOOD:

[Hell, who has never known a summer evening? But anyway:]

*from the distance, cowbells are dully clapping thing-thang in dewy fields
and shadowy thickets; evening milking is done, and the cows move back
to pasture.*

*From the yard grass, from all around, from everywhere up and
down the valley, chirps of bugs scrape cracklingly up, and croaks from the
creek, and peeps from the trees; you learn to recognize the instruments of
this chorus: the* tzeek-tzek-tzuk *of katydids, the* irdle dee irdle *of crickets,
the* tchung *of the tree frogs, and that old jug of rum by the bull frogs.*

*A watermelon seed drops on the porch floor, bounces twice. Sonora
smacks her lips and draws the back of her hand across her mouth.*

*The air is all blue. All the air is blue. The night is hot, more than
hot, but blue is cool.*

Latha tells Sonora that she looks very pretty tonight.

*My dog—Gumper isn't my dog, but he belongs to Uncle Murrison,
who is my host, and he follows me around—Gumper comes trotting up
and climbs the porch and slobbers on the floor. He is an ordinary hound,
and he smells. I am embarrassed for his smell. Sonora kicks at him, and
Latha swishes her arms at him and makes a noise in her throat, "Gyow
hyar!" which means, "Get out of here" but is the only way the dog would
understand that. Gumper puts his tail between his legs and bumps down
off the porch; he walks to the great oak in the yard and lifts his leg against
it and waters its roots profusely and audibly: another sound for the summer night. Later he sneaks back onto the porch from the side, and curls
asleep beneath the swing I'm sitting in.*

*Latha asks Sonora who does she think she might go out with
tonight?*

Sonora says we will just have to wait and see.

*Other sounds: someone, far off, trying to start a car. Farther off,
the bugle-baying of a treeing dog. And more crickets and katydids and
tree frogs, faster because of the heat, louder because it's hot.*

*The blue air carries all the smells of the summer night, which even
obliterate the powerful smell of Gumper sleeping below me. The blue
air is full of green things, strange wildflowers and magic weeds, and of
creekwater, and of some dust and motor oil mixed with the dust and wild
dew. Especially of the dew, which is the creekwater and dust and wild
green things all liquefied together and essenced and condensed.*

Gumper, in his torpid contentment, makes the mistake of striking the floor noisily with his wagging tail. Another thumping sound for the summer night, but because of it he is once again evicted.

"Git home, you smelly dawg!" I holler after him.

His disappearance brings out the cats. From all over: black and striped and marmalade, and gray and white and calico. I've never counted, but I think Latha feeds something like two dozen cats. They make no sounds to contribute to the summer night's chorus, but their indolent grace is a decoration, they festoon the porch rail and the porch and the shrubbery with their sensuous, writhing forms. Some people keep a lot of cats because they like cats, but Latha keeps cats because she likes to watch them fuck. I know this for a fact.

And now, as the blue of the air darkens, the lightning bugs come out. At first, as with stars, only one or two (and I would as soon wish upon a lightning bug as upon a star), but then, quickly, dozens and hundreds, until the air of the yard, of the road, of the meadow across the road, of the creek beyond the meadow, is filled with them. There are at least 35 different species out there, flashing their cold yellow-green light, and each species uses a different signal system of flashes. Contrary to popular belief, the purpose of the flashing light is not guidance, nor illumination as such, but purely and simply to make "assignations": the males fly around in the air, advertising their availability; the females wait immobile on leaves in bushes and trees, and if they spot a flash coming from an eligible bachelor of their own species, they return a flash whose signal has the same intervals.

[I was disturbed recently to learn from a fellow of my acquaintance, an intelligent person from Andover, Massachusetts, that he had never heard of a "lightning bug." When I described this creature to him, he replied, "We call those fireflies." This bothered me so much that, at considerable expense to myself, I asked the Thomas Howland Poll organization of Princeton, New Jersey, to conduct a nationwide survey. The results satisfied me: 87% had definitely heard of "lightning bugs," 3% had heard of lightning bugs but thought they were insects who made thundering noises, 7% had never heard of a lightning bug, 1% thought it was an automobile, and the remaining 2% had no opinion.]

What is most uncanny is that the interval of the flash is dependent not only on the species, but also on the temperature of any given night. The bugs flash twice as frequently on hot nights as on cool nights. Thus, the brilliant female must not only memorize the signal of her own species, but also know exactly what the temperature is. Otherwise, if she flashes the wrong response and attracts a male of a different species, the only thing she can do is eat him.

The male of the species is fickle. As soon as he engages the female in procreative recreation, she obligingly turns off her luring light. But if any other females happen to be flashing their lights in the vicinity, the busy male will quickly disengage himself, as per coitus reservatus, and take off after the competing lady.

Some species of lightning bugs do not eat at all after becoming adults; the adult stage is only for the purpose of procreation; they become adults, they flash, they fuck, they die. This has nothing to do with Latha. She lives.

The lightning bug, or firefly, is neither a bug nor a fly, but a beetle. I like bug because it has a cozy sound, a hugging sound, a snug sound, it fits her, my Bug.

Deep in the dark blue air sing these lives that make the summer night. The lightning bug does not sing. But of all these lives, it alone, the lightning bug alone, is visible. The others are heard but not seen, felt but not seen, smelled but not seen [I have bottled a sample of that air and sent it for analysis to the Meredith Olfactory Laboratories of St. Louis, whose Dr. S.I. Coryell is the leading authority in differentiation analysis, but his report is of little help: "This specimen is broken down as follows: 1.09% glucosides extract from chlorophyll of various field weeds, primarily *Datura stramonium*, or Jimson-weed; 2.03% fragrance of clover-blossom; .08% fragrance of alfalfa; .04% essence of hay, primarily Timothy and Johnson Grass, probably new-mown, but not wholly discrete from residues of same included in .009% bovine excreta; .0085% effluvium of stream water with traces of crayfish, bass and bream, and limestone; .00076% excretion from human sweat glands; .00034% miscellaneous excretions from a canine male animal, possibly a hound; .00026% excretions, mingled, from several diverse feline animals, male and female; .00017% traces of oestrus secretions in various mating reptiles and insects, including .000002% exudations of the insect, *Photinus pyralis* or other species of the Family *Lampyridae*, fireflies. There is also a trace of emanation from the rubber seal on the Mason jar in which you sent the specimen, but apart from this, Mr. Harington, I regret to say that I cannot positively identify the larger proportion of components, and I would be pleased if you would inform me where and when this specimen was taken."] *That air, that blue magical scented balmy air, is the world, the habitat, the home of the lightning bugs. And of my Bug.*

IT BEGINS:

one by one, or together in pairs or groups, the boys come. In his dad's car, a '36 Chevy coupe with rumbleseat, is Oren ("Junior") Duckworth, Jr., and his brother Chester. These are the best-looking. On foot, and separately from different directions, arrive the triplet sons of Lawlor Coe the blacksmith, Earl, Burl & Gerald. You should know that the way they say "Gerald," he rhymes with his brothers. Gerald will die a hero with the Marines at Iwo Jima in 1945. These brothers look just alike, which is not much to look at: inclined to pudginess, and over-freckled. Alone on foot comes John Henry ("Hank") Ingledew, Bevis's boy, nephew to dead Raymond Ingledew, who was Latha's beau a long long time ago. Then comes the W.P.A. gang, who are staying with the folks of Merle Kimber, who is a W.P.A. boy himself (and who rhymes with the Coe triplets, though he'd just as soon not); he and Leo Dinsmore are the only ones from this valley; the others are Furriners, which means that they don't come from this valley: Clarence Biggart comes from Madison County and is even a married man, so is J.D. Pruitt, who comes from someplace up north in Newton County, Eddie Churchwell and Dorsey Tharp are from downstate somewhere.

Here are a dozen boys. They have each said, politely, "Howdy, Miss Latha," and they have each said, warmly, "Howdy, Snory, honey," and a few of them have even said, "Howdy, Dawny." One of them, Eddie Churchwell, teases me. "The boogers are sure gonna git you tonight, Dawny boy. I seen one down the road, a-comin this way, and I figgered he was out after me, but he tole me he was comin to grab you." I titter.

They stand around. There are three empty chairs on the porch, but the boys do not sit in these. Some of them sit on the porch rail, brushing the cats aside, but most of them just stand around, some of them in the yard.

Merle Kimber spits. As if on signal, each of the others, in turn, spits. After a while Merle Kimber spits again, and one by one the others do. Clarence Biggart has a reason to spit, because he is chewing tobacco, but the others spit because…well, because I guess it makes them look manly, although you'd think that if they keep that up long enough, night after night, we would all of us drown in it by and by. Maybe the spit is a kind of advertisement, maybe a substitute for all the sperm they'd like to get rid of.

It is professional spitting. I have tried to do it but can't. A certain snap of the tongue squirts it out through a crevice between the front teeth, in such a way that it goes in a straight stream and lands intact and compact. When I try to spit, it splatters all over. Any one of these boys could hit a horsefly from five yards away. Naturally, they are spitting only into the yard, not upon the porch. Inside, over the post office boxes is a printed sign, KINDLY DO NOT EXPECTORATE UPON THE FLOOR, *but I don't think any of these boys knows what that means, even if they could read; still, they are gentlemen, and know where to spit.*

But Chester Duckworth, spitting, is momentarily careless: his blob alights on J.D. Pruitt's shoe. J.D. hauls off with his fist and clobbers Chester a good one; soon they are scuffling in the grass, putting up a scrap not really out of belligerence so much as ostentation: they are showing off for Snory. J.D. is older by several years, nearly 21, but Chester is bigger. They smack each other around all over the landscape; J.D. chases Chester up the road, and after a while he comes back, huffing and puffing and rubbing his wounds. Later, Chester too comes back, acting like he was just arriving. "Howdy, Miss Latha," he says, cool as buttermilk. "Howdy, there, Snory, honey. Howdy, boys. Howdy, Dawny, has that 'ere booger man not cotched you yet, tee hee?"

Merle Kimber spits.

J.D. Pruitt says, "Hoo, Lord, aint it a hot night, though?"

Clarence Biggart says, "Yeah boy."

Junior Duckworth says, "Hotter 'n Hades."

Hank Ingledew says, "Might come a rain tomorra."

Earl, Burl & Gerald Coe spit.

Eddie Churchwell says, "Well, now, boys…"

[Now if one has not been reading me carefully, one is antici-pating that pretty soon Latha Bourne will start selling tickets and each of the boys will take Sonora into the house. One is not reading me at all.]

Eddie Churchwell says, "Well, now, boys, why don't we just draw straws?"

John Henry "Hank" Ingledew slugs him square on the jaw. Then the big fight begins. Although Merle Kimber and Leo Dinsmore are local boys, they side with the Furriners because being a W.P.A. boy is more important than being a local boy. So it is six against six, our boys against theirs. Knock down, drag out, clear-to-Hell-and-back-again. Even though they are serious, and even though they are hurting one another, they are still essentially showing off for Snory.

I have watched this fight so often it no longer interests me. So I watch Latha and Snory watching it. Snory is feigning alarm, and even making little screaming noises. But Latha has the trace of a smile around the edges of her mouth.

What does she look like? She is dark, and of very fair skin. She is taller than average, and neither thick nor thin, but full-bodied, I sup-pose what you could call "shapely" though not in any way to make men whistle. [I cannot help but think of Vanessa Redgrave in *Blow-Up*, which of course is ridiculous, and possibly even an insult to Miss Redgrave, but I have no doubt that a highly paid make-up techni-cian could take Latha and after some diligent and thoughtful work transform her into the spitting image of Miss Redgrave. As a matter of fact, I have before me—on the wall—a poster obtained for $1.00 from Famous Faces, Inc., Box 441, Norristown, Pa. 19404, depict-ing Miss Redgrave life-size from the scene in *Blow-Up* when she is about to allow herself to be laid by David Hemmings in order to "buy" his roll of incriminating negatives. She is wearing a dark hip-hugging miniskirt with a wide black leather belt. But she is topless, and out of modesty has hugged her arms around herself to cover her lovely breasts. She is staring out of the picture (and into the eyes of Hemmings?) with large eyes—with the expression of a very sweet and good girl who has done a bad thing and is now getting ready to do another bad thing because of it. (My Aunt Murrison always said, "Two wrongs never make a right.") Not only have I seen Latha Bourne in that exact same pose, one afternoon when I barged in on her while she was dressing, but also I have seen Latha Bourne with that exact same expression…and, kindly believe me, that exact same beauty.] *I love to look at Latha Bourne, which is something I do more often than anything else, except sleep. Maybe I disturb her, looking at her so much. The fight goes on, with grunts and thuds and slams and rips, but I don't watch it.*

*Here are all of the known facts about her: she was born in Stay More, in a cabin on the east side of Ledbetter Mountain. (The post office is at the foot of the south side of the same mountain.) Her father, Saultus Bourne, was a subsistence farmer. He died of pneumonia in 1921 and lies buried in the Primitive Baptist Church cemetery on Swains Creek. Her mother, Fannie Swain Bourne, was descended from one of the original settlers of Stay More. She died of apoplexy in 1927 and is interred in the Church of Christ cemetery at Demijohn. Latha has two sisters, Mandy, who married Vaughn Twichell and lives in Little Rock, and Barbara, who lives in California but has not been heard of. Latha attended the Stay More grade school, first through eighth grades, then went to high school at Jasper. She was popular in high school, and at graduation she was unofficially engaged to Raymond Ingledew, a Stay More boy, but he joined the service and was killed in the Argonne—actually, he was only listed as missing, but he never did come back, although some people say that Latha is still waiting for him, which I doubt. Latha had already lost her virginity, at the age of eleven, to some third or fourth cousin of hers. (Well, as they say in this part of the country, a virgin, by definition, is "a five-year-old girl who can outrun her daddy and her brothers," so I guess Latha was a late-developer or else just lucky—or, from another point of view, un*lucky.) *There was some gossip that as soon as she learned that Raymond Ingledew was reported missing Over There, she began to carry on again with that same third or fourth cousin, but nobody ever caught them at it. In any case, shortly after the death of her father, in 1921, she moved to Little Rock to live with her married sister, Mandy. About nine months after that, in May of 1922, she was committed in the*

Arkansas State Hospital at Little Rock, where she remained nearly three years. Her escape, in March of 1925, attracted some attention in the Little Rock newspapers. Although escapes from the A Ward, the B Ward, and even the C Ward were relatively routine, Latha was (and today remains) the only patient who ever escaped from E Ward. She was never captured. Some folks insinuate that she lived thereafter as a prostitute in some large city, possibly Memphis or New Orleans or St. Louis, but nobody really knows. In any event, she was never seen again until June of 1932, when suddenly she appeared out of nowhere back in Stay More, with a deed to Bob Cluley's General Store which had recently been foreclosed by the bank in Jasper. Where she got the money nobody knows, though they've had a long lot of fun trying to guess. Two years after establishing herself as proprietress of the store, she applied for and obtained the post of postmistress, after the death of longtime postmaster Willis Ingledew, the father of Lola, who wanted the job and will always hate Latha for taking away what she thought was rightfully hers.

And that is all. Nothing has happened to Latha since. She has received, and rejected, proposals of marriage from the following: Doc Calvin Swain, Tearle ("Tull") Ingledew, our village drunk, and a five-year-old boy euphoniously sobriqueted Dawny.

The fight is over. Our boys, as usual, have emerged victorious, bloody but unbowed. The W.P.A. boys are shuffling off up the road, declaring that they are going to a square dance at Parthenon where the real *men are and the* real *gals are, and that besides you Stay More boys fight dirty.*

Junior Duckworth is inspecting his tattered shirt and his dirt-caked abrasions. In front of Snory he holds his arms out as if to display himself, and says to her, "Aw, shoot fire, Snory honey, aint I a sight? I was aimin to take you over to Jasper to the pitcher show, but now it looks like I got to go home and git cleaned up some, don't it?"

Junior and his brother Chester get into their car, and Junior sprays gravel letting out the clutch, and shows off some more turning the car around skiddingly like a maniac.

Earl Coe says to Burl Coe, "You want to see thet pitcher show?"

Burl Coe asks, "Is it Tex Ritter or Hopalong Cass'dy?"

Earl Coe says, "Hit's ole Hopalong."

"Sheeut," says Burl Coe. "Noo, son, let's see what's doing up to thet thar squar dance."

"Okey doke," says Earl Coe, then turns to Gerald. "You, Jerl?"

"Fine and dandy," says Gerald Coe.

The Brothers Coe say "See y'all around" to us, and amble off up the road.

That leaves Hank Ingledew. He spits, shuffles his feet, clears his throat. "Snory," he says. "You keer to watch that squar dance, or somethin?"

"Or somethin," she says, echoing, slightly teasing.

She stands up, walks down off the porch, takes Hank's hand.

"See y'all," says Hank.

"Night night," says Snory.

"Be good," speaks Latha. It is a formality; I do not believe she means it. In fact I think she means, "Be bad as you can!"

Hank and Snory walk off up the road, hand in hand.

It is easy enough to surmise that a girl of Sonora's temperament, appearance and popularity might be inclined to promiscuity, but this is not the case. Unless I miss my guess badly, her body, if not her heart wholly, belongs only to John Henry Ingledew. When the other eleven boys are around, he is merely one of them, a rather reserved and inconspicuous member of the gang, but when he is alone with Snory he is her lover. I have watched them make love three times, once in a thicket on the other side of Swains Creek, once in the abandoned tavern up the road from Latha's store, and once in the corn crib behind Latha's place. It is a sight to behold. It is beautiful, and it is awesome, and it is only faintly disturbing to a boy of five whose immature penis can only envy such voluptuous recreation.

I think Latha lives vicariously in Sonora. The younger woman appears, to all intents and purposes, to be the Lightning Bug, but it is the older woman who lives in her and really appreciates it.

Latha and I are alone now. I rock the swing gently, my feet not reaching the floor. Latha holds in one hand a lovely silk handkerchief, which she has been using for the purpose of blotting perspiration from her brow. She stares off up the road in the direction Hank and Snory have disappeared. She raises the handkerchief to her mouth and grips a corner of it between her teeth.

Clouds march past the moon.

The blinking, flashing scintillation of the lightning bugs seems to keep a beat with the music from the grass and trees.

The music runs, and if I listen very carefully I can separate the instruments. They speak to her, my Bug, who does not hear them.

Only I can.

The katydids:

Cheer up, cheer up, Bug. Cheap luck, Bug, Sit your seat, Bug. Sweet seat, seat you sit, Bug. Sitting sucking sweaty sweet silk, sighing, Bug. Sweet sullen suffering Bug, sitting swept by swift Swains Creek. Creak your seat, Bug. Swing, swivel, swoop, sway. Switch, Bug, itch, Bug, twitch, Bug, in this tweeting twangling twinkling twilight!

The bullfrogs:

Bug, O come! Bug, a crumb! Drug a mug a some scummy jug a rum! Hump a stumpy rump! Thrum, you smug dumb Bug! Shrug your chummy bumps! Jump the rug's numb lumps! Bug, Bug, O Bug, *become!* Hum, Bug, hum with your gums, you sluggish bummy Bug! O Bug, O Bug, O hugging, tugging, thumping Bug so mum!

The crickets and cicadas, in chorus:

Were you to stir your blurry fur and purr, O Bug, I would demur to slur you. Such verse is worse than Satan's curse, but terse as all the universe. Disgust you must such lusty crust, and fussed, and cussed me for it, yet still I trust you will be just, and never bust me for it. Enough rebuff will make me gruff, and puff my cheeks in stuffy huff.

Sick. sick. sicksicksicksicksicksick.

Cheap. cheap. cheapcheapcheapcheap dirt-cheap

Cheer up. cheer up. cheerupcheerupcheerup chirp chirp

Wish. wish. wishwishwish

crick critic critter crotch
O Bug

"*Tell me a story.*"

"*Sure, Dawny, but first I have to go out back.*"

She rises. The screen door WRIRRRAARAANGS. *She walks through her sitting room, through her bedroom. There is a faint distant wrirraanngg of the spring on the back door. She walks up the path, she climbs a few stone steps, she opens the door of the outhouse. It is, for some reason, a two-seater, I don't know why. I doubt that she and Sonora have ever sat there together. I have never found them there together. (Yea, in my watchings I have even spied once there. From behind. From below.)*

Tearle Ingledew comes staggering down the road. A man of 48, he is "The Bad Ingledew," the one out of six brothers who has gone wrong. He has what they call a drinking problem, which means he is never sober. To me he is the Good Ingledew.

He stops before the porch, spreads wide his arms, and in a thick gravelly voice declaims, "Behold, thou art fair, my love; behold, thou art fair; thou hast dove's eyes within thy locks: thy hair is as a flock of goats, that appear from mount Gilead. Thy teeth are like a flock of sheep that are even shorn, which come up from the washing; whereof every one bear twins, and none is barren among them. Thy lips are like a thread of scarlet, and thy speech is comely: thy temples are like a piece of pomegranate within thy locks. Thy neck is like the tower of David builded for an armoury, whereon there hang a thousand bucklers, all shields of mighty men. Thy two breasts are like—"

I interrupt him, "She's not here just now."

"Who's thet?" *he says, dropping his arms and squinting in the dark.* "Thet you, Dawny?"

"Yep."

He sits on the bottom step. "Whar's Lathe?"

"She's takin a pee."

"Oh." *He puts his elbows on his knees and cradles his chin in his hands.* "S'funny," *he muses. Soon he rises up.* "Wal," *he says,* "I jest drapped by to give her my love. I'm off up towards Right Prong, to see if Luther Chism's rotgut is done makin yet. Give her my love. You don't*

*let them fool ye, Dawny, about them boogers. They aint no sech thing.
I know."*

He walks away.

*Then—a moment later—what seems to be merely one among a
million lightning bugs grows brighter and brighter, coming up the road.
It is not a lightning bug but a flashlight. The light comes nearer; soon I
can make out the arm holding it and then the figure of a man attached
to the arm. The flashlight swings upward and plays for a moment upon
the center of the sign attached to Latha's store:*

ʾOST OFF
ƧTAY MOF
ARK.

*Then the flashlight beam swings along the porch until it comes to
rest on me. I raise my arms to shield my face from the glare. I cannot
make out the figure behind the flashlight, but something in me senses
that he is a stranger, and I am slightly frightened.*

*"Howdy there, sonny," his voice says, and it is unfamiliar but warm
and friendly. "You must be Bob Cluley's boy…or maybe his grandson."*

*"Nossir," I reply. "Bob Cluley don't live here no more. He sold out
back in 1932."*

"Do tell? Why, that was quite a ways back."

"Yessir."

*"I notice they've moved the Post Office to here. Is the Ingledew
Store gone?"*

"Nossir, but it's not the post office no more."

"Who owns this place now?"

"Latha Bourne does."

*Silence. Then in a very low voice, as if not talking directly
to me at all, he says, "You don't mean it." Then he says, "You don't
mean to tell me." Then he says, louder, but tripping on his words, "Are
you…are you her boy?"*

"Nossir. I live up the road at the next place."

*"The Murrison place? Then you must be Frank's boy. You kind of
favor him."*

"*He's just my uncle.*"

"*I see. Latha Bourne…she don't have any children?*"

"*She aint married.*"

"*I see. Well, tell me, son, where is she at, right now?*"

"*I thought she'd just gone to pee but I reckon she must be making hockey too.*"

He laughs and says, "*My, you sure talk brash, for such a little spadger.*" Then he seems to get rather nervous, and says, "*I reckon she'll be coming back directly, then?*"

"*I reckon.*"

"*Well, uh, tell me, is there anybody living on the Dill Place?*"

"*The Dill place?*"

"*Yes, it's up beyond your Uncle Murrison's, first house on the right up beyond.… Or it used to be, anyway.*"

"*You mean where that old blacksmith shop is?*"

"*That's the one. But it wasn't actually a blacksmith shop, but a wagonmaking shop.*"

"*That house has been empty since that blacksmith died, twenty year or more ago.*"

"*He wasn't a blacksmith. He was a wagonmaker. Well, I guess I'll just mosey up there and take a look around. See you later, sonny.*"

Quickly he walks away. Very quickly.

Scarcely are he and his flashlight out of sight when Latha returns from her errand of elimination. When she has seated herself again, I tell her,

"*There was a man here.*"

"*Who?*"

"*I don't know. He didn't tell me his name.*"

"*What did he want?*"

"*Nothing. Just wanted to know who lived here now. I told him. Then he wanted to know if anybody was livin on the Dill Place, so when I said no he headed off in that direction, said he was just gonna look around up there.*"

Latha stares in that direction. I detect a quickening of her breathing. "*What did he look like?*" she asks. I have never heard her voice quaver quite like that before.

"I couldn't much tell. He was on the other side of a flashlight. Sort of tall, I guess. Seemed like a nice man."

She is silent a long time.

Finally I have to remind her, you were going to tell me a story.

She comes back from her trance, and smiles, and reaches over and rumples my hair. "Sure, Dawny," she says. Then she asks, "Would you care to hear a strange tale about a dumb supper? Have you ever heard tell of a 'dumb supper'?"

"Caint say that I have."

"Well," she says. "Once upon a time, in a month of May long time ago, a bunch of girls who were just about ready to graduate from high school decided to set themselves a dumb supper, which is an old, old custom that must go all the way back to the days of yore in England.

"The idea [she, like all others, pronounces this "idee"] is that you take and set out a place at the dinner table, just like you were having company, except you don't set out any food. You put out the plate and the knife and fork and spoon, and the napkin. Then you turn the lamp down very low. A candle is even better. Then you wait. You stand behind the chair and wait to see what happens."

As in all her tellings of ghost tales, she says these words very somberly, and makes a dramatic pause, and I feel the thrilling chill that makes her ghost stories so much fun.

"Well," she goes on, "there were six of these girls, and they set out six places, and then the six of them stood behind the six chairs and waited, with only one candle to light the room. They waited and they waited. The idea is that if you wait long enough, the apparition—not a real ghost, Dawny, but a ghost-like image—the apparition of the man you will marry will appear and take his seat before you at the table.

"Oh, of course it was all a lot of foolishness like all that superstitious going-on, but these girls believed in it, and anyway it would be a lot of fun. So they waited and they waited.

"Sometimes, if a girl was wishing very hard that a particular boy would appear, somebody she was crazy wild about, then she might get hysterical and really believe that he had come! Imagine that, Dawny. But the other girls would just laugh at her.

"Anyway, these girls waited and waited, but of course nothing hap-

pened. Some of them closed their eyes and mumbled magic words, and some of them prayed, but no boys showed up, and no apparitions of boys showed up. Until finally..."

I suspend my breathing. It is as near to approaching an orgasm as a five-year-old boy could ever get.

"Until finally there was this one particular girl who was wishing very, very hard, and she opened her eyes, and there coming into the room was a boy! With his hat pulled down over his eyes, he came right on over to her chair and sat down in it! And then in the candlelight she saw who it was! It wasn't the boy she was wishing for at all! It was another boy, the one she had already turned down twice when he asked for her hand!

"And then she fainted dead away."

I wait. "Well," I say. "Then what happened?"

"Well, after they got her revived, with smelling salts and cold compresses, one of the girls explained it all to her. Somehow that boy had found out about the dumb supper. The boys weren't supposed to know, but somehow he had found out. And came on purpose. The other girls had thrown him out of the house, after this poor girl fainted, and told him he ought to be ashamed of himself. And maybe he was."

"Well," I ask, "did she ever marry him?"

"No."

"Did she ever marry the other one, the one she was wishing for?"

"No."

"That other one, the one she was wishing for, his name was Raymond, wasn't it?"

Latha makes a little gasp, and then exclaims, "Why, Dawny, I didn't know you knew about that!"

"What was the name of the one who came to the dumb supper?"

She does not answer.

I leave her alone, but I cannot leave her alone for long. "Latha," I say, sweetly as I can, "what was the name of the one who came?"

"Won't tell you," she says, and her voice is the voice of a child.

"Please tell me," I beg.

"No," she says. "You'll have bad dreams, and your Aunt Rosie will come down here and give me a talking-to again for telling you ghost stories."

"I will have bad dreams anyway," I declare.

"No."

"Please."

"No. I won't."

"Pretty please, with sugar and cream on it."

"No. Hush. You stop asking me."

"Was it Tull Ingledew?"

"Law, no!" she laughs. "Back then he didn't even know I existed."

"Was it Doc Swain?"

"He was too old, and besides, he had a wife back at that time."

"Then who was it? Was it anybody I know?"

"No."

"Please, please tell me."

"No."

"If you don't tell me, I'm going to go away and never come back, and I'll never ever love you anymore."

She laughs again. "Or, if not that, you'd be nagging me about it for the rest of my days, wouldn't you?"

"I just might," I say fiercely.

"All right," she says. "His name was Dill. Every Dill. Isn't that a queer name? It wasn't Avery, but Every. He was William Dill's boy, old Billy Dill who used to make wagons."

I break out in a rash of goose bumps. "What...whatever...what did ever...become of him?"

"Nobody knows, child."

"Maybe..." I say, pointing up the road toward the Dill place.

"Yes, Dawny, that's what I've been wondering about too."

I suddenly ask, "Can I sleep with you tonight?"

"Whatever for?" she asks, with a big smile.

"To protect you."

She starts to laugh but decides it might hurt my feelings, which it would've. Instead she says, "Your Aunt Rosie wouldn't allow it."

"Aw, sure she would. She don't care where I sleep."

"But I don't have any spare beds, except that one that Sonora sleeps in."

"Why caint I just sleep in your bed?"

She laughs. *"My, my,"* she says. *"I haven't ever slept with anybody in my bed."*

"Never?"

"Never not all night."

"Well," I promise, *"I won't bother you."*

She laughs a long gay lilting laugh. *"You'd have to let your Aunt Rosie know where you are, and I bet you she wouldn't want you spending the night down here."*

I stand up. *"I'll be right back, fast as I can."*

"Good night, Dawny," she says, and waves. *"See you in the morning."*

"I will be right back," I say.

I run all the way home, which isn't far.

I burst in upon Aunt Murrison, who is reading her Bible by coal-oil light. I have always been a good liar, even then. I tell her that a whole bunch of kids are having a bunking party at Latha's store; they've laid out a lot of pallets and are going to have a real jamboree of ghost-story telling and I will just die of heartbreak if I can't join in.

"Which kids?" she says, eyeing me with leaden lids.

"Well, there's Larry Duckworth, and Vann and Tommy Dinsmore, and Jack and Tracy and Billy Bob Ingledew, and—"

"I bet them kids don't want a little squirt like you hangin around."

"But Sammy Coe's there too, and I'm older'n him!"

"How come y'all are havin yore bunkin party at Latha's place?"

"Well, she's treatin us to free soda pop."

"Hmm," says Aunt Murrison. She mutters, *"That crazy gal…"* Then she says to me, *"Well, you behave yourself, you hear me? Be a good boy and don't bother them other kids."*

"Yes ma'am!" I cry, and rushing out, holler back, *"See you in the mornin!"*

So that is how I came to spend the night with my beloved Bug.

(There remains just another short piece of bug business, and then I am done with these over-long prefatory hemmings and hawings. Another image symbolically related to lightning bugs: that of a book of matches being struck, one by one. It happened like this: with my beard and my pipe and my Harris tweed jacket I was fool enough to think that I could pass for a visiting psychiatrist, but the Keeper of Records at the Arkansas State Hospital said to me politely, "It isn't that we are challenging your authority, Doctor, but our regulations require that we cannot give you access to our records unless we see something in the way of credentials, perhaps only your A.A.P.P. membership card..." So I went away and bought a doctor's white smock and came back in the middle of the night and snapped impatiently at the night clerk on duty, "The file on Latha Anne Bourne, please. B-O-U-R-N-E. 1922–25." But the night clerk looked at me and said, albeit pleasantly enough, "Which ward are you from, Doctor? I don't recall seeing you around before. But I suppose you're new. Perhaps your name is on my list here, let's see...." One would think that my nerve, which has never been distinguished for its intrepidity, would have failed at this point. But I was extraordinarily dedicated. I went upstairs and walked the corridors and read the names on the doors of doctor's offices, picking one at random. Then I went over to Ward A and read the list of patients, picking one at random. Then I went to a phone booth and called that same night clerk in the Records Office and said, disguising my voice, "This is Doctor Reuben. Please, would you very quickly get the file on Wilson Olmstead and bring it up and slip it under the door of my office? Thank you so much." Then I quickly returned to the Records Office. The clerk was gone. But he had locked the strong wire gate to the Records Room. There was, however, a small opening at chest-level for the purpose of passing documents through, and I managed to squeeze through this. I did not dare turn on a light. I used up three matches finding the 1920's section, and two more matches locating the B's, and one more finding Latha's file. Then I sat on the floor with it in my lap, and opened it, and used up the rest of my matches quickly reading it. It was a thick sheaf of papers, sandwiched between an Admission slip which said, "Committed, under protest, May 12, 1922, by married sister, Mrs. Vaughn Twichell," and a small piece of paper which summarily remarked, "Escaped E Ward, method unknown, March 23, 1925." Several times I burned my fingers because I was so absorbed with what I was reading that I did not watch the match closely. If there is no draft, a book match can be made to burn for a maximum of 36 seconds. This means that I had a total reading time of only about 7 minutes 45 seconds. But I am a relatively fast reader. And the glow of those matches, so help me, was quite uncannily akin to the pulsing flashes of a lightning bug.]

> *"Dawny, close your eyes."*
> *"Why?"*
> *"You don't want to watch me undressing, do you?"*
> *"But it's pitch dark, I caint see you noway."*
> *"Close your eyes."*
> *"Okay."*

Why is it, I wonder, that all those sounds of the summer night are louder indoors, when you're lying in bed, than they are outdoors, when you're sitting on the porch?

> *"Well. Now you can open your eyes. But don't look at me."*
> *"Why caint I look at you?"*
> *"Because it's so hot and we'd have to pull the covers up because I don't have anything on."*
> *"You mean you're nekkid?" I begin to turn my head.*
> *Her hand presses the side of my face. "Don't look."*
> *"But it's so dark I caint see nuthin noway."*
> *"Maybe you can. I can see you."*
> *"What's wrong with lookin at you? I like to look at you."*
> *"But I don't have anything on."*
> *"Who cares?"*

It is very hot, not a night for covers at all, not even a sheet. I look down at myself, at my undershirt, at my shorts. The faintest breeze comes through the window screen.

> *"Do you sleep nekkid all the time?"*
> *"Just in the summertime."*
> *"I never knew of anybody sleepin stark nekkid."*
> *"Most people don't."*
> *"I reckon it's a awful lot cooler, that way."*
> *"Oh, it is."*

"*Can I sleep nekkid too?*"

"*Dawny, I wish you wouldn't say 'nekkid.' It makes it sound bad.*"

"*Okay, can I sleep undressed too?*"

She does not answer for a while. Then she laughs a little and says, "Dawny, you're commencing to make me nervous. If you ever told anybody, your Aunt Rosie or anybody, that me and you slept together, let alone without our clothes, do you know they would cover me with hot tar and feathers and ride me out of town on a rail?"

"*Aw, Latha! Do you honestly think I would ever tell anybody? I aint ever gon tell anybody anything about me'n you.*"

"*Maybe,*" *she says,* "*maybe I better get a quilt and fix you a pallet on the floor in the other room.*"

I begin to cry.

"*Oh, shush, Dawny, a big boy like you!*" *she coos.* "*Lie still, and shush.*"

I keep crying.

She reaches over and grabs me by the undershirt, and at first I think she's going to fling me clean out of the bed, but she just tugs my undershirt over my head, and then pulls my shorts down and off my feet.

"*There!*" *she says.* "*Now shush.*"

I shush.

It is hard, from here, to see through the window and watch any lightning bugs. But I don't care. I have my own Bug beside me.

"*Close your eyes and go to sleep.*"

"*I'm not much sleepy. Are you?*"

"*Not much, I guess.*"

"*Tell me a story.*"

"*All right.*"

She tells me, not just one ghost story, but several, many. Some of these I have heard her tell before, but they are good ones, and the new ones which I have not heard before are very good indeed. They thrill me, they hold me, they seize me, they jolt me, they drain me. It is nearly as good as if I were full-grown and could mount her and ride her, over and over, again and again, till the last drop of my seed were draught off. Often, in the grip of a mighty story's climax, I have to squeeze her hand.

She likes her own stories too, and gets carried off by them, which is why she is such a good teller…and which is why she has not noticed that I am staring at her. The moon has shifted from behind a tree, and some of its light comes into the room. She lies staring at the ceiling as she talks, one of her hands gripped by mine, the other hand resting upon her white stomach. All creation does not know a sight lovelier than her breasts. How does Tull Ingledew say it? Yes: "Thy two breasts are like two young roes that are twins, which feed among the lillies." I do not know what a roe is, but it has a lovely sound.

"Latha," I say, "I love you."

She turns, and does not seem to mind that I am staring at her, and that there is enough light for us to see one another. "Oh, Dawny," she says. Then she reaches out her hand and rumples my hair and says, "I love you too, and if you were a growed-up man I would marry you right this minute." She pulls me to her and squeezes me and then puts me back where I was. "Now let's try to get some sleep."

We try to get some sleep, but we are both listening.

We listen for a knock, or for footsteps on the porch.

The night passes on. The symphony of the bugs and frogs never stops. The night cools.

Footsteps. My heart thunders. But it is not my heart, it is Latha's. I realize I am in her arms, my ear against her chest.

A voice. A girl's. It is Snory, coming home. Her screen door opens very slowly in a very slow WRIRRAANG, and light footsteps move across a floor, and to a room. She bumps against a table or something.

Then it is silent again, and stays silent a long time,

By and by I ask Latha in a whisper, "Do you think that it might really be him up there? Do you think it's really Every Dill?"

"Oh, I know it," she says, and there is no fear nor alarm nor anxiety of any sort in her voice, but almost a kind of thrilled anticipation. "I know it is."

We sleep.

MIDDLING

ONE: Morning

O n this day of days, she rose, careful to touch the floor with her right foot first—though this practice was habitual, spontaneous, she was conscious of it as her first waking thought. Her second thought was: *Today.* Then she slowly dressed, in her multipatched denims and her faded chambray shirt. She put on her heavy shoes, which the night before she had carefully left in the position of the shape of the letter T. That T, she realized, could have stood for *Tomorrow*, or, now, for *Today*, although this was not the reason she left them in that position.

Before leaving the room, she turned and cast an affectionate parting glance at the small boy asleep in her bed, and felt a momentary anxiety, a fleeting self-reproach: *I oughtnt've allowed him to do that. Fool girl, you are going to step too far sometime.* Then she turned back from the door and walked quickly to the big four-poster and leaned down to kiss the sleeping boy on his forehead. He did not wake; he would sleep a long time yet.

In the kitchen she took a platter of day-old pork-flavored biscuits from the food safe and carried them out onto the back porch and threw them one by one to her cats, saving the last one for herself.

She munched it slowly and lingered to watch the cats fighting over the biscuits. She stayed even longer to watch the cats loll in the early morning sun and lick themselves and each other, then she returned to the kitchen and got her milk pail and filled it a quarter ways with water dipped from the water pail. She carried this up the hill to the cow lot, pausing only briefly at her backhouse. She squatted by the Jersey's flank, not needing a stool, and after washing each of the teats carefully with the water in the pail, she swirled the rest of the water out of the pail and began to milk.

The milk was good; Mathilda had been grazing lately on the orchard grass, free of the lower pasture's bitter weeds that gave the milk a pungent taste. The pesky flies of July bothered Mathilda, and she fidgeted restlessly while she was milked. "Saw, Jerse," Latha would croon at her, "saw." Latha closed her eyes while she milked and enjoyed the feel of the long cool dugs. She filled the pail and carried it down to the springhouse to crock it and leave it to cool.

By this time her free-ranging chickens had assembled in a packed flock around the back steps of the house. She walked through them to the back porch and scooped into the feedbag and flung several handfuls into the yard. The chickens made a racket.

Then she took down the slop bucket hanging from the porch ceiling and carried it to the sty, for her four Chester Whites. Pigs were her favorite animal, not alone for the ebullient gratitude they showed for the garbagey swill she showered upon them, but for the noises they made, which seemed to her an expression of basic life forces.

Now for a moment she spoke with these hogs in their own language of intricate reiterated snorty grunts. Then she chanced to look up and catch sight of a redbird in a tree. Quickly she made a wish, and waited. Soon the redbird flew down to a lower limb. If it had flown upward, her wish would have come true. *But I really didn't mean that wish*, she decided, *I don't honestly want for that to happen*.

The animals all taken care of, it was time for the vegetables. She returned to the house and consulted her calendar and discovered it was turnip-planting day. Personally she hated turnips, but you always plant turnips on turnip-planting day. She entered her store and took a package of seeds from the rack. Then she gathered up her hoe and her rake and headed for the garden across the road. This land belonged to whoever still owned the abandoned house beside the garden, but she had raised a garden here every year for the past eight years, and nobody'd ever said anything about it.

Crossing the road she saw Penelope sitting in the road. Penelope was one of her cats, an all-white. To see a white cat sitting in the road is good luck. So *there,* that takes care of that down-flying redbird.

She planted the turnips, reluctantly. *Sonora likes turnips but she'll be gone back to Little Rock before they're ready. Well, I will make a turnip pie for Tull Ingledew. Or will Sonora be going back? I wonder if Every likes turnips.* After the turnip seeds were in the ground she took her hoe and chopped weeds out of the lettuce and cabbage and beans, chopping hard, working up a sweat, a real lathering sweat.

She began to sing:

Well met, well met, my own true love
Long time I have not seen thee
Well met on such a shining day

but stopped, shocked at herself, stopped hoeing too, stood still and remembered: *Sing before breakfast, Cry before supper. It means I will be crying before this day is out because I haven't had my breakfast yet. Well, it's likely I will. Serves me right. It's like as not I'll have more than enough reason for crying before suppertime.*

She resumed chopping weeds, with a vengeance. Accidentally she decapitated a cabbage. Still she kept chopping, until her shirt was soaked through with sweat. She grabbed up the cabbage head and ran back to the house. She went to her room and got a towel and a dress. The boy had rolled over, embracing the place she had left, but was still sound asleep. She left the house once more, crossed the road once more, entered the garden once more. At the end of the vegetable rows, beyond her tall corn, is a dense line of trees, bordering Swains Creek. She went into these trees.

She began to remove her sweaty clothes, but noticed for the first time that she had her chambray shirt on wrongside out. *Oh, great gracious sakes!* she sighed. *Isn't this just dandy?* Anybody knows that if you accidentally put something on wrongside out, the only way you can keep from having bad luck all day is to keep wearing it wrongside out until bedtime. But this shirt was all dirty and sweaty, even if it was fit to wear for company coming.

She continued unbuttoning it. *Latha dear,* she said resolutely, *once in your life you'll just have to quit being so all-fired superstitious.* And while she finished undressing, she reflected upon the nature of superstition, and remembered something that nut doctor in Little Rock had tried to get her to believe: "Superstition is the harmless but invalid attempt of the individual to cope with the unknowns and intangibles and the factors in fate and environment over which he has no control. Superstitions vanish as the person becomes more civilized and develops more sense of control over his fate and environment." Remembering this, Latha laughed, but reckoned it was true.

Now in her nakedness she stepped through the thicket and slipped into Swains Creek and lay down in the shallow water, and cooled. She loved her body; that was her one certainty; not the sight of it, nor even the feel of it, but the *it* of it, the itness of it, that it was there, that it was hers, that it could feel something like cool creek water swarming around it and washing the sweat from it, that it could sweat, that it could be cleansed, that it could tingle. *I am a jar of skin, a bottle of flesh, a container. All the things I contain....*

She leaned her head back and gazed up at the sun rising above Dinsmore Mountain, and gauged it. It was about five-thirty. Stay More was waking up. Tull Ingledew was just going to sleep, but the others were beginning to wake. Lola Ingledew with a goose feather was tickling the soles of the feet of E.H., her brother. Stanfield Ingledew was exaggeratedly imitating the snores of his brother Odell, in an effort to waken him. In another room, Emelda, the wife of Bevis Ingledew, was crowing into Bevis's ear an excellent imitation of a rooster. Their son, John Henry, would sleep for another two hours; he had been out past midnight, shagging Sonora Twichell three and a half times.

Retired physician John Mabrey Plowright was stepping out onto his front porch and hollering across the road at Doc Colvin

Swain's house, "How's yore goddam arthuritis *this* fine mornin, you on-scruplous young horse doctor?" And Doc Swain was stepping out onto his porch and hollering back at his nearest neighbor, "A damn sight better'n yore putrid rheumatism, I reckon, you frazzled old sawbones." From the creek Latha could hear the distant sound of their imprecations.

In the rough homestead in the timber atop Dinsmore Mountain, Selena Dinsmore, whose man Jake went to California three years ago and has not returned, was banging the dishpan with a large spoon, and with each clanging stroke calling out "Hubert! Sarah! Clovis! Lorraine! Tommy! Vann! Jelena! Doris! Willard! Ella Jean! Tilbert! Norma! And Baby! Y'all all tumble out!"

Luther Chism went out to his smokehouse where the revenue agent was tied, and asked him, "How you lak yore aigs cooked?" The agent complained, "How'm I gon eat any aigs with all this here rope on me?" Luther said, "My gal Lucy'll feed em to ye. How you lak em cooked?" The agent said, "Turned over." Luther said, "You take sweetenin in yore coffee?" The agent said, "Some, I thank you." Luther said, "Yo're welcome."

Oren Duckworth, finished with shaving, took down the leather strop and lined up his four boys, Junior, Chester, Mont, and Larry, ranging in age from 19 to 9, backsides to him, and tanned their hides. It was for whatever mischief they might have gotten into the night before. Then, because tomorrow was Sunday and he would not lay the strop to them on the Lord's Day, he tanned their hides once more, for whatever mischief they might get into tonight.

Frank Murrison woke to discover he had a morning hard, but Rosie protested, "It's Sattidy. My day off." He waited for it to subside, and when it did not he went to the barn and used a ewe.

Ella Jean Dinsmore came running into the kitchen, hollering, "Maw! Baby Jim fell through the hole in the outhouse!" Selena Dinsmore smiled absently and said, "Aw, just leave him go, Ella Jean. It'd be easier to have another'n than to clean that un up, even if we could git him out."

There are no morning bells, no matinals, in Stay More. Instead there came the chime of hammer and anvil in Lawlor Coe's blacksmith shop. This morning it was answered, once, by the distant anvil in Dill's wagon shop, deserted these many years.

Latha, in the water, sneezed. And recited to herself:

Sneeze on Monday, sneeze for danger
Sneeze on Tuesday, kiss a stranger
Sneeze on Wednesday, sneeze for a letter
Sneeze on Thursday, sneeze for better
Sneeze on Friday, sneeze for sorrow,
Sneeze on Saturday, a friend you seek
Sneeze on Sunday, the Devil will be with you all week.

What day's today? she asked herself. *Why, I believe it's Saturday. Yes, I'm almost certain it's Saturday.* She lay in the slow-running green stream but a few moments more, then got up and waded out, and toweled herself dry. She put on the dress, a blue one with small yellow daisies printed on it, and carried her work clothes bundled in the towel back to the house.

She started breakfast. The woodbox was near about empty. She went out to the backyard and chopped an armload of kindling slowly so as not to sweat again. She stuffed half a dozen sticks into the stove, poured some coal oil over them, and lighted it. She filled the kettle and put it on.

When the coffee was making, she noticed that the coffeepot was rattling on the stove. That was sure enough a sign that a visitor would come before nightfall.

She ate her breakfast alone, and left a platter of eggs and bacon and biscuits on the warming shelf for Sonora and Donny.

Then she unlocked the store from the inside. Jesse Witter was already sitting on the front porch, waiting to hire folks to help pick his tomatoes.

"Mornin, Jesse," she said.

"Fine mornin, Latha," he replied. Then he asked, "Could you let me have a plug a Brown Mule and I'll pay ye after I've took my tomaters to the cannin factry?"

"You want me to bring it out to you, or you want to go in and get it yourself?" she asked, smiling.

He snorted. "Aw, shoot, I can git it myself," he said, and got up off the nail keg he was sitting on and went into the store and behind the counter and reached up and got the plug of chewing tobacco and unwrapped it and bit off a chaw.

Then she took him by the hand and led him over to the corner where the feed bags were stacked and made him lie down on the pile of feed bags and unbuttoned his pants and groped around inside until she found his dood and pulled it out which was limp and floppy as a hound's ear but she worked on it with both hands and got it perked up enough so she could lift her dress and sit down on it and get it well in and then pretend she was on a galloping horse going faster and faster bouncing up and down and Jesse Witter had to turn his head to one side ever now and again to spit tobacco and she had to point out to him the sign KINDLY DO NOT EXPECTORATE UPON THE FLOOR *and he said* "Goll darn it, Latha, the least you could do is keep a spitoon over in this corner so a feller could take a spit while you was diddlin the daylights out of him" *and she said* "Shut up and wiggle your rump" *and he did and she galloped faster and finally came*

"How many hands do you need today?" she asked him.

"Aw, I reckon five or six ought to do her. Aint but about twenty short rows left in that patch."

"Those W.P.A. boys aren't working on the bridge today. Maybe a couple of them could use some extra cash."

"I wouldn't hire a W.P.A. boy to break rocks or tie string."

Latha went back into the store and got her turkey-feather duster, and dusted her three show cases. Her small store was stocked to capacity, using every inch of space. There was this difference between hers and Lola's; that Lola's seemed empty because it was so big for what little was in it, while hers seemed full because it was so little for what a big lot was there. There was also another difference, not to mention the post office: Latha kept a Coke cooler full of soda pop and ice, and on these hot days she made a good profit. Lola claimed it wasn't worth the cost of the ice, but she was wrong.

Latha's staples were lined up in neat clean rows: baking soda, sugar, salt, flour, crackers, and some canned stuff, Vienna sausages and such. She carried hardware too: files, and bolts, plowshares, axe handles, horseshoes, four different sizes of hemp rope in large neat coils. And fresh things: eggs, butter, bread (both store-boughten light and her own), and home-made sausage.

Things hung from the ceiling, like stalactites in a cave: lamp chimneys, hickory handles, horse collars, harness straps. And she kept things for the womenfolk too: all kinds of thread, needles, Putnam dyes, and several bolts of bright gingham and flannel and even rayon. And she dispensed Lydia Pinkham Remedies, and Carter's Little Liver Pills and other medicines. And four brands of snuff, six of chewing tobacco, seven of smoking tobacco. It was rare that somebody asked for something she didn't have.

Last year she had cleared a net profit of $438.

On the front porch were three of the Dinsmore children, with the oldest, Lorraine Dinsmore, as their spokesman, bargaining with Jesse Witter:

"How much you payin today?"

"Seven cents a bushel."

"Maw said not for us to do it for less than nine."

"Eight is the most I could ever hope to give ye."

"Is they first-picks or pickovers?"

"Some of it's pickovers, but they's a good few fresh rows."

"Enough for till sundown?"

"I reckon not, but leastways till six or so."

"Okay. We'll do it for eight. Miss Latha, you heerd him promise us eight, so we count on you to keep him to his word."

"Git in the wagon," Jesse said. "We got to see if two or three more show up."

It was nearly seven o'clock, and Jesse Witter was fidgeting with restlessness, before Dulcie Coe came and offered to pick. Right behind her came Estalee Jerram, the schoolteacher, unemployed for the summer.

"Doggone," said Jesse Witter, "I wush I had me a couple of stout boys 'stead of all you gals."

Lorraine Dinsmore said, "You aint payin us by the hour, noway. I kin pick fast as ary boy you'd find."

"Well, let's git on with it," said Jesse and the six of them got into his wagon and he turned it into the Parthenon road.

Then Latha was alone until eight o'clock, when the candy drummer from Jasper drove up. He was a new fellow. "What happened to Mr. Clinton?" she asked him.

"Aw, he got hisself into some trouble down towards Hunton, a-foolin around with the storekeeper's daughter. Only way to stay in this business is behave yoreself. But I *do* declare, lady, it's shore gonna be mighty hard for me to behave myself with a pretty thing like you." And he winked big before turning back to his car to get his sample case and order book.

A little while later, inside the store, he said, "I caint hep but notice, ma'am, that you aint wearin no weddin ring."

"And I cant help but notice that you, sir, are a good bit fatter and unsightly looking than Mr. Clinton was, and I will bet anything you cant last nearly half as long, but come on anyway," and she drew him over to the feed sacks and yanked down his britches and took a sad look at his sorry little pink dinger and had to gobble it and lap on it and draw on it and nearly swallow it for a long time before it got sturdy enough and him standing there eating one of his own candy bars and then when she'd gone to all that trouble to get it ready he wouldn't let go of her but grabbed her by the hair and dove down her throat and spewed a half-pint and shoved his candy bar up her thigh and into her Every Dill Every Dill O Every*

"I will take a box of Baby Ruths, a box of Butterfingers, a box of Powerhouses, and a box of those round pink-goo peanut blobs, whatever you call them."

"I couldn't interest you this mornin in some Tootsie Rolls or some Hershey Bars?"

"In this weather?"

"You could cool em in with your sody pop there."

"I'll do that when you invent a waterproof wrapper."

"Well, how bout some orange slices? They'll keep in any weather."

"They'll keep forever, too, because nobody around here eats them."

"All right. How bout me'n you seein the pitcher show over to Jasper tonight? That's my own car out there."

"I thank you. But I'm already set up for tonight."

"I bet he don't have his own car."

"No, but he's got something a durn sight prettier than any car."

The candy drummer stared at her for a moment, and then he blushed from his tight collar to his brow, and said, "Haw." Then he said, "Well." Then he closed his order book and headed for the door. "Feisty gal," he mumbled. "Good day, ma'am," he said and went to his car and drove off.

Donny came into the store from the side door, rubbing his eyes. "Could you tie my shoes for me?" he asked her.

"Hot day like this, you could go barefoot," she said.

"Okay," he said, and took off his shoes.

"Come and I'll set you out some breakfast," she said, and led him back to the kitchen. She poured him a tall glass of milk and gave him a plate of eggs and bacon. While he ate, she asked him, "Did you sleep all right?"

"Just fine," he said. "But I had a lot of bad dreams."

"What did you dream about?"

"You and that feller Every."

"What was bad about it?"

"I don't remember."

She washed some dishes while he finished his breakfast. Then she said to him, "You'd better go let your Aunt Rosie know you're okay. I imagine she won't like it that I fed you breakfast."

"She won't care."

"Dawny, you're not going to tell…"

"Course not," he said. "Never." Then he asked, "Can I sleep with you again sometime?"

She frowned. "We'll have to see," she said.

He went home.

There was nothing to do until the mail came at ten o'clock.

She sat in the rocker on the front porch. She had learned to sit quietly, doing nothing, she had learned long ago to keep company with herself. Infrequently a wagon would pass, or a rider, sometimes a car, and they would wave and she would wave back.

Sonora woke up around nine o'clock and got her own breakfast, then took a bar of soap and went to the creek to wash her hair. When she came back, she picked a sunny spot of the porch to sit in, to dry her red hair in the sun. After a while she began to comb it.

A car passed, its occupants waving. "Was that Merle Kimber in there?" Sonora asked.

"Looked more like Leo Dinsmore," observed Latha.

The cats crawled under the porch to sleep in the shade.

A wagon passed, and two boys on the buckboard waved. "Is that ole Ralph Chism from Sidehill?" Sonora asked.

"I believe."

"What's he doing around here?"

"Guess he's going up to visit his uncle."

A mild breeze came down Swains Creek, bearing the faint sound of the machinery in the canning factory, and the acid smell of boiled tomatoes.

Folks began to drift up to the store to wait for the mail truck to come. By ten o'clock there were nearly twenty people hanging around the store porch. A few of them bought cold soda pop.

Rosie Murrison asked Latha, "How was yore bunkin party last night?"

Latha studied the question for a moment, and studied Rosie's face before answering, "Oh, pretty good, I guess."

Sonora asked, "What bunkin party?"

Latha said to her, "Hon, you sleep so late of a morning that you miss pretty near half of everything that goes on in the world."

Some of the boys on the porch commenced to have a giggling fit, and Sonora pouted and said nothing more.

Across the road Sammy Coe and Donny were throwing rocks at each other.

"You, Dawny!" Rosie hollered. "You stop that this minute or I'll send you home."

Doc Swain chuckled, and remarked, "Puts me in mind of old Granny Price up on Banty Creek. Th'other day she come into the room where her granddaughter Sally was a-nursin that big overgrowed baby a hers, and she says, 'Why, law sakes, chile, when air ye ever gonna wean that youngun?' and Sally says, 'Grammaw, I've tried and I've tried, but ever time I wean him he throws rocks at me.'"

A small few of the men and boys guffawed, but the main sound was the prim gasps of the ladies.

The mail truck came at 10:08.

The driver opened the canvas flap at the end and unwrapped the canvas covering on the ice, and with his tongs lifted two 25-pound blocks of ice and carried them into the store and put them in the soda pop cooler, while behind him at the truck a mob of small boys were fighting over the tiny shavings of ice around the blocks and Donny was screaming because they weren't giving him a chance to get any.

"You boys!" Latha snapped at them and they stopped and looked at her. "Give Dawny a piece." One of the older boys reached in and drew out a big sliver and handed it to Donny, who began happily licking it.

"Takin up for him, are you?" said Rosie to Latha.

"Somebody ought to," said Latha, and turned and went into the post office part of the store.

The driver brought in two mail bags, and she took out her key and unlocked the collars on them. One bag was for Stay More, and she would sort that slowly later on, but one bag was for the south end of Swains Creek Township, and she had to sort the mail quickly for Demijohn, Hunton, Spunkwater and points beyond.

"Here you are, Ted," she said, and gave the driver the empty Stay More sack and the sorted sack for the other towns, as well as the sack of outgoing Stay More mail.

"Fifty pounds on Monday?" he asked.

"Better make it seventy-five, if this weather keeps up."

After he left she sorted the Stay More mail, while the folks congregated near the boxes, waiting. This morning there were two pieces of mail for herself, a letter from her sister, and some business from the Post Office Department. When she had finished all the sorting, she opened and read the letter from her sister. She was only dimly conscious of the sounds around her—other people opening their mail and reading it and sharing whatever news there was.

Dear Sister—

Sure is hot and dry here in LR. Wish I could come up to SM and cool off, but I just never seem to get caught up with all there is to do. We take the streetcar out to Fair Park just about ever evening to cool off, but sure is crowded out there.

Hows my little girl? Sure do miss her. Latha, me and Vaughn have been talking. You know she is all we've got in this world. If it doesnt make a whole lot of difference to her or you, I wish she could just come right on back to LR right now, instead of waiting till late August. Do me this favor, and just take her into Jasper and put her on the bus.

Latha, I sure wouldn't hurt your feelings for anything. So I dont mean we dont trust you. You swore what you swore, and we took you on your word. So thats that. But I just dont sleep good nights worrying about her. She's really *my* little girl, after all, who I brought up and reared with a true Mother's Love. No telling what all kinds of trouble a girl of her age might get into without proper supervision.

Also, me and Vaughn dont much like the way she changes after staying in SM. You remember last summer. She come back here to LR talking and acting like a ignorant hillbilly, and it didn't do her much good at LRHS, the other kids poked fun at her, the way she talked. And she didn't even seem to care! So me and Vaughn oftentimes have wondered, is SM a bad influence on her. Just another year or so and our baby will be leaving us to get married, and I mean to see to it that she marries the right crowd.

So I hope you dont think I'm a Indian Giver or

Double Dealer or nothing, but I just think we'd all of us be a lot more happy if she come on back home now. Say hello to everbody for me. Hope you are all well.

Your loving sister, Mandy

Latha laughed, and she crumpled the letter and dropped it into the scrap box, singing to herself under her breath, *Too late, too late, you're way too late, My darling sister dear....*

Then she opened the other envelope. Usually she never even bothered to read any of the duplicated stuff the Post Office Department was always sending to her, but something in this one caught her eye. It was duplicated too, just a form letter, but there were blanks that had been filled in.

POST OFFICE DEPARTMENT

Regional Operations
Headquarters Office

Postmaster:

You are hereby directed to discontinue the post office at *Staymore, Ark.* on the day of *August 1, 1939* , and required to account for the fixed credits, all funds and all Government property in your possession. Your final postal account should be forwarded to the Regional Controller's office at *Little Rock, Ark.* .

You shall deposit all surplus funds, including paid money orders, redeemed saving stamps, and funds remaining in your various fixed credits in the Federal Reserve Bank, P.O. Box *2744, Little Rock, Ark.* .

You shall render a final postal savings report on Form PS 704, The Division of Postal Savings will instruct you as to the disposition of postal savings certificates, records and active accounts.

Upon receipt of your acknowledgment of this order (please sign enclosed Form OC 526 and return promptly) this office will forward instructions regarding disposition of postage stamps, revenue stamps, money order forms, post office scales, other Government property, as well as your current account book, any cashbooks, bond records, and the mail keys.

Mail for the patrons of your office, all records on file pertaining to forwarding addresses, and all records pertaining to registered, insured, and COD mail will be sent to the post office at *Parthenon, Ark.* at the close of the date set for discontinuance.

You and your sureties will be held responsible under your bond for the proper execution of these instructions.

The enclosed notice shall be placed in some conspicuous place available to the public. The post office sign must be removed from the building.

Form B/A-201, Report of Separation, must be completed and forwarded to Regional Controller.

Sincerely yours,

Blakely F. Lucas
Operations Manager

Sing before breakfast, Cry before supper. Is that what I am fated to cry about? But she did not feel like crying. She felt like swearing. So she did. "Goddamn those bastards!"

Doc Swain stepped over. "Which bastards?" he asked. "What's wrong?"

She handed him the enclosure. "Here."

He read it. Then he read it aloud to the others in the store, his voice quavering:

NOTICE TO THE PATRONS OF THE U.S. POST OFFICE AT *STAYMORE, ARK.*

By order of the Postmaster General, effective *Aug. 1, 1939* this post office is discontinued. Patrons may

43

arrange to receive their mail and contract business with the Post Office Department through the post office at *Parthenon, Ark.* .

At first there was no response from the gathering. The first person to speak was Larry Duckworth, who asked his father, "What does 'discontinued' mean?"

Oren Duckworth looked down at the boy with contempt, and answered, "It means they are closing this here post office, son." Then to the company at large, he said, "By godfrey, they caint do this to us!"

"Hell fire, no!"

"Dadburn em, they caint!"

"I swan, they'll never!"

"Judas Priest, *naw!*"

"Who do they think they are?"

"I, for *one,* shore don't aim to walk all the way over to Parthenon to get my consarnit mail!"

"Nor me neither!"

"What d'ye reckon has gave them people such a notion?"

Rosie Murrison pointed her finger at Latha and declared, "It's her fault! She aint been runnin this post office proper, so they're closin it on account a her, I just know it!"

"Now, Rosie," Doc Swain said. "More'n likely the reason they're closin it is because this town is simply got too small to have one."

"*Small,* my hind foot!" said Oren Duckworth. "Why, we got a cannin factry, aint we? Do them Government bigwigs know that we got a *industry* in this here 'small' town? How'm I gonna conduct my business, I ask you? Naw, I won't stand for it!"

Rosie said, "Let's have a 'lection, and vote for Lola Ingledew for postmaster, and then tell them people we've done cleaned the corruption out of the post office, so's they'll let us keep it."

"Good idee!" said another woman, but Doc Swain said, "Aw now, postmasters aint ever elected, and besides it wouldn't make no difference to them people. If they've made up their minds, their minds is made up."

"You kin talk big, Colvin Swain," said Woodrow Kimber, "'cause you got a fine automobile to ride over to Parthenon and git yore mail, but most of us folks is gonna have to wear out shoe leather gittin thar!"

"Not me!"

"Nossir!"

"I won't stand for it!"

"They can just *keep* their dadgummed mail!"

"Keep it till they drown in it!"

"Aw, listen, folks," Doc Swain said, "like as not they'll be sendin out a mail carrier from Parthenon, and all we got to do is each of us get us a mailbox and set it up out front of our house. We'll just be a rural route instead of a post office."

Oren Duckworth moved into the doorway and pointed up the road. "By jiggers, lookee out there! Does that look like any *rural route* to you? Does it? Don't it look more like a town to you? Lookee out there, goddammit, and tell me what you see!"

Sadly Doc Swain said, "I see an old bank building with its window lights bustid out, and I see a few old houses mostly without anybody livin in em, and I see a big old Gen'ral Store that don't do much business any more, and I see a old barn that somebody has tried to turn into a tomato cannin factry…"

Oren Duckworth came out of the doorway and thrust his nose up against Doc Swain's. "Doc, boy, you makin light of me?"

"Naw, Oren, I'm just makin light of this town."

"If it's too light fer ye, you could just git out of it."

"Been here all my life, Oren. Same as you. Gonna be here all the rest of my life, the Lord willing."

Latha went into her bedroom and closed the door behind her to muffle the noise of all the bickering going on in the store. She sat at her dresser and got out her stationery box and wrote a pair of letters:

Dear Mr. Lucas:

Your communication, incorrectly addressed and mailed, has been forwarded to this office. As there is no "Staymore" post office in the state of Arkansas, an order discontinuing same is invalid and will therefore be disregarded.

Yours respectfully,

(Miss) Latha A. Bourne, Postmistress

Stay More, Arkansas

Dear Mandy:

I doubt if Little Rock could be any hotter than Stay More has been lately, around 95° in the shade, so you aren't missing anything. We are all well, and hope you are the same. Sonora seems to be having a good time. John Henry Ingledew, Bevis's boy, seems to be her special "beau." I am sure she would not consider, for even a moment, the dreary prospect of returning to Little Rock prematurely, and I seem to have no inclination toward urging it upon her. Sorry.

Your loving sister,

Latha

P.S. Every Dill showed up in town last night. What do you know!

She read this letter over again, and decided to remove the postscript. She took a pair of scissors and snipped it off. There would be, she decided, time enough for that news later.

She returned into her store and mailed her letters at her post office but realized that they wouldn't be picked up until Monday, because on Saturday afternoons the mail truck did not come back down Swains Creek but went on back to Jasper by way of Highway 7. *I might as well go fishing this afternoon,* she thought. *If Every Dill doesn't ever show his face, and I could get Sonora to mind the store again, I'd just go up Banty Creek and fish awhile, and I might even run across that fellow Dolph Rivett again.*

Most of the folks had taken their mail and gone on home. A few were still sitting on the porch, arguing about the closing of the post office and wondering what the world was coming to. Latha looked out the window at the road for a while, thinking of nothing, then she got down the big book, U.S. POSTAL CODE, and blew the dust off of it, and read for a while.

The Coe triplets came in to get the mail for their father, and then they each bought a Baby Ruth bar and a Dr. Pepper soda pop, and stood around silently munching their candy and sipping their pop.

Donny came running into the store, yelling, "He's coming down the road!"

Earl, Burl and Gerald Coe said together, "Who is?"

"*Him!*" Donny yelled at her. "It's him, I seen him, and he's coming this way."

"Just be easy, Dawny," she said, and moved along behind the counter to the window, and furtively looked out. The Coe triplets crowded into the doorway, and watched the road. The men sitting on the porch stopped talking.

And then he came into view, and it was sure enough him, though you'd hardly know it. He would be almost 40 years old now, and he looked it. He was wearing eyeglasses, too, and with his long sideburns and his hair parted in the middle he looked like…like a drummer, or maybe a preacher, or a county judge or something. But even with those glasses and that hair and those sideburns he was more handsome than he'd ever been, and Latha heard herself sighing at how sightly he was.

He did not approach the store, though. He just stopped, out in the road, nearer the far side, and after a quick glance at the store he turned and looked at the bank building. She could not see his face then but she could imagine what thoughts might be going through his head as he stared at the empty old bank building with its broken window and its door sprung loose. I bet he is thinking, she said to herself, *Did I do that?*

He was carrying in his hands a sheaf of papers. He was wearing a light summer suit, gray-colored, with a white shirt and a necktie. He was a tall, lanky man and the suit hung loosely on him. His brown hair, even though it was greased and parted down the middle, was thick and long, even the heavy sideburns. He had not shaved this morning, and there was a stubble of beard on his strong firmly chiseled jaw. She strained her eyes to see if there was any glimmer from a gold band on his ring finger but that hand was wrapped around the sheaf of papers and she could not tell.

"I aint scared," Donny declared, and he ran out of the store and down into the road, and began talking to him.

From inside the store Latha could not hear what they were saying to each other, but her left ear was burning and that was a sure sign that somebody was talking about you.

He gave Donny a sheet of the papers he was carrying, and said something more to him, and then Donny turned and came back into the store.

"Here," he said, and gave the sheet of paper to Latha. "He wants to know if you would mind puttin this up on the store."

Latha looked at it. It had a printed photograph of him, like on the Wanted posters that the Post Office Department sent out, but underneath the photograph it said:

BROTHER EVERY BANNING DILL

EVANGELIST

Revival Meeting at *Stay More, Ark.*
Week of *July 26–Aug. 2*

EVERYBODY WELCOME!

*"Preaching the kingdom of God, and teaching those
things which concern the Lord Jesus Christ with,
all confidence, no man forbidding him."*
—*Acts 28:31*

Latha broke down and had a long fit of laughter. She couldn't hold it back, and the sound of it reached him out there in the road, and he turned his face away. Woodrow Kimber came in off the porch and asked her, "Who's that feller out there? I seen him somewheres before." Latha handed him the poster. He read it, and it took a long time for the name to register. Then he said, "Well, strike me blind! If that aint the—! Can you feature that!" Then he began hobbling quickly toward the rear door, saying, "I got to tell Bertha. She won't believe it."

Donny said, "He wants you to sell him a box of tacks so he can nail these up on trees and places, all around."

Latha, still laughing, said, "Well, if he wants to buy something he can darn well come in here and get it!"

Donny returned to the man to tell him this. The man seemed to fidget, and he said something to Donny, and Donny came back into the store and said, "He doesn't know if you want to see him or not. He says he don't want to cause you no embarrassment. Latha, he's a awful nice man."

"The only embarrassment he's causing me is standing out there in the road like a fool," she said, and then she took a deep breath and walked out onto the porch and stood on the edge of the porch and stared at him. He stared back at her for a brief moment, then he looked down at his shoes and began to kick at the dust in the road. He looked like he was about to wet his britches.

"Howdy, Preacher," she said, still laughing, but with gentle mirth, not malice.

He looked up. He started to say something, but choked. He coughed and then he said, "Howdy, Postmistress."

"Come in out of the boiling sun," she said, "before you get stroke."

"Thank you," he said and began walking toward her.

I must hold my hands at my sides, she warned herself. *I must keep them tightly against me. I must will them to stay put. I must not allow them to reach out.*

He came up into the shade of the porch, and faced her. For a moment there his hands seemed about ready to spring out and grab her, but he stuck one of them into his pocket and the other one, the one holding the posters, behind his back.

"Have a chair," she offered. She deliberately pronounced it "cheer."

49

"Thank you," he said, "but I caint stay but a minute. I've got to get these here posters tacked up all around, if you'd kindly sell me a box of tacks."

"Sure," she said. She pronounced it "shore." She went inside and got a box of tacks and brought it out to him.

"How much?" he asked, fishing in his pocket.

"A nickel."

He gave her a nickel, then he said, "I hope you'll come to the meetin too." Politely, a little formally, but still with some warmth in it.

"I haven't been to a church meeting in twenty years," she said, and he frowned, and she added, "but I'd like to hear you. Where's it going to be at?"

"Well, I don't rightly know...yet," he said. "I was wonderin who's the head deacon in charge of the meetin house, and I'll ask him for permission."

"That would be Oren Duckworth," she said.

"Oh," he said. "Well."

"But ask him anyway. He might let you."

"Well," he said.

She noticed for the first time Sonora sitting there on the porch, watching and listening, and she said, "Sonora, this is Every Dill. Every, this is my niece Sonora."

"Howdy," he said. "Barb's girl?"

"No, she's out in California and none of us have heard from her in a coon's age."

"Then..." he said, "is she Mandy's?"

"Yes."

"Mandy?" he said, and stared at the girl. "Don't favor her too much."

"Favors her dad," Latha said, and looked at him.

"Oh," he said, and stared at her some more. Then he said, "Sure has been a lot of water flowed under the bridge. I'll have a lot of catchin up to do. Well, I got to git these signs tacked up. Do you reckon you could loan me a hammer?"

"You sure travel kind of light," she said, and laughed, but

fetched him a hammer from the store. Then she walked as far as the road with him, out of earshot of the others, and she asked, "Do you suppose folks are going to let you get away with it?"

He wrinkled his fine forehead. "Get away with what?" he asked.

"*You,*" she said, "giving a revival meeting."

His face flushed. "Well, my goodness," he protested, "I've given meetings for the last eight years, in hundreds and hundreds of towns all over the—" His voice faltered, and he stopped, and he resumed in a weak voice, "Latha, could I come and talk with you?"

"Any time," she said. "*Any* old time. I've been here nearly eight years."

"See you later, then," he said. "Soon," he added, and walked away.

She tacked up his poster on the front of her store, and stood back and studied the photograph. My, he was distinguished-looking.

Sonora was looking at it over her shoulder. "I've heard Mother mention him," she said, "but I didn't know he was a preacher."

"I didn't either," Latha said.

"He's awful good-looking," Sonora said, "even with those glasses and that hair."

"He didn't used to be," Latha said.

"Is that why you never married him?"

"Maybe. I don't know."

Donny asked, "Are you going to marry him now?"

Latha laughed, and she said, "Well, not this afternoon, Dawny." Then she added, "And probably not ever." She rumpled his hair. "I'm going to just wait until you grow up."

At noon Donny went home for dinner, and the few others on the store porch got up and went home for dinner. Sonora offered to fix dinner—just some sandwiches and milk—so Latha sat on the porch alone while Sonora was back in the kitchen.

While she was there alone a man rode up on horseback.

She recognized him even before he got down off his horse.

She wanted to run and hide.

More than that, she wanted to go off into the woods with him and spend the whole afternoon making love, again and again.

He had said his name was Dolph Rivett and he had said he lived the other side of Spunkwater. Sometimes she had seen that name on the mail that she sorted out for Spunkwater.

She had told him her name was Sue McComb and she lived down below Demijohn.

Now he was saying, "Howdy. There aint any Sue McComb anywheres near Demijohn."

She did not comment on that.

"But," he said, "I figgered if I just kept lookin hard enough, I'd find you. So this is where you live, huh?"

She nodded.

"Well, Sue-or-whatever-yore-name-is, I been doin a lot of thinkin lately. Matter a fact, I aint hardly been able to think of nuthin else. And here's what I've decided: I've just got to have you. I don't keer whut it takes. I will leave my wife and kids. I will sell everthing I own. I swear, they aint nuthin on this earth that I ever liked as much as that little hour me'n you spent in that cave up on Banty Creek. I swear, they aint nuthin in this world that I want to do any more, exceptin that. I know you liked it too. I swear, they's not nuthin for me to do but have you. I mean to have you, and I aim to tear the clouds out of the sky to git you."

I am not imagining this, she realized. *He is a real man, and he is really standing there and talking to me. He is really saying what he is saying.*

SUB ONE: *Recently*

That summer you often could have gone fishing, Bug, not because the sport of it held any particular fascination for you, nor even because the fish supplemented your larder (although you have confessed to a weakness for sunperch fried in cornmeal), but only because it could have been your one legitimate excuse for escaping occasionally from the store, from the town, and getting up close to the Nature which was what you loved most. In blackberry time and gooseberry time, you could have donned your old clothes (tight at the neck and wrist to keep out chiggers and ticks) and gone off with your pail on your arm and without an excuse for anyone, but berries don't come in all summer long and you could have needed another reason to tell Sonora where you were going.

Because you were required to sort mail twice a day except Saturdays and Sundays, the only time you could have gone fishing would in all likelihood have been Saturday afternoons or any time on Sunday.

It could have been a Sunday morning in late June or early July, when most God-fearing people were at church and you, Bug, could not have feared God if he had appeared in a burning bush before you and called you dirty names. It could have been that you rose just before dawn and quickly tended your chores then dug a bucket of redworms out of the compost pile and pulled your cane pole out from under the porch and took off, up the creek. It could have been Banty Creek that you chose, because there were a couple of deep holes in deep-forested timber up below the south side of Dinsmore Mountain.

You could have taken your time getting there, because you liked to stop and identify the wildflowers. You could have known them all by name: Beebalm, Mallow, Lady Slipper, Bouncing Bet, Fleabane, Loose Strife, Bluecurls, Lobelia, Dayflower, Mullein, Saxifrage, Bedstraw—you might have known a hundred other names. You could never have picked one.

It might have neared seven o'clock before you finally reached that one cove of stream known as Ole Bottomless. Previously some time ago you could have touched bottom yourself to give the name the lie—it was from five to six feet deep almost everywhere except for one small drop-off that went down to about twelve feet. You could have unwound your line and baited your hook and thrown—

No, probably first if the morning was warm and you felt like it you could have taken off your shirt and jeans and plunged into the—But if you had done that it might have scared the fish off and besides if all you wanted to do was swim you could have done it in the privacy of Swains Greek right behind your own garden.

So you could have begun fishing right away, and because of the time of the day the fish would have been hungry and you could have caught, say, five sunperch, three crappie, two catfish and a trout within the space of an hour, as well as several redtails and hogsuckers which you threw back in.

For a stringer, you could have taken your jackknife and stripped a thin branch from a sapling and sliced the bark off of it. While you were doing this you could have leaned your back against the sapling and have been a little amazed to notice how the sapling quivered with your body, and it could have made you feel very much like a live, live thing. You could have strung the fish on that branch and kept them cool and alive in the water.

Sometime around eight o'clock the man could have come downstream, carrying his fine store-bought rod and reel and his tackle box. A dog could have followed him, a mongrel whelp, black and tan.

"Why, howdy do, ma'am," he could have said, surprised to find you there fishing, because it is a very rare thing for a grown woman to be found fishing in these hills, let alone a grown woman all alone. Fishing is the preserve primarily of young boys and an occasional grown man. You, Bug, would have been the first grown woman fishing he had ever come across.

And you could have returned his greeting, saying, "Howdy do, sir," but more likely you would not have. More likely you could have simply smiled and kept on fishing. Voices scare the fish away. *Fish in silence, get plenty; fish talking, don't get any.*

Then he could have stepped to the edge of the bank and pulled up your sapling branch and taken a look at your string and exclaimed, "My, my, what a purty mess of fish! What you usin for bait?"

"Worms," you could have replied.

"Well now, that shore is one of the purtiest mess of fish I ever seen," he could have continued, lowering the string back into the water. "All I got is spinners and flies, no live bait, but we'll just see if them fishes is in the mood for teasin. I do hope you don't keer, ma'am, if I just throw my line in there too."

You could have shaken your head to signify that you did not mind his sharing the pool with you. Your feeling might have been that you had caught enough fish already and perhaps had even been on the verge of leaving when this man showed up. You might still have been planning to get up and go at any moment, but something could have been holding you back.

The man could have lashed his rod and cast his lure way out to the far edge of the pool and have slowly begun retrieving it, while you could have been slyly scrutinizing him. He could have appeared to you to be tall, sturdy, obviously a hard-working farmer, with skin browned and wrinkled by the sun, and a sun-bleached shock of light hair, and small eyes the color of mockingbird's eggs. He might have been about your own age, which could have been 38; possibly he might have been a year or two younger.

He could not have had much luck; you could have had told him that, that these Banty Creek fish in Ole Bottomless did not seem to care for any bait but worms or grasshoppers or crawdad tails. After he had failed to get a strike during his first ten minutes of fishing, you could have given him a worm. He could have at first rejected it, but then have accepted it.

"Aw heck, I aint never fished this creek afore," he could have said, as if that explained something. Then, casting the worm and letting it sink, he could have turned his glance on you and asked, "You live roundabouts?"

Now you could have been asking yourself why you had decided to lie to him. You could have shaken your head and have answered, "No, I'm from down towards Demijohn." *Now why did I tell him that?* you could have wondered immediately, *Why didn't I just tell him that I'm the Stay More postmistress?*

"Demijohn," he could have responded. "Well, now, I caint say I know anybody from that part of the country, though I've been there a time or two. I'm from up beyond Spunkwater myself. You know whar that's at?"

"I've been there a time or two," you could have answered, truthfully.

"Dolph Rivett's my name," he could have offered.

"Sue McComb's mine," you could have returned, and could have said to yourself, *There! Now I know I'm lying.*

"Mighty pleased to meetcha, Miz McComb," he could have said, and added, "It is 'Miz,' I reckon."

"Miss," you could have corrected him, and in all the trees all kinds of birds could have been singing.

"Do tell?" he could have remarked, beaming. "Why, how come such a keen-lookin gal like yoreself happened to turn out a maiden lady?"

You would not have liked that expression, "maiden lady," although you would have preferred it to "spinster" or "lone woman" or even to "bachelor girl," and you could have felt vaguely grateful for his tact.

"Nobody ever asked me," you could have lied to him.

"Aw, I aint about to swaller *that*," he could have objected. "Such a peachy dream as you, them fellers down to Demijohn must all be old men or else their eyes is all on the wrong side of their heads."

"They are just all already married," you could have pointed out and have added, "like you."

"Why—!" he could have exclaimed. "What gives you the idee I'm married?"

"I haven't yet met a good-looking man who wasn't."

He might have blushed and have asked, "You think I'm good-looking?"

"Oh, yes indeed," you could have affirmed, but have cautioned yourself, *Easy, girl. You are supposed to let him do the courting.*

He would have blushed even deeper, and coughed, and hemmed and hawed, and said, "Well, let me tell you something, honey, and I don't keer if you believe it or not, but *you* are the most scrumdidliumptuous lookin creature I ever seen in all my born days."

You could have laughed at length and have said, "Nobody ever called me that before."

And he could have joined your laughter and have said, "Well, they just aint any words. You're cute as a bug's ear."

So saying, he, Bug, would have been the first to sense your bugness.

You could have liked him from the word go. Whether he was married or not—and that could not have mattered anyway because you could have been lying to him—you could have sensed something in the simple kinship of the situation: that he and you alone could have happened to be fishing at this spot on this morning when all God-fearing people were getting ready to go to church.

There would have been an easiness about him that could have helped you feel at ease. This would have been important. For you could have begun to entertain a thought, a thought so serious that the only way to tinker with it would have been with easiness.

Your problem, Bug, your long-standing and nearly hopeless problem could have been this: that being a woman, and a woman still relatively young, you possessed a woman's body, and a woman's reproductive system with all its nerves in full function, a woman's sex and a woman's (no *average* woman's, granted) desire, and capacity for passion. It had gotten you into difficulties in the past…the distant past. Now, what opportunities could there have been in Stay More? Tearle Ingledew, one night when he was so drunk that he would mercifully have forgotten it the next morning had slipped his hand up your dress and toyed briefly with your pudendum. Colvin Swain, after writing out a prescription for some anodyne to help you sleep better, one time, had questioned you in a halting and roundabout manner as to whether or not your life had enough "satisfaction" and then he had taken a heavy swallow of some nerve-giving medicine and announced, "By God, Latha, I may be gittin on in years but I swear I can still coax a respectable stand out of the ole dingbat down here, so if there ever comes a time when you feel like you just got to have it, then I'll gladly be at your service." But the effort of this announcement had cost him so much—he grew red as a beet all over and had a terrible coughing fit—that you never got a chance to answer him, even if you had been able to.

Oren Duckworth had tried for two years to seduce you, but had given up several years ago. Shy, homely Stanfield Ingledew had broached the subject in a very tentative and inconclusive way. Six assorted drummers, two traveling salesmen, a county road agent, and three random "tourists" had all, within the last eight years, flirted with you with intercourse as their object.

Had you submitted to any of these, Bug, you might well have

achieved some of that "satisfaction" that Doc Swain had alluded to, but the price you would have paid for it would have been the disrepute of a "loose woman" and all the concomitant opprobrium that would have ruined you as far as Stay More was concerned.

A man who needed it badly could have gone up to Eureka Springs and bought it at a whorehouse. There was nothing anywhere for sale for women, and even if there had been you could not have paid cash money for it, Bug.

The only way open to you, and this is what you could have been thinking about on this morning at Ole Bottomless, would be a chance encounter with a stranger in some remote place, under an assumed name, so there would never be any fear that he might tell on you or that anyone might ever trace it to you if he did. This situation, now, this meeting with Dolph Rivett, could have been virtually perfect—the answer, if you'll pardon the expression, Bug, to a maiden's prayer.

It has been so *long!* you could have been shouting to yourself. *I can't even remember what it's like.*

Dolph Rivett, by this time, could have seemed to have lost his interest in fishing, and could have appeared to have been more interested in talk, a loose, easy, bantering kind of chitchat.

"I declare," he could have remarked, with a wink in his voice if not in his eye, "aint you a little bit skeered to be way out here in the woods all by yoreself?"

"No more scared than you," you could have rejoined.

"Some old goat might could come along and try to lead you astray."

"I expect he'd find me hard to *lead.*"

"Never kin tell when there might be one of these here *sex fiends* a-runnin around loose."

"Life is full of dangers."

"Why, for all you might know, I might even be one of them myself."

"You sure don't much look like one."

"Caint never tell. Them that don't look it is probably the most likely."

"Do you *feel* like a sex fiend?"

"Well, by nature I gen'rally feel pretty harmless, but any man would get to feelin kinda roosterish after lookin at you long enough."

"Now that's too bad, because roosters can't last more than a poke or two."

He would have blushed, but have said, "Haw! I happen to know one particular rooster who kin shore last a lot longer than that."

"Braggart," you could have teased.

"I'd be right glad to prove it to you."

Your wit could not have come up with a good retort for that.

"How about it?" he could have asked, no longer joking, and you would have had to say something to that.

"Fast, aren't you?" you could have managed finally.

"Thank you. Folks up home is always sayin that Dolph Rivett is slow as molasses in January."

You might have been desiring to say, *"Then let's see if you can be slow enough for you and fast enough for me!" Why am I being coy?* you could have been asking yourself, in view of your decision to go through with it. What did it matter? Perhaps you simply could not have wanted to seem too easy. Or perhaps there could have been still some reservation in your mind, which, however, would have been dispelled when you now remembered that it had only been the night before when Sonora came home and confessed to you that she had lost her virginity and you, after assuring yourself that the girl was smart enough to have been careful against the possibility of impregnation, had received from her a rather frank sketch of the experience, which not only had cemented forever a bond between the two of you but also had left you feeling for the first time envious of her youth and position and popularity.

"All right," you could have said.

He could have looked at you strangely, not understanding, uncertain, and then have asked, "All right *what?*"

"All right prove it."

"You honestly mean it?"

You could have nodded.

"You mean…" he would have been suddenly uncomfortable, not expecting you to give in so readily "…you mean me and you…I hope you understand what I'm talkin about…now do you honestly mean that it's all right with you if I…if you would…if me and you were to…to sleep…"

"Not sleep."

"Naw, I mean…you know…"

"I know."

He could have stared at you for another moment, and then asked, "You're not a…you aint…you've done it before, have you?"

You could have nodded.

"I—" his voice would have been apologetic, "I aint got no…none of them…them things, you know, them safes…you know, them rubber—"

"It's all right," you could have assured him.

"Are you sure?" he could have persisted. "If you wanted me to I could…I could…stop beforehand…before…the seed…"

"I just finished my monthlies," you could have prevaricated.

"Well now, that's just jim dandy," he could have said, beaming, and begun to look around him, as if looking for a nice spot to do it on. He would not have noticed that a fish had taken his bait and was pulling it down into a hole at the bottom of Ole Bottomless.

"You've got a bite," you could not have helped pointing out to him.

"Huh?" he could have said, a little panicky, perhaps thinking you had made some accusation which precluded the anticipated tumble.

"There," you could have said, pointing out the line being unreeled and disappearing into the water.

"Shoot fire!" he could have exclaimed, and grabbed up his rod and begun reeling it in. After a minute's work, a large fish could have appeared at the surface, a gollywhopper, the biggest catfish you'd ever seen, thrashing around and trying to pop the hook loose from its lip. Dolph Rivett would have been as a man torn. He would have wanted to land that prize cat, but have feared that during the several long minutes it took him to play the fish out you might change your mind. You could have been tempted to assure him, *"Take your time. We've got all morning,"* but somehow this would not have seemed a decent thing to say.

Dolph Rivett could not have taken his time. "Aw dad hackle it," he could have said, and jerked the line hard in order to remove the hook from the fish's mouth. "What's a ole fish at a time like this?"

He could have reeled in his line and have put down the rod, and have asked you, "What about that willow thicket over there?"

You could have shaken your head. "The chiggers'd chew us alive." Then you could have pointed up at a ledge on the side of the mountain, "There's a little cave up there," but have regretted this: being from Demijohn, you would not have been supposed to have been familiar with the local terrain.

"Just lead me to it!" he could have enthused.

The two of you could have climbed up to the ridge, a hundred feet above the creek, and walked along beneath the overhanging ledge until you came to what was not actually a cave so much as a nook, a recession in the rock where ancient Bluff Dwellers had a shelter. The dirt floor of this cavern was still littered with the fragmented relics of this strange non-Indian tribe that had owned the Ozarks in the time of Christ. With his foot Dolph could have swept an area clean of bones and shards.

His black and tan mongrel could have followed you. "Go tree a bird!" Dolph could have commanded it, but it could have sat firmly on its haunches with its head cocked to one side, curiously watching these two crazy people. You would not have minded, but Dolph would have, and eventually he could have thrown a piece of 2000-year-old pottery at it, and have hit it, and it could have yelped and dragged itself out of sight.

You could have unbuckled your belt and unbuttoned your jeans and sat down on the dirt floor to tug them off your legs, and then have sat upon them as a mat of sorts.

The light in the cavern would have been dim, but not dark, not really dark enough. For this reason, Dolph Rivett could not have removed his trousers; he merely could have unbuttoned his fly.

You could have had a fleeting glimpse of his privates before he knelt before you: one of the heavy hirsute stones would have been still inside the fly, the bolt swollen and bolt upright, taut and straining.

He would not have bothered with any preliminaries, assuming you were already aroused and ready. The sight of his equipment would have anointed your passage with some erotic dew, but not enough, not enough to ease his sudden hard deep entrance.

It could have hurt. You might even have cried out. It would have had been so long since you last harbored a bloated penis within you that there simply would not have been room.

He could have stopped. But only for a moment. Yet a moment of welcome respite that would have given you time to expand and to lust and to seep.

Then he, having groaned repeatedly and having mumbled "Ah, Lord Jesus," could have begun to pump, from the first stroke driving at full speed, an unvarying tempo of banging jolts. You, Bug, would have wanted to churn in response, but because of his weight upon you and the hard earthen floor beneath you you could not have. So all the work would have been his.

And he could not have lasted very long. Just as you could have begun to hope that you might be plugged to that peak from which you could soar free, he, crooning "Goody" to the beat of each shuddering sock, could have disgorged his gob into you, you would have been able to feel the pulsing spasms of the unloading, the throbs shortening and weakening, until there was no movement or sound remaining but his breathlessness.

He could have rolled off of you, and lay by your side.

After a while, you could have said, not bitter nor even teasing, but dispassionate: "Rooster."

"I beg pardon, Sue," he could have responded. "I reckon I just had it stored up too much."

Then he would have talked to you about his wife, who, it seemed, would only let him "bother" her about twice a year.

The two of you could have lounged for a while on the dirt floor of that rock shelter, talking to each other about yourselves. You would not have learned much of consequence.

Then you could have talked, idly, about various things. He

could even have talked about politics. "I been readin in the papers about this here D.A. feller up to Noo Yark, fergit his name, but they say he could shore give old Franklin D. a run fer his money."

"Dewey," you could have said.

"Yeah, that's the one. I heerd tell that one of them gallop polls says that Dewey'd git 52 per cent of the vote right now. 'Course, I've voted Democrat all my life."

By and by, Bug, you could have impulsively reached out and wrapped your fingers around his drooping piece. It would have been what you thought was the first time you had ever touched one. And because it would also have been what you thought was the first time you ever had an opportunity to take a good look at one in the light of day, you could have begun to study it while you fondled it. He would have been fidgety at first, because it would have been the first time anyone had ever fondled, let alone studied, his member. But then he would have become less fidgety and more fiery as he felt himself beginning to stir beneath your touch.

You could have been thinking that it was a durn shame that society compelled a man to keep his genitals always covered, because there was something uniquely handsome about a smooth, sleek, sinewy, tall-standing stalk of healthily pink flesh. There was a carnal grandeur about it unequaled by any of Nature's other deliberate inventions.

And you could not have needed to have told him that you needed it.

He could have started to bestraddle you again but you would have asked him if he didn't mind taking off his pants. Blushing deeply, he would have.

Then he would have been into you again, and this time, because there was no great pent-up gism thrashing to break loose, he could have lasted a good bit longer, his strokes steady and not quite so violent—a mechanical piston, a skin-sheathed ramrod. If you could have bothered to have counted, you would have found that he kept this up for nearly three minutes before reaching that point where he quickened, and his breathing began to puff "Goody, goody, goody" to the beat of his beats, and your cinctures expanded and contracted with the throbbing of his spewing.

But this time, when he rolled off of you, you could have rolled with him and have pinned him down and have climbed aboard, and in the brief minute left to you before his magic wand lost its turgid magic you could have ridden upon him, tilting and pitching your hips, fashioning your own elaborate alternating measure, with irregular stresses that sung a cadence of touch and sensation your strings could be moved by. You would have been so busy constructing this great resplendent convulsion that you would not have noticed that Dolph Rivett could have been beginning to say "Goody goody" again. All that you could have been conscious of, as you closed your eyes and wildly wrenched your bottom, was the surge of your substance merging with all nature, while in the background the cockles of your heart rollicked and roistered. I confess, Bug, it gives me one just to think of yours.

When you could have come to, some time later, you would have found that Dolph had soaked his handkerchief in cold creek water and spread it over your brow and was fanning you with a frond of fern.

"Why, I declare, Sue, darlin," he could have declared when you opened your eyes, "if you didn't just pass plumb dead out. Give me kind of a skeer. But, boy golly, I liked to of passed out myself."

You could have risen and put your jeans back on, and have gone down to the creek and found a spot along the bank where a spring flowed into it, and have cupped your hands and lapped up a refreshing drink.

"You know somethin?" Dolph, at your side, could have said, "That there was the first time in my life I ever let off even twice, let alone *three* times. Holy snakes! Who would a guessed I had it in me?"

You could have retrieved your fishing pole and your catch, and then have asked him a test question: "I wonder how far it is from here to Stay More?"

"Couldn't rightly tell," he could have replied, to your relief. "If we was up on the road I might could spot a landmark, but it's hard to say from here. I reckon it aint more'n maybe three, four mile at the most. You aimin to head that way?"

"No, I'm just going on back over the mountain to Demijohn."

"Sue...could I...I got me a horse...could I sometime maybe ride down to Demijohn to see you?"

You could have pretended shock. "Lord have mercy! Dolph, my daddy and my six brothers would shoot you on sight if they even caught you talking to me!"

"Well." He would have seemed dejected for a moment but then have brightened. "Is there any chance you might be comin back here fishin again?"

"More than likely," you could have replied.

"Then maybe me'n you might could...might could *get together* again.

"Sure."

"Then I'll be lookin fer ye, Sue. I shore am much obliged. You'll never know what a good turn you did me."

Then he would have been gone, and you could have heard him off up the creek whistling for his dog.

You could have started home, reflecting, *But he didn't even kiss me.*

TWO: *Noon*

WRIRRRIRRAAANG! sounded the screen door, and Sonora came out, carrying a plate of chicken-salad sandwiches and two glasses of milk. She gave her a glass and a sandwich, and then, because it is very rude not to offer something to another person present, even a stranger, she held out the plate to him.

"Thank you kindly, I aint et since five this mornin," he said and took a sandwich from the plate and bit a large bite out of it and studied Sonora while he was chewing.

"This is my daughter," Latha said.

He chewed quickly and swallowed down the bite half-chewed. "You tole me you wasn't married," he said.

"Reckon I must've been telling you one."

"Miss…" he said to the girl, "…would ye mind too awful much if me and yore Maw had a couple words private?"

"That depends," said Sonora.

"'Pends on what?" he asked.

"'Pends on whether them two words is nice or nasty."

"I promise ye, gal, they'll be nice as I kin make em."

"'Maw,'" said Sonora to her with a smile, "you want me to leave?"

"Just for a minute or two, hon," she said, "if you don't mind."

"Okay," said Sonora, and took her glass of milk and her sandwich and went back into the house.

"Now," Dolph said, as soon as the girl was out of sight, "kindly tell me: whar's yore man?"

"He's working over at the canning factory," she answered.

"I'd be pleased to meet him," he said challengingly.

"He'd make worm food out of you so fast you wouldn't know it."

"Naw, now, I don't 'low he would. Leastways, not 'less you'd done already tole him bout me'n you, and I reckon you wouldn't never a done that or else you'd already be worm food yoreself. I figger yo're smart enough not to tell him, 'less you aim to persuade him I raped ye." He paused and took a deep breath and then resumed, speaking rapidly. "But even if you had tole him, he'd never whup me with his bare hands, he'd have to use a gun, and if he did that I wouldn't keer, because I'd just as soon be daid as not to have you. But may be I could persuade him anyway, if you'd just tell me where to find him. But maybe he aint even there. Because maybe he just *aint.*"

"Don't you be talking such foolishness, Dolph Rivett," she said sternly. "I'm a respectable married woman and here you are coming around to try and start a scandal and I won't stand for it. Now you just go right back where you came from."

"No, honey, I reckon I caint do that. I been roamin around these hills for the last week or more, looking for you, and now I've found you I aint gonna quit so easy. I shore don't aim to go home. I've seen all I'm gonna see of that wife of mine. So I will just tell you plain: I aim to have you for my own, and if I caint git you then I'm better off daid. Now'f you'll just kindly tell me whar that cannin factry's at...."

"Just right up the creek there and take the first road to your right."

"Thank you. Now, you mind tellin me yore man's name?"

She thought. What would his name be? Then she thought of something and smiled and said, "Luther Chism."

"And yore real name aint Sue, but—"

"Sarah."

"Thank you. And yore gal's name is—"

"Lucy."

He climbed on his horse. "Well, Sarah, my darlin, I will see you later, or else you will see me later, in a coffin." He began to ride away.

"Don't be a fool, Dolph!" she yelled after him. "Don't do anything rash!"

He kept on riding away. She did not watch him ride out of sight. It is bad luck to do so, to watch somebody go out of sight. Sometimes it means that person will die.

But would he die? Of course not. She smiled as she envisioned the scene;

"Which one of you fellers is Luther Chism?"

"Whut d'ye keer to know fer?"

"I'd just keer to know, just lak to ast him a question or two."

"Mister, if yo're another revenuer, I kin tell ye y'aint gonna leave this valley alive."

"Sheeut far, do I look lak a revenuer to you fellers?"

"I seen all kinds of lookin revenuers. You caint never tell. I seen a old lady schoolteacher who was a secrit revenuer."

"Boys, I swear on a pile of Bibles, I aint no revenuer. I'd jist lak to ast Luther Chism a question or two, and it aint got nuthin to do about no moonshine or nuthin. Strak me daid if I'm a revenuer."

"We will strak ye daid."

"Lord tear my tongue out if I'm lyin to you boys."

"All right, mister, I'm Luther Chism. Whut d'ye aim to ast me?"

"Sir, hav ye got a black-haired wife name of Sarah?"

"Yeah, I happen to. Whut about her?"

"Hev ye also got a growed daughter name of Lucy?"

"That's right. Whut about her?"

"Then yo're the feller I'm a-lookin fer."

"Mister, if ye've went and got Lucy inter trouble, I'll—"

"Naw, naw, this don't concern her."

"What are you laughing about, Latha?" asked Sonora.

"Him," she replied.

"What did he want with you?"

"Oh, he's just another one of those cagey fellows with snatch on his mind," she said, and both of them laughed.

"Is that why you told him I was your daughter?"

"Yes, and it worked."

"Did you have much trouble getting rid of him?"

"Not much."

"I *am* your daughter, aren't I, Latha?"

"Why land sakes, honey! What makes you say that? Just because I told that feller—"

"I don't much favor Mother at all. I look a lot more like you than like her."

"My goodness, that doesn't mean anything! Why, I favor my Aunt Robie more than my mother, but that doesn't mean I ever thought Aunt Robie was my mother. Whatever put such a notion in your head?"

"I don't know. I've just been thinking. Folks say I resemble Daddy, but I don't especially think so. Gee, I don't look any more like him than like...like...like somebody like that fellow Every Dill!"

"Now, Sonora! People can't help who they look like. You're a very, very pretty girl, and it might be a wonder how Mandy and Vaughn Twichell could have such a pretty girl, but you ought to just let it go at that."

"How come I don't have any brothers or sisters?"

"Hasn't your mother ever told you?"

"Never a word."

"Well, when you were born it was a bad delivery so the doctor tied up your mother's tubes so she couldn't have any more children, for fear they couldn't've been delivered."

"Well, okay, but how come Daddy's first wife didn't have any children?"

"I didn't realize you knew your father'd been married before."

"I found some old letters."

"Well, you nosy kitten, I reckon you're going to find out every-thing by and by."

"Will I find out who my real mother is?"

"Mandy Twichell is your real mother."

"Will you look me in the eye and swear that you are not my mother?"

"I will look you in your eye and swear that I am not your mother."

"Cross your heart and hope to die?"

"Sonora, what's got into you? Your mother would be hurt if she could hear you talking like this."

"I think she *can* hear me talking like this, and she does not look very hurt," Sonora said, and then she turned on her heel and went back into the house.

My, my, thought Latha, *what could I say?*

A while later Luther Chism walked up and asked, "Store open?"

"Just finished my dinner," said Latha.

"Need me a bag a Bull Durham," he said.

She got it for him and made change for his quarter.

He stood on the porch and rolled a cigarette and lit it.

"How's things over to the factory?" she asked.

"Slow. Aint many termaters been comin in today," he said. He took his cigarette out of his mouth and frowned at it for a while. Then he said, "Latha, you happen to know any fellers named Rivett, any chance?"

"I might," she said.

He shook his head, back and forth. "Funniest durn thing," he said. "We'uns was sittin under a tree over to the cannin factry just a little while ago, eatin our dinner, when this here stranger rode up. He got off his horse and ast which one of us was me. Said he wanted to ast me some questions. Well, we took him fer a revenuer at first, but I figgered I'd jist find out what he wanted. So I tole him who I was. And he ast me did I have a wife named Sarah, and I says yes. And you'd never believe whut that feller said then!"

"I can imagine," she said.

Luther stared at her. "You mean you put him up to it?"

"I wouldn't say it like that. Anyway, just tell me: what happened to him? What did he do?"

"Well, one of the boys said to Bob Witter, he said, 'Bob, you git in yore car and ride over to Parthenon and tell em to let you use the telephone, and you telephone the state loony bin and tell em to git up here quick, cause we've caught us a feller who thinks he's fell for ole Sarey Chism!' And everybody just belly-laughin fit to bust a gut.

"And this feller got right pervoked, and he says, 'I don't aim to let nary man make fun out a my true love, and I'll whup ye one at a time or all put together, come on, ye bastuds, and put up yore dukes.'

"Well, some of the boys was about to take him up on it, but that'ud spiled the fun. Most of em was jist hollerin, 'True Love! True Love!' in prissy voices. And Fent Bullen was a-slappin me on the back and sayin 'Aw, come on, Luther, and be a sport. Give ole Sarey to this feller. You've had her long enough.' And other boys sayin 'Charge him fifty dollars!' and 'Swap him for his horse and saddle!'

"Well, I got that stranger calmed down and tole him none of us wanted to fight with him, and then I ast him, 'Mister, jist tell me, how long has this been goin on?' And that set all the boys to splittin their sides again.

"And he says aint been nuthin goin on. And I says, 'Well, mayhap ye jist seen her ridin by on her mule and was smitten at fiist sight?"

"He says naw, he'd jist seen her twice, wunst up fishin on Banty Creek and wunst just now on the storeporch.

"So I knew fer sartin right then and there that it warn't nuthin but a bad case of mistook identity. Fer one thing Sarey aint never been fishin on Banty Creek, leastways not that I ever knowed about, and fer another thing she'd have no business to be on no storeporch today. So I says to the feller, 'Would ye mind tellin me what this Sarey a yourn looks lak?'

"He got plump rapcherous. 'She's got eyes like a startled doe's,' says he, 'and a mouth like a pink morning-glory just openin, and hair like the smoke in a kerosene lantern, and she's nearly tall as me and built like a young cat.'"

Luther Chism chuckled and flicked tears from his eyes. "Well, I tell ye, I said to him, 'Mister, I know of jist one gal hereabouts who'd fit that description, but it sho aint Sarey. My Sarey's got eyes like a sow's, and a mouth like a dried persimmon, and hair like a black rooster a-sittin atop her haid, and she's half as short as you and built like a brick outhouse.'

"Well, by this time I figgered that pore feller had reckoned somebody'd put him on a false trail, and he says, sour-like, 'Thank you. I'm sorry to've bothered ye.' Then he turned and got on his horse. Then he ast me, 'Could I trouble ye to tell me the name of that one you mentioned that fits the description?'

"'I could, but I won't,' I says to him.

"'Thank you, anyhow,' says he. 'I reckon I kin find it out someway.' Then he spurred his horse and rid off. But he didn't turn his horse down this way. Headed up the creek. So I come right on over to see if you was the one he had in mind."

"Guess I am," she said.

"Well, if he shows his head again, you just let me know, and I'll round up the boys and run him clean out a the country."

"Thank you, Luther. I just might have to do that."

He turned to go, but turned back again. "Say!" he said. "Did ye know who's all of a sudden turned up again?"

She pointed at his poster tacked on her store.

"Yeah," Luther said. "He come and put one up on the cannin factry this mornin. Everbody over there aint stopped talkin about it since. What do you make of it?"

She shrugged. "He's the last person I would have taken for a preacher."

"Yeah, that's what I been thinkin." He moved closer and lowered his voice, although there was nobody around. "You don't suppose he might could be a revenuer?"

"It wouldn't surprise me as much as him being a preacher."

"Hmmm," said Luther. "We'll have to keep a sharp eye peeled.

Every always was kind of ornery and standoffish, just like his dad. Them Dills never did seem like true Stay More folks."

"Nobody ever gave them much of a chance to."

Luther was squinting out at the road. "Speak a the Devil!" he said. "Yonder he comes."

Down the road Every came walking, holding the hammer she'd loaned him. He approached the store, and stopped at the steps and looked up at them. "Howdy, Luther," he said.

"Howdy, Ev. We was just talkin about you."

"Nothing bad, I hope."

"Not exactly. Just been wonderin if yo're really a genuine preacher or not."

"Well, Luther, actually I'm a special agent of the United States Revenue Office, and they sent me out to find one of our men that you've got locked up in your smokehouse."

Luther turned purple and his legs gave away and he sat down on a chicken crate. "Great jumping Jehoshaphat!" he croaked.

Every smiled. He pointed the hammer at Luther and said, "This here Colt revolver is loaded and ready. Will you come along peaceable or do I have to shoot you?" he laughed.

"Dangdarn ye, you varmint! Are you a-pullin my laig?"

Every reached out and pulled his leg.

"But dadblank it all!" said Luther. "How did you know I got a revenuer in my smokehouse?"

"Everybody knows it. You told Fent Bullen and he told Bob Witter and he told Lawlor Coe and he told somebody else who told his wife who told me."

"Dodgast that Fent Bullen! I got a mine to go wring his neck."

"What are you going to do with your revenuer, Luther? Train him to tree squirrels?"

"I'm still studying on it. I aint figgered out nuthin yet."

"Why don't you bring him with you to my revival meeting tomorrow?"

"I aint a-comin myself."

"Why, Luther, you yourself just said you were wondering if I'm a genuine preacher or not. Why don't you just come and find out. I might even save your soul for you."

"You just might even try to talk me out of moonshinin, mightn't ye?"

"Why, no, that aint part of my business, Luther. I hear tell you make some of the finest whiskey to be found. I imagine you'd rather die than make a run of bad whiskey, am I right?"

"You bet yore boots."

"I really doubt that anybody's ever got fusel-oil poisoning from drinking your whiskey, have they?"

"Nary a soul."

"If I were a drinking man, I'd even be mighty proud to be your customer myself."

"Aw shucks, preacher, I aint all that good."

"Making pure whiskey's your business, Luther, and making pure souls is mine. If I would go to you for whiskey, you ought to come to me for religion."

"Well, uh, look, I got to git back to the cannin factry," Luther said, and began walking away. "I just might," he said. "I just might come, Brother Dill." He went on off.

Every called after him, "Tie a collar on your revenuer and bring him along!"

Latha, laughing, remarked, "If you can get religion into Luther Chism, you might even get it into me."

He smiled. "I'd sure like to try."

"Pull you up a chair," she offered.

They sat together on the porch, he in the straight-backed chair, she in the rocker. A long moment of silence drifted by. Then he clapped his hands together, once, and said, "Well, well, well." Another moment of silence passed before he said, "Sure has been a right smart spell." Then he turned to her and said, "I'll swear, Latha, I'm pleased as punch to see you looking so good. You haven't changed a smidgin." At length he asked, "How you been?"

"Tolerable," she said with a smile, pronouncing it "tobble." "How've you been, Every?"

"Tobble too," he said. "I've sure seen some places. Been all the way to California and back."

"And been all the way to Heaven and back too?" she said.

He looked at her, momentarily puzzled, then said, "Oh," and laughed mildly. "No, I haven't had a chance yet to inspect the Kingdom, though I've had a couple of words with the King."

"Really?" she asked.

"Believe it or not," he said.

"It is a little bit dubious," she said.

"Remind me sometime," he said, "to tell you how I got converted."

"I suspect there are a lot of things I will have to remind you to tell me how you got."

He did not comment on that. He was not looking at her but at the old ruin of the bank building across the road. "You've not changed at all," he said, "but this town sure has. This old place is sure dead on the vine." In a reminiscent tone he continued, "Last time I was through here was back in the spring of '25, and it was late at night and I didn't stay very long at all. Just made one stop. Just dropped in for a few words with Lawlor Coe." He dropped the reminiscent tone; his voice became earnest. "You recall Lawlor used to be just about my only pal back in the old days, so I didn't mind talking to him. There was only one reason I had for talking to anybody. I want you to know what that reason was, Latha. I will tell you: the only reason I come through here that night was to try and find you."

He stopped. After a while he said, quietly, "Lawlor told me they'd had you locked up down there in that state hospital for going-on three years. Three whole years. So I reckon there are a lot of things I will have to remind you to tell *me* how *you* got."

She did not comment on that.

"Latha," he said, "you and me are going to have to do an awful lot of talking, sooner or later, but there's just one thing I've got to ask you right now: are you boiling mad at me, or just plain mad at me, or just peeved at me, or what?"

She smiled. "A little bit burned, maybe."

"Well, is it just a first-degree burn that I could put some ointment on, or is it a hopeless fourth-degree burn?"

"Hard to tell, Every. It's an old burn with a lot of scar tissue grown over it."

"I will heal it," he declared. "I promise you."

"All right," she said.

"Last night…" he said. "Last night I couldn't hardly believe it when I found out you were back here again. I went up to the old home place and tried to sleep on an old pile of straw in the corner, but I couldn't. Not a wink. I swear, I had a hard enough time talking myself into coming back to Stay More in the first place, to give a meeting. But after I found out you were here, I just didn't know if I could ever get up my nerve to go and do it. I tossed and turned till the crack of dawn, and then I got up and went out into the yard and asked the Lord if He could give me any help, but He just said to me, 'Son, this is something you'll have to settle on your own. This is your Big Trial, and you'll—'"

"Horsefeathers," she said. She said that and he hushed, and she said, "Every, if you're asking me to believe that you actually heard a voice saying those words, then you are crazier than I ever was."

He looked hurt for a moment, but then he grinned and asked, "When you were down there at that state hospital, did you ever hear voices?"

"I don't recall," she said. "I suppose I did."

"I'll bet," he said, "that you even hear voices once in a while even still."

She shook her head, but he was right.

"Aw, come on, I'll bet you do," he insisted.

"Okay," she said. "So both of us are crazy."

He shook his head. "No, you don't have to be crazy to hear a voice. Now I don't mean for you to believe that I heard some actual *sound* coming out of the Lord's mouth and into my ear. I don't hold with that prodigy hokum myself. But a true Christian has got his Lord *in* him, and can talk with Him *subjectively*, in his mind or in his heart's core. Likewise, some crazy people might have the Devil in them, and hear *subjective* voices of evil."

"So you believe in Satan too?" she said.

"I believe in Evil," he said, "just as I believe in Good. I don't believe in any fiendish-looking brute running around in his red underwear with a long tail and a pitchfork, just as I don't believe in any old white-bearded Grampaw a-sittin Up Yonder on a cloud. But I believe in Forces. Powers. Causes. Agents. Movers, even if all they move is people. I believe in Light and Darkness, in Right and Wrong, in True and False, in Sickness and Health…"

"You've got it all spelled out, have you?" she said, with sarcasm, but then she softened her tone and said, "Preach to me tomorrow, Every. Go ahead and finish telling me about this little chat you were having with the Lord."

"Well, He just wanted me to know that He was trying me out on my own, that I couldn't be hanging onto His apron-strings during this particular time of trial. But He left me with the notion that He wouldn't think too highly of me if I was to back down."

"Maybe that Mover inside of you isn't the Lord," she said. "Maybe that thing talking to you was just your guilt."

He thought about that for a while. Then he asked, "How do you mean that, Latha?" There was that sudden nervousness in his voice again.

"You feel the Lord has deputized you to come and save Stay More," she said, "to save the town you nearly ruined!"

He was stricken. "You mean you—"

"I don't mean *me*," she said.

"Then I don't know what you might mean," he said.

"I think you do," she said.

Impulsively his eyes shifted to the old stone edifice across the road, and then he seemed to realize that she had caught him glancing at it, and when his eyes returned to hers they were thoroughly sheepish. He asked, "Does everybody think that I—?"

"Nobody thinks anything," she said. "Nobody even knew that you were back in town, remember?"

"Then why do *you* think it was me?"

"Think what was you?"

"Think it was me that robbed—"

"How did you know it was robbed?"

"You just said so."

"No, I didn't. I didn't say a word about it."

"Well, somebody told me, then. But why do you think it was me?"

"Good Lord, Every, who else could it have been? And even with that get-up you were in, that hood with the two eye-holes cut in it, and those outlandish clothes, I knew it was you, Every. Have you forgot it was *me* that you robbed, not just the bank? Have you forgot that *I* was the poor scared teller you held up? And even though you didn't even speak to me, even though you didn't want me to recognize your voice so you just passed me that note, I knew it was you. But I almost didn't believe you, I almost felt like testing you, to see if you really would kill me, but I figured that if you were desperate enough to hold up the bank, you were desperate enough to kill me. You would have killed me, wouldn't you have?"

"Did you ever tell anyone you thought it was me?"

"No."

"Why not? Didn't the sheriff ask you who you thought might have done it?"

"Yes, but I told him I thought it must've been some foreigner because there wasn't any resemblance to anybody I'd ever seen."

"Why'd you tell him that?"

"Why, to protect you, of course, you fool. See? That's what I did for you, after you'd gone and threatened to kill me. And you would have killed me, wouldn't you have?"

"I still haven't said it was me," he said.

"Then don't say it! Keep it a secret to your grave! I don't need you to say it, because I know it was you!"

"Shhh, Latha. No call to shout. Somebody might hear."

Quietly and wearily she asked, "Why did you do it, Every?"

"It wasn't me, Latha, Not *me*, the *me* that I *am*. Not the me that I am *now*. I'm a Christian, and a good man. That job was pulled nearly twenty years ago by a mean young hellraiser."

"All right, why'd *he* do it then?"

"Pure meanness. He hated Stay More. Those Ingledews had

already run him out of town twice, hadn't they? And after all he'd gone and done, getting in trouble with the Army and court-martialed, trying to rescue Raymond Ingledew from the Huns. And coming home to find his dad dead and finding out nobody'd even gone to the funeral. And finding the girl he'd loved all his life was still pining for Raymond that wasn't ever coming back…"

"And raping her."

"Yes, and ravishing her out of despair, and doing all kinds of mischief, and making all kinds of trouble, until the only mean thing left for him to do was take the bank's money and—"

"And go away forever."

"No. He never meant to do that. He meant to go down to Little Rock and buy an automobile and come back and get that girl."

"And why didn't he?"

"Because being a mean young hellraiser, you see, wouldn't he just have to go and get himself into a gambling game down there in Little Rock and get himself drunker than a boiled owl and lose most of his money, and get in a fight, and get picked up by the police and handed back over to the Army to serve out the rest of his court-martial that he'd broken out of Leavenworth to go back home and ravish that girl and rob that bank, and be locked up for three more years before he could break out again and go back to Stay More once again long enough to find out that she herself was locked up down in the state hospital in Little Rock."

"She broke out too," Latha said.

"Does she remember how she broke out?" he asked.

"No, she just woke up one morning and discovered that she wasn't in the state hospital but in a hotel room in Nashville, Tennessee."

"That," he announced, "was the same hotel room where that mean young hellraiser got converted into a faithful Christian."

SUB TWO: *Twenty and Eighteen Years Ago*

For a while yet, Bug, I cannot permit you to discover what he meant by that. You will find out in time. And when you find out it will heal that scar tissue which you spoke of. But until then I cannot let you love him as you had when you were a child.

He had been your first lover, we know that. His mother was a second cousin of your own mother, whose grandfather was the great-uncle of his mother, and when this old man lay dying in his home down at Demijohn, when you were only eleven and Every was twelve, you had been left at the Dill cabin one night when the grown-ups went down to Demijohn to set up with the dying man, and although you had been left in the bedroom of the cabin's east wing, separated by the dog-trot from the west wing where he was to sleep, you crossed this separation out of loneliness and fear of the night and out of curiosity, and although he was shy and awkward, just as virginal as yourself, he was just as ripe as yourself, and the two of you tried. You tried long enough, and it worked.

From then on he considered you his girl, and he planned to marry you as soon as the two of you came of age. But when your mother learned of your attachment to him, she talked you out of it. It took her a while, more than a while, but she did. The Dills, she thought (and said) were trash, even if Every's mother was her own second cousin. Every, she thought (and said), would never amount to anything. She wanted you to marry an Ingledew. Presumptuous of her, that "social climbing"—upon a ladder with so few rungs, and those broken or cracked, that it was not fit for any ascension. The Ingledews were, by and large, wealthier than most people in Stay More, since John Ingledew owned the bank, and they were certainly wealthier than the Dills, who were quite poor indeed, but I have never been able to figure out why your mother sensed any sort of social or economic strata in a town where nobody had any great wealth to speak of.

Still, Every was the closest thing to a beau you had for several years, although you had to keep it hidden from your mother. But when you started high school it was Raymond Ingledew who sat beside you on the school wagon into Jasper, you and he the only two graduates of the Stay More school to be sent into town for the last three grades. Every didn't go; instead, like most others, he went to work. Now your mother really had a reason for rating Raymond over him.

And Raymond was very good-looking, which Every had never been. But that itself was what was wrong. He was too much interested in girls to give all his attention to you. Like the fickle male lightning bug, he was all too ready to forget you whenever anybody else wearing a dress came into view. Even after he had asked you to marry him, and you had agreed, he still courted other girls. You pretended not to notice, but Every, who never gave up trying to get you back from Raymond, would make you notice; he would rub it in.

One night when Raymond was away keeping company with Wanda Dinsmore, who everybody knew was a loose girl, you, in bitter retaliation, gave yourself to Every again, for the first time in years. When Raymond found out about this, his strict double standard tore him up. He and Every had a fist fight, which did not last very long. When Raymond picked himself up, he ran off to Jasper and enlisted in the Army. You blamed yourself more than you blamed Every, but still you would not let Every become your beau again, although he tried very hard—until Raymond's brothers ganged up on him and told him he had better go and join the Army himself, or else.

They were both gone nearly two years before you saw one of them again, and the one you saw again was not the one your heart had grown fonder over the absence of.

He comes: the horse galloping madly, down the road from towards Parthenon; he jerks up on the reins and brings the horse to a stop, and is leaping down and hitching the reins to the post even before the horse can cease all its momentum. Then he takes all of the steps of the porch in one bound.

You are in the first month of your new job at the bank and you are still not accustomed to John Ingledew's habitual noontime parting, made with a grin, "Watch out for robbers"—you don't know yet just how much he means it or not, and thus, alone in the bank, you are frightened at the dashing speed with which this man arrives.

You do not know him at first. He struts boldly up to the counter, dressed in a soldier's uniform with the red chevrons of a sergeant on his sleeves, and a broad and flat-brimmed doughboy hat cocked down over his eye. He thrusts the folded note at you. With trembling hands you take it and unfold it and read it.

THIS IS A STICK-UP. FORGIT THE MUNNY, BUT HAND OVER YOURSELF. *ALL* OV IT. P.S. I LOVE YOU MOAR THEN ENYTHANG IN THE HOLE WIDE WURL.

You look up, and he is grinning big at you, and you recognize the grin before you recognize the face: the old familiar, half bashful, half-mischievous expansion of the mouth with just a thin line of the white teeth showing. You are about to exclaim his name, but instead you wad up the note and fling it at him and say, "You gave me a bad skeer. I ought to get the sheriff on you."

He holds up his hands as if you were pointing a gun at him, and says, "Aw, please, Latha, the only crime I've done was borry a horse from a feller without him knowin it so's I could come and see ye."

"Your're looking right good," you say. "How come you're wearing that fancy uniform if you're out of the service?"

"I ain't out yet," he says. "Matter of fact, I aint even on a proper furlough, but I was gittin to where I was gonna kill me a couple of majors or colonels, 'less I could come and see you."

"How'd you know I was working in the bank?"

"Mandy tole me."

"Where'd you see Mandy?"

"Well, my train ended up in Little Rock, and this buddy in my outfit was a cousin of Vaughn's and he'd given me their address, so I figgered I'd just drop by and ask her how-all you was doing."

"You tell her you were coming up here?"

"I did."

"What'd she say?"

He laughs. "Said she aimed to write Tull or Bevis and warn em I was a-comin. I aint skeered a them, though. I'd walk through hell barefoot and blindfolded to see you."

You do not smile. "I tole you last letter I sent you," you say, "that you better just put me out of your mind."

"Yeah, you did, but that was before—"

"Before what?"

"Before Raymond was listed missing."

"I don't care," you say. "He's just missing, and he'll find his way out of there one day…unless…unless, and this wouldn't surprise me a bit, unless you killed him yourself and hid his body somewheres."

"Latha," he asks, "when do you git off work? I got to talk to you."

"Four o'clock, but I won't see you then."

"How come?"

"I don't *want* to see you. Can't you get that through your big dumb head?"

"My head may be big, but it aint so dumb. It knows a few things that might be of interest to your ears."

"If you have something to say, then say it."

"Not here. Standing up like this. We got to sit down someplace private."

"I don't want to be anyplace private with you."

"Latha, why do you hate me so?"

"I don't hate you. I just don't want to have anything to do with you."

"All right," he says severely. "I'm going up to visit with Mom and Dad for a little spell. Then I'll come and talk to you. Then I'll go." He turns on his heel, a soldierly about-face, and marches out.

At four o'clock, Mr. Ingledew closes the bank, and you walk with him down to his brother Willis's post office and store, but you do not tell him that Every is back in town. It is for nothing that you withhold this information, for as soon as you arrive at the post office, Willis says to his brother, but glancing at you, "John, Tull says he got word Every Dill's coming back to town."

"No!" John Ingledew says. "Where'd he hear that?"

"A certain gal wrote him and told him she'd heard it from Every hisself."

Mr. Ingledew looks at you. "Just let us know," he says to you.

You decide not to keep it. "He's back, all right," you say. "He came in the bank at noontime while you were out."

"No," says Mr. Ingledew.

"Aint he got a nerve, though?" says Willis Ingledew.

"What'd he do? What'd he say to you?" Mr. Ingledew asks.

"I reckon he's still after me," you tell him.

"That bodacious rasper!" says Willis. "He wouldn't dast!"

"What'd you tell him, girl?" Mr. Ingledew asks.

"Told him he was wasting his time," you say.

"Where's he now?" Mr. Ingledew asks.

"Said he was going up to visit his folks."

"Come on, Willis!" he says to his brother. "Where's the boys?"

"I don't know. Over to the mill, maybe."

"Never mind em, then. Me'n you's enough."

"Lola!" Willis hollers. "Mind the store, I got to go out."

They stalk off up the road at a brisk pace, and after a moment you follow. You are going that way anyway; it is necessary to pass the Dill place to reach your own house. But that alone is not why you are following. There is an imp of perversity in you, Bug, that makes you want to witness the confrontation between these two angry men and Every. *Well,* you say, justifying it to yourself, *if I can't make him go away and leave me alone, then somebody else has got to do it for me.*

The Dill place is a wattle-and-daub log cabin of two rooms connected by a dogtrot, set back up on the hill a short way from the small clapboard shop on the road where William Dill makes and repairs wagons. The cabin is nearly choked up by a lush growth of vines and trees surrounding it. The two men pause at the shop and, finding no one there, head on up toward the house. You leave the road and cut through the woods, to eavesdrop from the side of the house without being seen.

Old Billy Dill and his ugly wife and son are sitting together in the dogtrot.

Mr. Ingledew addresses them. "Howdy."

"Howdy, John. Howdy, Willis," Billy Dill says. "What brings y'all way up to my digs?"

"*Him,*" Mr. Ingledew says. "What's he doing here?"

"Wal," Billy says, "I caint see none too good 'thout my specs, but looks to me lak he's jest lollygaggin thar and airin his heels."

"Don't ye trifle with us, Billy," Willis Ingledew says. "Whut'd he come back to Stay More fer?"

"Damn 'f I know, really now," Billy says. "Reckon maybe the durn idjit got some fool notion ter drap in and see if his ole folks was still above ground."

"I got a powerful hunch," says Willis, "that his ole folks aint the main party he's interested in. I got a idee he's maybe sniffin around after a sartin gal, and me'n John is wonderin if he aint complete disremembered that that gal belongs to John's boy."

"She caint belong to no boy who's six feet under," Billy says. "John, when you gonna git that through yore noodle?"

"I don't feature that," John says. "Aint nobody said he was officially dead. For all anybody knows, he could still be in some hospital over there, banged up bad maybe but still kicking. I don't aim to hold with him being dead till I git the word from Uncle Sam."

Every speaks up. "Might have to wait forever for that, Mr. Ingledew."

John's voice bristles. "Then by God I'll wait forever, but I shore don't aim to 'low no unprincipled cur-dawg to swoop down like a vulture the minute Raymond's gone and try to take his bride away!"

"Why'ntcha lock er up in yore bank vault, John?" Billy says. "That way ye'd keep her a ole maid till the Judgment Day when her and Raymond could finally tie the knot."

"I don't have to take no sass off you, Billy Dill!" John says. "You're fergittin somethin I already got in my bank vault, and that's the mortgage on your shop!"

"How 'bout that, Ev?" Billy says to his son. "Kinder looks lak this son of a bitch is threatenin to run us up a stump, don't it? I'm jest skeered shitless, aint you?"

Mrs. Dill speaks up. "Such language, Bill," she says. "Is that any way to talk in front of these sons of bitches?" Then to John

Ingledew she says, "Why'nt ye take that mortgage to yore outhouse and use it for wipes?"

"By God, you don't think I might?" John demands.

"Beats corncobs a real sight," she says.

"Naw," says Billy. "That mortgage paper's too slick. It'd slide right off ole John's bung-hole and leave him nasty as ever."

"Shoot," says Every. "When God made old John, he plum fergot to give him a bung-hole."

John says to his brother, "Willis, I've had all I can stand. Remind me tomorrow to foreclose on these riffraff." He turns to Every. "Now you listen to me, boy. And listen good. You kin visit yore folks all you want, but if you aint out of this town by noon tomorrow, you're gonna have an escort party of about seven fellers to see you out. Noon tomorrow. And if you come anywhere near the girl before then, you'll be leavin all the sooner."

"Well, I'll tell ye, sir," Every says. "As far as gettin out of town's concerned, I got to go back in the mornin anyhow. As far as seein that girl's concerned, hell and high water aint gonna stop me. But I'll tell ye why I got to go back in the mornin. I got to face court-martial. Want to know why they're court-martialin me? Cause I knocked a lieutenant flat on his ass. Want to know why I knocked him flat on his ass? Cause he wouldn't let me crawl fifty feet through the woods to untie Raymond from a tree. Want to know why he wouldn't let me? Cause the Germans had tied Raymond to that tree for a decoy, to ambush us. Want to know what Raymond said to me after I'd knocked down that lieutenant and went to him anyway and tried to untie him? Said to me, 'Get away from here, you fool!' Want to know what I said back to him? Said back to him, 'Naw, Ray, I done writ yore sweetheart and tole her I'd fine you by and by and git you out alive or else die tryin.' Want to know what he said to me then?"

Every's voice chokes, but he clears his throat and continues in a fierce, quivering tone, "Said to me, 'Ev,' said to me, 'Ev, no sense in both us gittin kilt! Clear the hell out a here while ye kin! It's a trap!' But I started untyin him anyhow, and I said to him, 'I don't see no trap. Reckon if it's a trap, they aint about to settle for just me. They're waitin to git a few more before openin up.' But just then I 'spose they got tired of waitin and figgered I was all they'd ever git. They opened up. See these here red scars on my laigs? Them's machine gun bullets. I couldn't stand up. I couldn't no more of stood up and finished untyin him than I could of took off and flew. And him screamin at me, 'Ev, you fool, clear the hell out a here!' So I did. My boys was brave enough to come down and open fire on that machine-gun nest long enough for me to drag myself out of there."

There is a long silence. Eventually John Ingledew asks in a quiet voice, "Was Raymond hit. Did they hit him?"

"I don't know," Every says. "Some a that spray that cut me down might've hit him, but then on the other hand maybe that tree he was tied to was shieldin him. I don't know. The next thing I knew a couple a my boys had tuck me under the arms and dragged me clean out a there afore I could take a good look back. Then that lieutenant I'd clobbered came up mad as a rattlesnake and kicked me in the face. I woke up in a field hospital."

"So you have no way of knowing that Raymond's dead," John Ingledew said.

"Naw. But the war's over, dammit. If they'd kept him alive as a prisoner, he'd of been liberated, and he'd of showed up by now, wouldn't he?"

Willis Ingledew says to his brother, "You know what I think, John? I think maybe this rascal is just makin up a tall tale. I think maybe the real reason they're court-martialin him is that he killed pore Raymond hisself."

"Hmmm," says John Ingledew. "I wouldn't be too surprised."

"Goddammit," Every says. "Come to the trial with me and hear the story from somebody else, then."

"Still and all…" John says, and then he says, "How do we know you aint even makin up the whole story about the court-martial? If they really meant to court-martial you, they wouldn't be lettin you run around loose like this."

"They sure wouldn't," Every agrees.

"You mean you're—what's it called?—you're—"

"A wall," Every says. "A.W.O.L. I broke barracks."

"But you're going back to face up to it?"

"In the morning."

"Well, even if the court-martial don't put you in the hoosegow, they'll put you away for being A-wol, won't they?"

"More'n likely."

"So you aint gonna have no chance to be foolin around with that girl for several years maybe."

"That's right. So I've got to do all of my foolin around while I'm still here."

"Naw you aint neither. You leave her alone. Time you git out a jail, Raymond'll be back."

"Maybe not. Time I git out a jail, maybe some other feller who aint got any right to her is liable to've took her away from me."

"Then good for her, sonny boy, cause she'd shore be a lot better off with just about anybody 'ceptin a devil lak you."

Billy Dill speaks up. "If you disparage my boy just once more, you bastard, I'll come to the bank tomorrow and wipe my own ass with that mortgage and make you a hat out of it."

"Come on, Willis," John Ingledew says. "Let's leave these scum." To Every he says, "But I'm tellin you for the last time, if you even dare look at that girl again, they'll be eight going out and seven coming back!"

John and Willis turn and stalk quickly away.

You leave too, Bug, but you are left with the feeling that somehow the Ingledews have not sufficiently intimidated the Dills, and that Every probably would not heed their threats. Thus you are anticipating that he might present himself to you again, and you are wondering what you can say to get rid of him. You are also in deep distress from hearing him tell how the Germans had caught Raymond and had used him. When Every had written you that letter claiming that he would find Raymond "for you" and get him out alive "for you," you had considered it merely more of his vainglorious boasting, just as he had boasted when leaving to enlist, "I'm gonna go over there and protect him for you," and just as he had later boasted by mail, "Here I am a sergeant already, and he aint but a corporal still," and "Killed me two Boches barehanded today," and "Tole Raymond that when I get to be general I'll make him a colonel if he'll let me have you; he said he'd think about it," and "Today they pinned the Craw de Gur on me—that's one of the medals the Frenchies give out—the only decoration Ray's got is the Dose of Clap—the Frenchies give that one out too." You are inclined, like John and Willis Ingledew, to be skeptical of his story, although you cannot quite accept the possibility that he would actually have killed Raymond…unless his desperation to have you was so great as to drive him to it.

But for the first time you begin to realize that Raymond might actually be dead. Before, you have not been able to accept this. And if he is dead? Would you have Every? Certainly not. He is the last man you would have. Indeed, even if he did not actually kill Raymond, he was responsible for Raymond's joining the service in the first place.

This is what you are going to remind him if he bothers you again.

But the afternoon passes on without his showing. You have returned home and have eaten supper, waiting, expecting him any minute, but he does not show up. After supper you sit on the cabin's porch until full dark, waiting, but he does not appear. "Lookin fer cumpny?" your father asks. No, you say. "Reckon I'll turn in," he says, and leaves the porch.

You are alone for several minutes in the dark, before you hear the whippoorwill. It is a good whippoorwill, coming from the woodlot, but, real as it sounds, there is an edge about it that tells you human lips are making it, and for a moment you are washed with a flood of old memories, some sweet but mostly bitter. When you were twelve and he was thirteen the whistle of the whippoorwill had been his signal, coming from that same woodlot, to tell you he was there. It was a near-perfect imitation; one night your mother had said "That shore is purty," and had listened sweetly entranced for a moment to what she thought was a real bird. Many times, all but the last time, you had heeded the signal and gone to the woodlot. Now again you do not heed it. It comes twice, thrice, four times, at one-minute intervals, but you remain seated. When it sounds the fifth time, you turn you head toward the woodlot and say, "Go away," not loudly, not loudly enough for anyone in the house to hear, nor anyone in the woodlot either. When it sounds the sixth time, mournful as the dancing of dead leaves, you cannot stand it. You leave the porch and walk out through the yard to the very edge of the woodlot, and you peer into the black mass of trees and say, "Go away!"

"Thought you'd not remember," his voice says softly. You cannot see him in there at all. He makes the whippoorwill whistle once more, just loud enough for you to hear. "The whippin of ole pore Will," he says. "Means you'll be making a journey in the direction it was heard. Remember? This way's northeastwards from your house. We was gonna head northeast. Remember? Well, I got to go northeast myself now, tomorrow. Wonder could I say anything to get you to go too, to bear me out, to stand by my side. Guess I caint, but I'll try anyhow."

"You're not a real whippoorwill," you say, needing to say something, even to assure yourself that he is not, despite the eerie resemblance between the plaintive tone of his words and the cry of that bird. You still cannot see him, though you know where his dark form stands.

"Am too," he says. "Me all over, I'm one. Same habits. Same lonesomeness. Just a-lookin everwhere for my mate. Caint find her. Keep a-callin and a-callin for her. Keep—"

"Please go," you say. "Please, Every."

"Got to tell you somethin first, Latha. Want to tell you about ole Ray. I'm shore abashed if any of them smart-alecky letters I sent ye gave ye any offense. Didn't mean em that way. Didn't mean to make em look lak I considered myself a cut above him, no. Naw, he was second to none, Latha. He was a real brave boy, lots more of a man than me. I want to tell you what he done."

"I've heard your story," you tell him.

"Oh," he says. "Them Ingledews tell ye?"

"No," you say. "I was there. You didn't see me, but I was listening in."

"Oh," he says, and his voice loses its gentle plaintiveness, sharpens. "I reckon you put em up to pay in a call on us."

"No," you say. "Mandy's letter put em up to that."

He comes nearer to you, out of the woods; you can see his dark shape clearly before you, although you cannot see his eyes. He is still wearing that Army uniform with the round-brimmed doughboy hat. "Latha," he says, "I let down on you. I let down on the promise I made ye. I *couldn't* get him out. But I tried my best."

A laugh escapes your throat. "Too bad you couldn't've got him out as easy as you got him in," you say, with sarcasm.

"You still blaming me for that?" he asks, hurt.

"I'll forever blame you for that," you return.

"You don't hold yourself none to blame?" he demands.

"A little," you admit. "Not much."

"All right," he says. "But listen, Latha, he's *not* coming back. I would bet almost anything on that. Now if you were hearing me when I tole them Ingledews about the court-martial, you know I aint in any position to ask you to marry me. So I'm not. But could I just ask you to wait just a little while, to see what the Army's gonna do to me? Could you just not marry nobody else for a little while, till I get some word to you?"

"The word I want," you tell him, "is a word from the government saying that Raymond is dead and buried."

"You might never get that," he says. "Then what?"

"Then I'll wait," you say.

"You might wait forever."

"Then I'll wait forever."

His hands come up and grip your arms. "Latha, don't you want a man?" he reasons with you. "Do you want the coldness of being a maiden all your life? Was Ray so important to you that you'll wait forever, lonely and cold, for him to come back? Won't you ever long for somebody to be close to?"

His words more than the grip of his hands grip you, and draw you for an instant to him, and you are about to say, *Oh yes, Every, I will long even for you,* when a lantern suddenly flares up to illuminate the two of you, and a voice says, "Okay, buster, git yore goddamn hands off that gal before I blow yore gizzard out!"

The voice is Tearle Ingledew's and you turn and see him aiming a shotgun at Every's heart. Bevis Ingledew is holding high the lantern in one hand, a pistol in the other. Stanfield Ingledew and

Odell Ingledew are each holding rifles. E.H. Ingledew is holding a pitchfork.

Every does not relax his grip on your arms. He glowers at Tearle.

"You think I don't mean it?" Tearle snarls. "Well, just hold on till I count three, and then you kin count the number a buckshot sprinkled through yore innards! One…Two…Thr—"

You break away from Every and stand back from him. He remains there with his hands still gripping the air where you had been. "Goddamn ye," Every says to Tearle, "I aint armed. Lay down yore yellow-livered shotgun and I'll take ye on man for man!"

"And I'd whup the shit out a ye so fast," returns Tearle, "thet you'd think ye was a freshed-up stable! But I aint gonna bother. I'd jest as soon blow off yore haid as look at you. And I reckon I will!" He raises the shotgun toward Every's head.

"Drop it, Tull!" comes another voice, from the woodlot. "All you fellers lay down yore arns! You heerd Ev, it aint fair he aint got a gun."

Tearle does not lower his shotgun. "Who's thet?" he demands, squinting into the woods. "Who's thet in thar?"

"Drop it, I say!" the voice persists.

"Thet you, Lawlor?" Tearle demands. "Lawlor Coe, thet you in thar?"

"Yeah, and if you fellers don't lay down yore arns and fight fair, they's gonna be a big gatherin up at the cemetery tomorrow."

"Lawlor now, you lissen a me," Tearle says. "This aint none a yore business. You butt in whar ye don't belong, yo're liable to git hurt yoresef!"

"Nobody's gonna git hurt but y'all, 'less y'all lay down them guns right now, and I don't mean maybe! My Winchester's on yore heart, Tull, and my finger's giving me trouble!"

"I see ye *now,* sonny boy," comes still another voice from the woodlot, and you realize with alarm that it is your own father, "and I got a right fine Springfield a my own that's ready to handle the likes of Lawlor Coe meddlin whar he don't belong!"

"Saultus Bourne!" comes a voice from the path to the road. That white nightshirt a yourn makes a fine target fer my old flintlock!"

Bevis Ingledew with his pistol says, "Naw ye don't, Billy Dill! I got the drap on ye!"

Then there is a long moment of complete silence.

Tearle finally breaks it. "Somebody better git a drap on ole Bevis, he's the only one aint got a drap on im." Then he says, "Well, all right, we might as well all fire together, and the devil take the hindmost. Aim good, everbody, 'cause the only one dead sartin to be kilt is Every, and I've got him."

A shot explodes—Lawlor's?—a shot is fired, and the lantern in Bevis's hand shatters and after a quick burst of flame it goes out. In utter darkness, other shots are fired, matched by violent curses.

You run to the cabin, where your mother is standing on the porch. "Maw!" you yell, "get a lantern, quick! Light a lantern!" She runs into the house and you stand waiting, trembling, listening to the shots fired and the curses screeched. When she returns with the lantern, the shooting has stopped but the curses are roaring louder then ever. You take the lantern and run bravely with it back out to the midst of the fight at the edge of the woodlot.

Every has his arm in a stranglehold on Tearle's neck and is choking him to death. Your father has a stranglehold on Lawlor Coe but Lawlor is breaking loose. Bevis Ingledew has clubbed Billy Dill over the head with his pistol butt and is standing over his unconscious form. Stanfield Ingledew with his rifle and E.H. with his pitchfork are taking aim at Every, while Odell is taking aim at Lawlor Coe.

"Let him go, Ev!" E.H. snaps, and pokes Every in the back with the sharp tines of the pitchfork. Every continues choking Tearle. E.H. thrusts forward with the pitchfork. Every lets out a yelp and releases Tearle and grabs himself in the small of the back.

"Goddamn ye, you punctured my backbone!" he yells at E.H.

"Yeah, and I might put yore eyes out too!" E.H. replies.

Tearle, freed, grabs up his shotgun, howling, "By God, now I'll plug holes through the bastard!" and he raises his gun at Every again, but Stanfield puts his hand on the barrel and forces it down.

"Naw," Stanfield says to Tearle. "We aint gonna kill him. We're jest gonna give him a head start afore we start firing."

"And *you* too," Odell says to Lawlor Coe. "You kin jest keep him company on that head start, Lawlor, and both you sonsabitches kin git clean out a town."

"My dad's hurt," Every says. "If you fellers've hurt him—"

"He aint hurt," Bevis says. "Might have a knot on his head when he wakes up, but he aint hurt."

"Now listen, Every," Tearle says. "Yo're leavin town fast, kin ye understand? Yo're leavin town fast as yore two legs kin carry ye, and ye aint *never* comin back. Never! Ye understand! If you ever show yore hide in this town again, we'uns will shoot you down afore ye could git word to God! We won't speak fust, we'll jest fire. I swear that to ye. Now march! You too, Lawlor, start marchin, and I don't keer to see ye again neither."

The Ingledews advance on Every and Lawlor and prod them with their weapons. They begin moving.

"Latha!" Every hollers. "Come with me! Please come with me!"

There is a brief thoughtless instant when you are tempted to yield to this pathetic request, but you do not move. The Ingledews would not have let you go with him anyway. You shake your head.

"Then wait for me, Latha!" he hollers. "I'll come back!"

"You'll never come back, I told ye," Tearle snarls. "If you come back, it'll be to git yoreself measured out fer a coffin. We'll be lookin at each other, and one of us won't know it. Now march! Run! We start shootin any minute! You too, Lawlor! Get a move on there!"

Every and Lawlor trot down the path to the road. When they reach the road, the Ingledews begin firing. They reload and fire several times.

You do not watch Every run out of sight. It is bad luck to watch somebody go all the way out of sight. It means they might die.

But maybe you should have, Bug. There would come many a time when you would wish that you had watched him walk out of sight, so he would have died and never returned. Because he did return, once more.

Another two years pass; you forget him; it is when you have completely forgotten him that he comes again, again by surprise.

It is after supper again, it is a summertime evening after supper again, and you are doing your evening chores. You are feeding the hogs. You have thrown their slop to them and are turning around with the empty slop bucket in your hand when he comes out of the woods. You drop the slop bucket. It rolls down the hill. You watch it roll away.

"No, now," you say, as if to the bucket. "Go away. You will be killed."

"He hasn't come back, has he?" he says. "I told you he wasn't coming back. He won't ever come back."

"How did you get out?" you ask. "They told me you were locked up in that Army prison."

"I broke out. I had to talk to you, Latha. I had to tell you that I could stand being locked in there for two more years if you would just tell me that you will wait for me."

"I won't tell you that."

"Who are you going to marry, then? Has somebody spoken for you?"

"No."

"Raymond's never coming back, I told you. I *know.* Believe me, he's dead."

"All right, but I can't marry you, Every."

"Why not, Latha? What's wrong with me?"

"They wouldn't let me marry you. Not just the Ingledews. There's nobody in this town who would let me marry you."

"We could run away."

"I don't want to run away. Stay More's my home."

"Then I'll come back here, and mend my ways, and *make* folks like me. I'll make em *all* like me."

"You forget the Ingledews have sworn to kill you if you ever come back."

"They got no right to."

"That won't keep them from it."

"I'll talk to them! I'll try to get em to understand!"

"They'll shoot you before you get a word out of your mouth."

"Then, Latha, you talk to em! Try to get em to understand!"

"Understand what?" you say. "Understand that you're still stubborn enough to want to marry me still? After all that's happened?"

He clenches and unclenches his fists. Through clenched teeth he says, "Latha, put yourself in my place! What would you do? What *can* I do?"

"The first thing you better do is give yourself up, and tell them you're sorry you broke out. Then if they ever do let you out, you ought to look around for some place to go, some place except Stay More."

He pounds his fist upon the rail of the hog pen. "All right, goddammit!" he says. "Looks like there's nothing I can do, is there?"

"No."

"All right, Latha. Goodbye, then, I'm going. Tell Mom and Dad I said hello. Tell em I'm all right. Tell em I'll be back one day, tell em to keep their chins up."

"Your dad's dead, Every. He died last winter."

"Naw!" he says. "Please don't say that's true! What'd he die of?"

"Stroke, I guess," you say. "I'll tell you one thing I did, Every. I went to his funeral. I don't know why, but I went. Nobody else did. Just me and your mother."

He pounds the fence rail with his fist so hard he breaks it. "By God!" he screeches. "I got a mind to kill everybody in this town! I got a mind to get me some dynamite and blow the whole motherfucking town sky high!"

"I'm sorry," you say. "You can't blame everybody."

"I caint, huh?"

"No," you say.

He hangs his head. For a moment, you want to reach out and touch him; more than that, more than touch him, you would like to make love to him once more; but even if you could do this, it is not the right time of the month for you, and you know it; and even if you could do this, it would make it all the harder for him to leave.

You cannot touch him. You cannot allow him to touch you. You must not. A touch would ruin it all.

He raises his head. His eyes are damp. *But do not touch him!* "Well, so long, Latha." *You must not touch him.* "Be seeing you some day, I reckon. I'm bound to, I reckon." *Then some day touch him, but not now.* "Do you suppose you could give me a goodbye kiss? I aint never even kissed you for nearly five years." *You cannot, you must not.*

"No," you say. "Don't you touch me."

He starts to reach for you; you pull back. "Just a kiss," he says. "I aint even had a kiss in nearly five years. I bought a woman, once, over in France, but I never kissed her." He comes after you, but you back away. *You must back away.*

Your backing alone does not stop him. *You must say something.* "If you touch me," you say, "I'll holler, and Paw'll come up here and shoot you himself."

Your threat changes him, angers him. "He will, huh?" he says. "Well, we'll just see about that." He clamps his hand over your mouth and with his other hand forces you up against a tree and presses you against it with his body. He whips off his belt and uses it to tie your hands together behind the tree, holding you to the tree. He whips out a handkerchief and gags your mouth with it. Now you cannot holler, you cannot even speak, you cannot even tell him that you are in the wrong time of your month.

He yanks up the hem of your dress and stuffs it into your collar. He tears away your panties with one strong pull and flings them aside. You squirm and try to bite through your gag; you cannot holler, but you can squeal; you squeal as loud as you can; the hogs watch you curiously.

He bends at the knee and then straightens up, and when he straightens you feel yourself entered, and all your squirmings cannot dislodge him. You feel the bark of the tree biting into your back as he thrusts and thrusts violently against you. You pray that he will come, and leave you, but he is holding himself back, and then you are praying that he will not come.

You hear a whippoorwill warbling shrilly, but realize it is your own bird within you.

You are still squirming, but in a rhythm to match his own.

You know he has come but has not stopped; you are glad; you hope he will go on, but he does not he comes out of you, he leaves you and flings himself back from you just as you reach the edge, when you want to cry out: *Oh, stay, Every, stay, stay more forever and have me forever* but he turns and begins running into the woods, and you realize he is disappearing into the woods and if you watch him go all of the way out of sight he will die, and you must not do that, and you must get over the edge.

You close your eyes to keep from watching him disappear all the way out of sight. You go over the edge.

It is full dark when you come to, and at first you do not know whether the blackness is of the night or of your passing out. Your first thought is *I have swooned.* And you wonder *Have I swooned so's not to watch him go, or so's not to feel him come?*

Your wrists are still bound by his belt behind the tree. *Maybe this is the way poor Raymond was strung to that tree.* You wriggle your wrists, for a long time you twist them and tug them before you can slip the belt off them. Then you are free. You pick up the belt and keep it.

You return to the house and build a fire in the kitchen stove to heat water.

Your mother comes and says, "Law, whar you been, gal?"

"Walkin," you say.

"Whut you fixin to do?" she asks, pointing at the kettles of water on the stove.

"Take a bath," you say.

"A hot bath this time a year?" she says, but it is not really a question, it requires no answer. She goes.

It is a hot bath you take, Bug, a scalding hot bath in which you sit and soak a long time, thinking *But it's too late, this isn't doing any good.*

The next day at noon when Mr. Ingledew says, "Watch out for robbers" before leaving to eat his dinner, you want to say, "Don't leave me" but you cannot.

You hear the approach of horse's hooves, and you start to

think *He is sure enough going to do it* but you do not think this yet. You do not think it until he comes through the door, carrying the empty toe-sack in one hand and the revolver in the other. He is fully disguised: strange, old-fashioned clothes, a queer hat, beneath the hat a pillowcase covering his head with two slits for the eyes. He does not even walk like Every, but you think *It must be him.*

He comes quickly to the counter and passes you the note; you know then; you have seen a note before, the same handwriting:

CLEAN OUT THE SAFE IN 2 MINITS OR
YOU ARE A DEAD GIRL

"Haven't you done enough?" you say to him.

He raises the pistol point-blank to your nose.

You do not move.

He cocks the hammer. He hands you the sack.

You take the sack to the safe and stuff it. You take the sack back to him. Then you hand him his belt, rolled in a neat coil.

He looks at the belt but does not take it. He refuses it.

He backs out through the door, holding the pistol on you until the last moment, when he turns and leaps from the porch to the back of his horse, and gallops quickly away.

You turn aside to keep from watching him go out of sight.

THREE: Afternoon

W hy, land sakes, Every!" she exclaimed. "Whatever do you mean by that?" But before he could begin explaining himself, they were interrupted by the approach of a man on horseback. "Uh-oh," she said, and in an aside to Every she said, "Listen. Just pretend you're my husband, all right? I'll explain it to you later."

Dolph slowly climbed down off his horse and tethered it. "Howdy," he said to them. "Shore is one hot day, aint it?" He came up onto the porch and sat in the swing. He began to swing gently. To her he said, "Would you like to hear a funny story about what happened to me over to the cannin factry?"

"I've already heard it," she said. "From Luther Chism."

"I bet it liked to tickled the daylights out of you, didn't it?"

"It *was* pretty funny."

"Wal, now that you've had yore fun, would ye keer to tell me who you really are?"

"I'm Latha Dill," she said and was surprised at how much she liked the sound of that, "and this is my husband Every."

Dolph looked at Every and then extended his hand and said, "Pleased to meet ye, Mr. Dill." He shook hands with Every and said,

"Or I reckon I should say *Brother Dill*. Yore pitcher's been starin me in the eye from every tree and fence post in town. Come to Stay More to give a revival, have ye?"

"That's right," Every said, "And I'd be happy to have you come."

"Reckon I might just do that, preacher. Reckon I'd shore lak to hear you explain to folks how you managed to hit town one night and git married to Latha Bourne the very next day."

A long and awkward moment of silence followed that. She wondered how he knew her real name, but she realized it wouldn't have been much trouble to have made a few inquiries here and there.

Every said to him, "What's your interest in this matter, sir?"

"Wal, I'll tell ye," he said, "I aim to marry Miss Latha myself, and if it's shore enough a fact that you've done beat me to it, why, then I reckon I aim to kill ye."

"Those are strong words, my friend," Every said, and stood up. Dolph rose with him. "What do you aim to do it with?"

"My bare hands," Dolph said, holding them out.

Every looked at his hands and said, "Them's right powerful-lookin biscuit hooks you got, my friend. Well, if you'll just step down into the yard we'll find out just how powerful they are."

"Glad to," Dolph said, and jumped off the porch.

"Boys!" she snapped at them.

"Well, it's him or me, isn't it?" Every asked, taking off his coat and his glasses before jumping off the porch to face Dolph.

"No," she said. "Dolph, you just clear out of here and leave him alone."

"He's done already challenged me," Dolph said, "and I shore aint one to back down from a challenge. Come on, preacher, and let's see how long you kin last."

Every asked him, "You mind if I pray, first?"

"Go right ahead," Dolph said. "Matter a fact, I advise ye to."

Every knelt in the dust. "O Heavenly Father," he said in a loud voice, "Thou knowest that when I killed those three fellers in that barroom up in Springfield, Missoura, I done it in self-defense. Thou knowest, too, Lord, that when I splattered Carl Rawley's brains all over his corn patch that it was forced upon me. And it was sure self-defense when I had to strangle those two Germans in that trench in the Argonne forest. So now, Lord, Thou has heard this here pore wretch threaten to kill me, and when I put him in his grave I ask Thee to have mercy on his soul. In Jesus Name, Amen." He stood up and presented his fists to Dolph.

"Haw," Dolph said nervously. "Tryin to git me skeered, huh? Wal, fer one thing I don't skeer easy. And for another thing I don't believe ye. And for yet another thing, you aint a goddamn bit bigger'n me." And he swiftly lashed out a fist and caught Every a blow that sent him sprawling backward into the dust.

Every scrambled to his feet but couldn't get his hands up in time. Dolph pummeled both sides of his head with several hard blows, the last of which sent him into the dirt again.

She yelled, "Dolph! you quit that! you hear me?"

"Had enough, preacher?" asked Dolph, standing over him.

"Enough?" said Every, "Why, my friend, we've not truly started yet. I'm just testing your punches out, to see how hard they are. I'd say they were about medium, maybe a little on the light-to-medium side."

"Then git on yore feet and I'll show you some heavier ones!"

She did not even see Every rise, he was up that fast, and the first thing she noticed was Dolph's head whipping from side to side as Every drove him with quick drubbing smashes out toward the road. Now Dolph was reeling groggily, and Every could have flattened him with one more punch but he stopped and said, "Those were what I think of as *my* light-to-medium punches, my friend. Are you still game for some *medium* ones?"

This pause gave Dolph time to clear his head. "You talk too much, preacher," he snarled, and sprang at Every with his head down and butted him in the stomach hard enough to lay him on his back. Then Dolph knelt over him and began pounding his face with short blows. Every arched up suddenly with his hips and threw Dolph off him.

Oh my, she thought, *there's so many fights in that yard I ought to set up a booth and sell tickets.*

They both got to their feet and squared off again. Dolph swung and missed; Every missed his first swing but connected with his second, which caught Dolph's shoulder and sent him staggering back. Then Every hit him two tremendous punches on the jaw, the second one actually lifting him off his feet and laying him flat out.

Every stood over him. "Those two," he said, "were of the *medium* variety. I'm afraid that the *heavy* variety are going to bust your head clean open. Git up."

Dolph could hardly move but he managed to climb slowly to his feet, and he even took a couple of wild slow swings, saying, "If yo're gonna kill me, preacher, then kill me, cause I don't keer to live without Latha!"

Every drew back his fist for a roundhouse wallop, then swung it mightily forward—and wrapped Dolph around the neck in a hug. Holding his neck that way, he led him toward the porch, saying, "Let's have a little talk. Might could get more accomplished that way." He put Dolph in a chair, and said to her, "Latha, could we have us some liniment?"

She went into the store for the jar of liniment and when she came back, Dolph was saying, "Not very long, but long enough to know I love her."

Every took the jar and opened it and dabbed into it and began spreading the liniment on Dolph's face. "And you?" he said to her. "How do you feel about him?"

"I hardly know him," she said. "I like him, but I think he's a fool to leave his wife and kids and come over here making trouble."

"Is that a fact?" Every asked him. "Have you left your family?"

Dolph, hanging his head, nodded.

"Why?" Every asked.

Dolph raised his head. "*Why?*" he said. "Why, because I aim to marry her, that's why."

"Has she given you any cause to think that she would marry you?" Every asked.

Dolph nodded.

Every looked at her and asked, "Have you said you'd marry him?"

"No," she said.

Every asked her, "Have you led him on, at all?"

"No," she said,

"That's a durn lie!" Dolph said to her. "Have you forgot about that time me'n you—"

"Hush," she said.

"I won't hush!" he said. "I don't keer if he knows it whether he's a preacher or yore husband or who he is. Me and you laid together lak husband and wife, and that's the whole truth, so help me, and if he's gonna kill me for it because yo're his wife then lak I said before let him kill me 'cause I don't keer to live without you!"

Every stared at her, and she had to turn her eyes away. Damn Dolph for telling on her!

"Maybe," Every said in a sort of choked voice, "maybe I better go off and let the two of you talk this out between yourselves."

"Don't go, Every," she said. "I don't have anything else to say to him. I won't marry him, and that's that."

Every laughed, rather hollowly, and said, "You know, this whole situation has a kind of painful familiarity for me. I recall when I was a young fellow I had a mighty powerful crush on a certain gal, and I kept asking her to marry me, but she said 'no' every time. I was stubborn as all get out, too, and I wouldn't take 'no' for an answer."

"Just like me," Dolph said. "That's the exact same way I feel, preacher. So what did you finally do?"

"I never *finally* did anything. I reckon I'm still trying."

"You mean you been a bachelor all your life, on account of that girl sayin 'no' ?"

"That's right, my friend."

"Did she get married to somebody else?"

"Not that I know of."

"But she still says 'no' when you ask her?"

"I've not had much of a chance lately to ask her. Too much excitement going on."

"What do you mean?"

"Well, just recently when I was getting ready to ask her I found out she'd been laying in fornication with some other fellow. What would *you* do if you were in my shoes?"

"Why, I'd kill that—" Dolph started, but stopped, and stared back and forth between Every and Latha.

"Yes," Every went on "that's what I was thinking. In fact, I had already come pretty darn close to killing him even before I found out what he'd done." Every re-opened the jar of liniment and began smearing some of it on his own face. "But, you know," he went on, "since I've been thinking about it, I've decided she wouldn't have laid with him if she didn't want to."

"That doesn't follow," Latha put in. "She'd been raped once before in her life."

"I didn't rape her!" Dolph said.

"We understand that," Every said, and with sarcasm in his voice he said, "After all, you can't begrudge a spinster *needing* it ever once in a while."

"Every!" she said.

"Well," he said, standing up, "I've got to go look over my sermon notes or something," He shook hands with Dolph and said, "Hope you'll come to the meeting too. Looks like me and you are rivals, but I've had rivals before, and if this rivalry ends in disappointment for me, why, I've had many a disappointment before, including some recent ones." He turned and walked down off the porch and began walking away.

"Every!" she called after him. "You come back here and stop acting like a hurt child."

He pointed one finger heavenward and said, "The Voice of God is calling me to Meditation. See you later."

He walked on away.

"Now see what you've done!" she said to Dolph.

"Hell's bells," he said, "if you really keer for him so darn much why do you keep saying 'no' to him?"

"I haven't said 'no' to him for nearly twenty years. Like he said, he hasn't had a chance to ask me lately because of the trouble you're making."

"You mean today's the first you've seen of him in twenty years?"

"Pretty nearly."

"And you mean you been waitin all this time for him to show up again?"

"Maybe I have, now that you mention it."

"Snakes alive, gal! Why didn't you just say 'yes' the first time he asked ye?"

"Now that is a long, long story."

"Shoot, I got all kinds of time to listen to it. Why, I got *scads* of time on my hands! Aint a blessit thing on earth for me to do no more except wait and see if I caint out-spark that preacher."

"Then you're wasting your time. I'd marry him the minute he asked me."

"What's he got I aint got?" he asked. "—Other'n quicker fists."

"Well," she said, thinking, "a job, for one thing."

"A *job?*" he asked. "Heck fire, you call preachin a *job?* Why, I bet he don't make enough money to pay for his shoe leather. And *me*—anybody kin tell ye that Dolph Rivett's one of the hardest-workin farmers in Newton County!"

"Except when he's out stirring up trouble," she said.

"Why, I've got one of the purtiest spreads a land y'ever laid eyes on, eighty acres of good bottom and a hundred twenty acres of upland, and a herd of fifty Angus and—"

"Who's been feeding those cattle lately?" she asked.

"They're out to pasture," he declared. "If you mean who's been milkin em and other chores, my boys is big enough for that."

"Do you plan on taking me to that place?" she asked.

"Sure do."

"Do you think your other wife would stand for it?"

He mulled that one over for a while, and finally he said, "I'll work out somethin."

"I can't see how you could work out anything that wouldn't leave somebody pretty badly hurt."

"Latha, I've already been hurt pretty bad myself," he said. "By her. I reckon *you* of all people kin understand what's it like to be desperate to…to…you know, to *get together* with somebody ever once in a while. Now I aint one of these twichet-struck tomcats who's got it on his mind day in and day out, but I'm a *man*, goddammit, and you showed me what it's like for the first time to *enjoy* bein a man. That's the honest truth. That time in that cave on Banty Creek—that was the highest old goluptious time I ever had. Why, it was lak barbercued sidemeat to a man dyin a hunger, lak ice-cold sarsprilla to a man dyin a thirst, lak a easy chur to set in after plowin all day, lak Christmas mornin after a good year, hell, they aint no words for such a hunkydory jubilation. I feel lak clawin myself just thinkin about it."

"Oh, Dolph—" she protested, sighing, but she felt like clawing herself too, and she wished he had not reminded her of the exhilaration of it with such rapturous terms. Now there were stirrings in her which she didn't want.

He suddenly asked, "Why'd you do it to me?"

She said, "It was more like you doing it to me."

"All right. Darn. Why'd *we* do it, then?"

"Craziness, I guess," she said, and reflected upon the truth of that answer. It had been crazy of him to do something that would lead him into abandoning his family. It had been crazy of her to think that the situation was a foolproof escape for her. But despite the trouble that had come of it, she realized that she was actually a little pleased to find herself in such a situation. *It's passing strange,* she thought, *that I've been sitting on this porch for eight years, and now all of a sudden two men are fighting over me. I feel like Sonora.* Maybe this was all happening because of a configuration of those signs that morning: the redbird flying downward, the white cat in the road, singing before breakfast, the shirt on wrong side out, sneezing on Saturday, the coffeepot rattling on the stove…*And Every home again! And making a preacher of himself! And saying he'd been converted in that same room where I woke up?* What was he doing there? What was *she* doing there? Oh, there was plenty of time for plenty of answers; she was not impatient; she was curious, and expectant: something, good or bad but *something,* was finally going to happen to her. It was good to be *fought over* again, and Dolph even reminded her in a way of Raymond. And for that matter, was Every any better than him? Getting peeved and insulting, like that, just because she'd made love with another man four weeks before he had suddenly shown up again. *The preacher in him,* she thought. Any sex is sin. More than likely his religion had half-castrated him. More than likely, if she married him, he could only do it once a month with his pants on after asking the Lord's blessing. *I could never be a preacher's wife,* she decided.

"Latha," Dolph asked softly, "have you got the heebie jeebies over that preacher?"

"I've barely had a chance to talk to him," she said. "It's been so long since I saw him, and way back *then* I sure didn't have the heebie-jeebies over him."

"You turned him down because you were struck on somebody else?"

"Yes."

"What became of the other feller?"

"He was killed in the war."

"And even after that you still turned him down?"

"I didn't believe the other one was dead. I thought he might come back."

"You mentioned somethin about bein…bein took against your will. Was it the preacher who done it?"

"He wasn't any preacher back then."

"But *he* done it?"

"Yes."

"And you're still glad to see him, after that?"

"I guess…I don't know…it's been so long."

"Would you really and truly marry him the minute he asked ye?"

"Maybe not the same minute."

"Latha, have I got even a ghost of a chance? If you say I've got at least a ghost of a chance, I will tear down mountains to persuade you to have me. But if I aint got even a fighting chance, I will just go off and find me a good spot to lay down and die."

"I don't want you to die, Dolph."

"Then give me a chance!"

"All right, Dolph, I will give you a chance."

He grabbed her head with both hands and kissed her.

It made her head swim, and her heart pound.

When he released her, she said, "You didn't even kiss me, before, that other time...."

"I know, goshdarnit, and I been cussin myself for it ever since. I reckon I just got so carried away I plumb fergot how to act. But I'll shore make it up to ye!" And he kissed her again.

She felt herself melting away, but she pushed him off and said, "That's enough, now. Somebody might come along."

"Aint nobody come along yet but me," he said. "On a dull Saturday afternoon like this, why, me'n you could take our clothes off and do it right here on the porch for the next three hours, and nobody'd ever see us!"

She laughed at that image. "I think Sonora's in the house," she said.

"Who's Sonora?"

"My daughter. —I mean, my niece. You met her."

"Oh," he said. He got up and walked over to the door and yelled through the screen, "Sonora, honey, you in there?"

There was no answer. He opened the door and went in. "Oh, cut that out!" she called after him, but he wouldn't mind her. A little later he came back.

"Not a soul in sight," he said, and came and gave her a third kiss.

That third kiss nearly undid her, but she said, "Stop it, now."

"Let's go inside," he said.

"Heavens, no, Dolph! I've got to mind the store."

"*Mind the store?*" he said. "Who's been comin to the store lately? Any fool in his right mind wouldn't come out of the shade this time of day."

"Somebody might come," she said lamely.

"Aw, if they did, you could git up and go tend to them," he said.

All right, all right! she said and grabbed his hand and led him to her bedroom and closed the door and didn't bother to take off her dress but just got her panties down and lay back on the bed in the hot room not as hot as she was and all soaked in the hairs of her crotch so that he flowed right easily into her and although it had been pent up in him since that last time he'd had her he managed to last and last and thrust and thrust so she could nearly feel him in her womb and she knew if she fainted this time there'd be nobody to mind the store Every O Every. Every?

He was kissing her neck, like a lover, and whispering into her ear.

"You're ruining me," she said. "You're making me into a bad woman."

"You don't really think it's bad," he said. "Do you?"

"No, but everybody else does."

"Not me," he said. "Come on. It'll just take a minute."

"I don't want for it to take just a minute."

"Then three hours if you want. Come on."

"No."

Uncannily he seemed to sense what was on her mind. "If you...if you were to pass out again, I'd just mind the store for you and tell anybody you'd gone visiting and would be back directly."

That wilted her resolve.

She looked up the road in each direction and then she pointed and said, "That room."

He lost no time going into it, and she followed and latched both doors from inside. She climbed onto the fourposter and lay back and arched her hips to remove her panties. He unbuttoned his fly and came after her.

"Take off your pants," she said.

"But what if somebody comes," he said.

"Indeed, what if somebody comes," she said, and began putting her panties back on.

He lay his hands on hers and stopped her. "Okay," he said, and quickly removed his trousers and hung them on the bed post.

She was very warm and very open and very wet, and he went right in and began his mechanical ramming.

"You're like a machine," she told him.

He stopped plunging. "How do you want me to do it?" he asked.

"Hold still, and I'll show you," she said.

He held still. She showed him.

Then for a long time they were a team of grindings and flexings and kneadings and smackings, and his heavy breathing in her ear began to groan "Goody goody go—"

"Don't say that," she sighed in his ear.

He hushed, but kept groaning.

"Now," she said. "Be your machine. Quick."

And he became again his repetitious pounding machine, and she pounded with him and no longer tried to keep from even thinking about fainting.

"Latha?" a small voice said.

She started so hard she jerked clean off his end, and scrambled out from under him, and got up and smoothed her dress and smoothed her hair and opened the door a crack and looked out. It was Donny.

"Hi," he said and held out his palm to reveal a coin in it. "I got a nickel for some soda pop."

"Just help yourself, Dawny," she said. "I'll be right out."

"Gee," he said, "you're sure all sweaty. Are you doing some hard work in there that I could help you with?"

She laughed. "I'm all finished, thank you. I'll be right out."

"Okay." he said, and headed for the soda pop cooler.

She closed the door and turned to Dolph. "Listen," she whispered, "you go out that back door quiet as you can. I don't want him to see you."

"Aw," he said, "it's just a kid. Come on and let's finish."

"No," she said. "You go on now."

"But he's just a little bitty sprat, and I'm so close to lettin off that just one or two more pokes would do it for me!"

"Shh, hold your voice down."

He got up off the bed and came to her and wrapped one arm

around her back and lifted her dress with his other hand, and jammed himself between her legs. "Please," he pled.

"No. Get on out of here now, Dolph."

"Just one or two pokes," he pled, poking.

"I *mean* it!" she said, and shoved him away from her.

He turned toward the rear door, buttoning his pants, and grumbling, "I'll fix that durn kid."

"You touch a hair on his head and that's the last of you, buster," she said.

He stared at her for a moment. Then he turned and walked out, slamming the door behind him.

She went to the dresser and brushed her hair, then waited a while longer and went back out on the porch. Donny was sitting in the swing, drinking his soda pop. She sat down in the swing beside him.

"Who were you talking to?" he asked.

"Why, nobody, child," she said.

"I heard voices," he said.

"Must've just been me, talking to myself."

"I heard a door slam," he said.

"That was just me, going to the kitchen."

"Why'd you slam it? Are you mad at somebody?"

"No, just careless, I guess." *I am indeed right careless.*

"Are you mad at me?"

"'Course not, Dawny." She rumpled his hair.

He sipped a sip of soda. "You smell kind of funny," he said.

"You mean like I need to take a bath?"

"No, not a bad smell. Like…sort of like creek water with fish."

"Oh," She said, "I'll go put on some rose water."

"No," he said. "I like the way you smell."

"Thank you," she said. "I like the way you smell too."

"How do I smell?"

"Like a five-year-old boy," she said. "Milk and honey and grasshoppers and skinny skin skin."

Donny laughed, and she laughed with him. A mad thought seized her. She was still feeling wild, and frustrated, after that interrupted tumble with Dolph. She'd already made such a mess of things. She would take Donny into the bedroom and let him take up where Dolph left off. Would it scare him, or would it tickle him pink? Would his little thing be able to rise up? Maybe it wasn't so little. She'd like to look. Maybe it was big, and could even shoot his juice. Wouldn't that be fun? And if he went and told his aunt and they came and ran her out of town it would serve her right. She'd already made such a mess of things.

"There was another man asking about you," Donny was saying.

She didn't know at first what he meant, then she asked, "When was this, Dawny?"

"Right after dinner," he said, "up at Aunt Rosie's."

"Oh," she said.

"He was riding a horse," Dawny said. "Just like that one." He pointed at the roan mare tethered in the yard.

"Oh?" she said.

"Yes. He asked Aunt Rosie what was the name of the lady who ran the post office, and Aunt Rosie told him, and then he asked when would the lady's husband be coming home, and Aunt Rosie said you never had no husband, and he said 'Thank you ma'am' and rode off."

"Oh," she said.

"And after he rode off Aunt Rosie said to Uncle Frank, 'Now I wonder what he's after?' and Uncle Frank said, 'Moosey, maybe.' What is moosey, Latha?"

"Oh," she said, "it's...it's just a brand of chewing tobacco. I know the man you mean. I sold him a plug of Moosey."

"Why did he leave his horse?"

"Well, Dawny, he said he wanted to hike up the mountain and look for wild turkeys."

The boy seemed to accept that. But after a while he smiled and said, "You tell better stories than I do." Then he got up and said, "That reminds me, Aunt Rosie told me to come right back and help her shell some beans." He walked down the porch.

"Dawny…" she said.

He stopped. "Huh?" he said.

"You're not…you won't…tell on me, will you?"

"Aw, Latha," he said. "I told you I won't ever, *ever* tell on you." Then he went on towards home.

She was alone then, and stayed alone a good long while. She wondered where Dolph had gone off to, without his horse. She wondered when, and if, Every would be coming back.

So much excitement in one day, she thought. She was used to sitting alone, oh, she had so much practice at it, but somehow it was hard to sit still after the excitement had started.

I am still slated to bawl before supper, she realized, remembering: Sing before breakfast, cry before supper. *When will it be?*

She had not wept since her father died, eighteen years ago.

As the afternoon was waning, Tearle Ingledew came walking—tottering—down the road. Climbing the store steps, he tripped, but staggered onward and grabbed hold of a chair and got himself into it.

"Good momin, m'love," he said to her. "Real fine and fragrant mornin, aint it?"

"It is," she agreed.

"I'm clean out a aspreens," he said, "and my ole noggin feels lak two dozen dawgs fightin over a rutty gyp. Reckon ye could lend me the borry of a couple a aspreen?"

She got up and went to the kitchen for a dipper of water, then came back through the store and picked up a package of aspirin and opened it and went back to the porch and ministered to Tearle's hangover.

"Jesus Christ A-mighty, that's fine water," he said. "Cool dipper a water from yore well's the best drink on earth. Wush I could stick with it."

She wished he could too. No, she realized, she *used to* wish he could; now she knew he had only one liberation. There were three, she reflected: drink, madness, religion. Tearle had chosen wisely. Without the whiskey he had been the most handsome of all the Ingledews, and he wasn't a man who had any use for being handsome.

"You know what, by jimminy cricket?" he said. "Ole Luther Chism's done went and caught hisself a revenuer! A real live one, too! Got him locked up in the smokehouse." And Tearle had a fit of laughter that became a fit of coughing.

"I heard about that," she said. "What does he plan to do with him?"

"Whut *kin* he do with him, fevensakes? He shore caint let him go. Reckon he'll just have to slice the pore feller's throat and bury him some'ers."

"He'd better not do that. Too many folks already know about it."

"Wal, he'd better do somethin quick. Old Luther don't know it, but that revenuer is a-tryin to sweet-talk his gal Lucy. I heerd im. I was up thar last night when he cotched that revenuer, and when I woke up this mornin I was in thet same smokehouse, and thet gal Lucy was feedin thet revenuer with a spoon, and he was shore a-sweet-talkin her. But I reckon Lucy's old enough to take keer a herself."

"Tull," she said, "have you heard Every's back in town?"

"Who?" he said.

"Every," she said. "Every Dill."

"Naw," he said. "Naw, now. NAW!" He stood up, unsteadily, and began looking in all directions. "Whar is the low-down dawg? Jist let him show hisself!"

"He's a preacher now, Tull."

"A *whut?*"

"He's come to Stay More to give a revival."

"Latha, hev you maybe been out in the sun too much today? I seen them bills tacked up on trees along the road but I never bothered to read one. Are you sure you wasn't imagining things when you read it?"

"There's one right there," she said, pointing. "Read it for yourself."

He did, squinting fiercely at it for a long time. "Hmmm," he said. "Must be somebody with the same name. Don't look lak ole Every a-tall."

"It's him, Tull. I met him."

"You *did?* What did he say?"

"Oh, we just had a little chat. Seems like he's honestly reformed, and he's been a gospel preacher for about eight or nine years."

"You don't mean to say. Does he have any family with him?"

"No. I don't believe he's married."

"How d'you know? Did he tell you he wasn't?"

"No, but I just—"

"Did he *perpose* to ye again, right off?"

"No, but—"

"But whut?"

"But he might."

"Wal, if he does, you jist let me know, will you? If he even mentions anything about marriage, you jist tell me and me and the boys will run him clean out a the country this time."

"Why, Tull! He's not the same old Every. You'll get used to him."

"Dang if I will," he said. "I won't ever in my life git used to Every Dill."

Tearle stayed on her porch for the rest of the afternoon. Countless times he had spent the whole afternoon on her porch, but today he seemed to have a special reason for it, as if he were waiting to see if Every would dare appear before him. Every wasn't mentioned again; they talked idly of matters general, nothing significant, the weather, the bold capture of the revenuer by Luther Chism, the mess those Germans were making again over there, E.H. Ingledew's own teeth falling out after thirty-five years as a dentist, the relative merits of the Dinsmore corn and the Chism corn for the production of Luther's liquor, the progress of construction on the W.P.A. bridge. Latha did not tell him that the post office had been ordered to close down. No need to send him to the bottle over *that.*

Dolph's horse, tethered to her hitching post all this time, began to fidget and whinny. Tearle noticed it and asked, "You or Sonora got company?" No, she said, the horse belonged to some surveyor who had hiked up the mountain. *When's he coming back to get it?* she wondered.

Late in the afternoon Every reappeared. One of his eyes had

turned black from his fight with Dolph and he had red bruises on his jaws and temples.

"Howdy," he said, studying the creased face of the man scowling at him. Then he said, "Why, I do believe it's ole Tull! How you doing, Tull?"

Tearle only scowled.

"Well, I declare," Every said, smiling, "your face is sure a lot friendlier than the last time I saw it, on the other end of a shotgun barrel. Latha, is this really ole Tull?"

She nodded.

Every wagged his head and said, "I swear, it's good to see you again after all these years, Tull." He held out his hand for a shake. "What do you have to say, you ole cuss?"

Tearle continued scowling. He did not take Every's hand.

"Come on, put er there, Tull," Every said. "Bygones are bygones. Let's forgive and forget. The past has passed like yesterday's snows. Come on and press the old flesh with me."

"I aint so damn sartin I'm ready to," Tearle said. "Whut hev ye come back fer?"

Every withdrew his hand and sat down on the porch rail. "My third chance, Tull. Everything comes in threes. I've been run out of town twice. I'd like to see if anybody wants to run me out once more."

"Boy," said Tull, "you've fergot whut you was tole the second time you was run off. You was tole you'd be shot on sight if ever you come back."

"You're right, I forgot, Tull. I forgot because it was such a long time ago. Long enough for a man to forget all kinds of things. But I'll tell you something I aint forgot, Tull. I aint forgot how it took five fellers ganging up on me to get me out of town. I aint forgot that no one man could have done it all by himself without his brothers. But I've forgot everything else. I don't harbor any grudge against you, Tull. I've made my peace with the Lord and I'm ready to make it with you."

Tearle broke his scowl long enough to make a short laugh.

"Hoo," he said, "it'll be the day if I kin ever feature *you* havin anything to do with any Lord."

"I'd be right proud to have you come to the meeting tomorrow and see for yourself."

"Not me," he said. "Never been near a churchhouse, nor never will."

"Now that sounds like a 'shiner I knew once who was offered a taste of eight-year-old store-boughten bottled-in-bond real McCoy, and he said nearly them said words, he said, 'I never drunk government stuff, nor never will.' Have you ever sampled the pure quill, Tull?"

"Naw, and I aint got no use for that neither."

Latha said, "If you boys will excuse me, I've got to go start supper."

She went to the kitchen and left them talking—and bickering—on the porch. From time to time, as she rolled out dough for a pie, she could hear their voices raised against each other, but after a while it grew so quiet that she thought one or both of them had left. She wiped her hands on her apron and went through the store to peer out the window. They were still there. Every in a quiet voice was telling some kind of anecdote to Tearle, and Tearle was grinning fit to split his jaws.

After she had all of supper on the stove or in the oven, she rejoined them.

"...during that big freeze last winter," Every was saying, "I was at this big revival over in Kentucky, with preachers there from all over the country. Well, there was a boy staying in one of the boardinghouses over there and he told everybody that he'd had a dream of hell. One of the preachers kind of smirked and said, 'Sonny, what is it like in hell?' And the boy answered him, all right. 'Just about like it is here,' says he. 'I mighty nigh froze. The preachers was so thick, I couldn't get near the stove.'"

And Tearle let loose one of his pealing guffaws, pounding his knees with his fists.

Every wrinkled his nose and said, "I'll wager my shoes that

there's a wild cherry pie baking in Latha's oven, and it sure smells good. Tull, if me and you just hang around long enough, she's bound to invite us to stay and eat."

"Sure," she said, "Both of you boys stay more and eat supper with me."

"Supper?" said Tearle. "Shoot, I aint even et my dinner yet. Anyhow, thank you kindly, but I tole Lola I'd eat with her this evenin." He stood up, placing a palm on the storefront to steady himself. "Well, Every," he said, "I reckon maybe I'll just go and have a little talk with Oren Duckworth, and if he won't let ye use the meetin house, why, then I'll just come early in the mornin and help ye cut branches to make a brush arbor."

"That's awful good of you, Tull," Every said, emotion in his voice. "I'm much obliged."

"S'long," Tearle said, and shuffled off.

When Tearle was out of sight, Every exclaimed, "Good land! He sure has changed. I'd hardly know him. Makes me feel old, to think he's not but eight or nine years older'n me."

"He's mellowed considerably, too," she said.

"You're telling me. When I first saw him, I started quaking in my boots. I never told anyone, but he used to be the only feller in this town I was ever afraid of. When did he start drinking so hard?"

"Right after he lost most of his money when the bank was robbed."

"Oh."

A full minute passed before another word was spoken. She sat down in the rocker, thinking, *Supper's nearly ready, and I haven't felt anywhere near like crying yet.*

"You know," Every said, "I just took it for granted that that mare there was his. When he walked off on foot, then I recognized the mare. Has Dolph moved in on you?"

"No," she said. "I don't know where he is."

"Why'd he leave his horse, then?"

Is this what I'm supposed to cry about? she wondered. *Is this going to lead up to me crying?* If so, she decided, then supper was going to be awfully late. "I don't know," she said. "Really, I don't have any idea."

"Have you invited him to supper?" he asked.

"No, and I don't intend to. I reckon it'll be just you and me and Sonora, when she gets back. I think she went swimming with some of her friends up the creek a ways."

"Latha—" he said.

"Yes."

"I've been wanting to ask you—"

"Yes?"

"Who is Sonora's father?"

"Vaughn Twichell, who used to live at Hunton. I thought you knew Mandy had married him. They live in Little Rock now. You used to know him, didn't you?"

"Knew him right well. Knew his first wife too."

"Really."

"Yes, and I wonder why Mandy married him. She used to always brag so about how many children she was going to have when she grew up. Wonder why she settled for just one."

"Well, maybe she thought Sonora was enough, or too much."

"Latha, are you *positive* she's theirs?"

"No. Maybe they adopted her."

"They must have. Did Mandy know why Vaughn's first wife left him? Did she know that Vaughn was sterile?"

She did not answer.

"Latha, I've got a strong suspicion that that girl is yours."

"I swear she's not!" she said, and realized, *Oh no, it's coming.*

"And maybe mine too," he said.

"You're mistaken! I swear she's Vaughn and Mandy's!"

"'Thou shalt not bear false witness…'"

"I swear it! I swear it!" she said, and felt the first hot tear drop down her cheek, and then another from the other eye. *I am going now.* "I swore to them I'd always swear it!" She collapsed in sobs.

SUB THREE: *Seventeen Years Ago*

Cry, Bug. This is a happy story, and at first glimpse your tears would seem most unwelcome, but I've persuaded myself that they are called for, even required. Let them flow. I'm sorry you had to wait so long before you could have a good cry, with a strong man beside you to comfort you through the deliverance.

I'll tell you about the last time I myself shed some tears. It was during my last visit to Little Rock, a few days after that evening I had clandestinely found my way into the Records Office of the State Hospital. On foot I went out and located 2120 West Nineteenth Street, that Taft era bungalow in the shotgun style. A family of blacks is living there now, as I discovered when a large and kindly woman came out and said to me in a mild voice without any indignation, "White man, whut you standin out here fo and gawkin at my house fo and waterin yo eyes so fo?" I told her a friend of mine had lived there long ago, and asked her if I might come in for just a moment. "My house a messy wreck," she protested, "but if it make you dry yo eyes, you jus come on in." I went in, but it did not make me dry my eyes. I found the room which I was almost sure was the room.

You were sitting in a chair with your feet propped up on the window sill; your legs were aching painfully again and you were trying to rest them. The view through the window was of a vacant lot next door [door? no door] grown high with rampant weeds. You had counted all those weeds; had you the desire you would have given a personal name to each. Your hands were together in your lap, almost out of sight below the bulge, your fingers were stripping tiny shreds of flesh from around your fingernails.

Beyond the field of weeds rose a single large sycamore tree; you had studied the configuration of its branches endlessly and you were beginning to read the language hidden in that wild calligraphy. God or Whoever It Was had been putting up these trees as signboards, as posters, for millions of years, but nobody until now had learned how to read the script of the twisting branches. You were finding a long message there, and understanding it; without that message you could have closed your eyes and ceased to exist.

You were three weeks overdue, and Vaughn had begun to make smart remarks. "It's just costiveness. Let's dose her with a big gulp of prune juice and she'll unclog."

That man, he was needing to be spiteful. For seven months now he'd been unable to forgive you for so violently rejecting his charitable offer to screw you on the sly for mercy.

Your sister was not being much better. At first, when you were very happy to be carrying a child, she had hated you bitterly for it, and abused you constantly and said things to you like, "If you had any sense at all you'd run a coat hanger up you and rip it out." Her real motive had been that she was maddeningly envious of you; but she pretended that you were bringing disgrace on your whole family, even though she was the only one of your family who knew about it. "If I were in your place," she would say, "I would just wear my head in a sack."

She had made you do the next best thing to it. She had kept you confined to the house for the past five months.

"Why couldn't," you would ask, "why couldn't I just wear a ring and you tell people my husband's in the service?"

"Too late," she'd say. "All my friends already know."

"But they're *your* friends, not mine. I don't care what they think."

"But I do, and I'm the one with a position to keep in this town."

"But," you'd say, feeling as if you could not even think straight any more, as if you were unable to grasp the slightest bit of logic, "if your friends already know, what's wrong with anybody seeing me?"

"You don't have to make a public spectacle of your sin!" she'd shout.

"But," you'd persist, clutching at one receding straw of logic, "what does my condition have to do with *your* position in this town?"

"You're my sister, aren't you? You think I want everybody to know I've got a whore for a sister?"

"But if you've already told your friends—" you'd say, and stop and wonder if you were making any sense at all, if you weren't perhaps just babbling some blathering rubbish.

Now things were turned around, and this was more confusing yet. You were hating that creature inside you and wishing you could kill it without killing yourself…or both. Once when it was kicking violently you had pounded your fists on it until you had become quite dizzy and it had stopped and you had thought it was dead.

But Mandy was taking a loving interest in it all of a sudden, and when she had found out you'd been pounding on it, she had upbraided you.

"What're you trying to do, for Chrissakes, *kill* it?"

"Yes."

"*Why,* for the love of Pete?"

"I don't want it."

"*You don't want it?* Are you out of your mind, girl? What have you got against babies? Pore defenseless little thing…. Pore, pore sweet little thing." And she would even stroke and pat your belly till you felt like screaming.

"It will be a cute little boy," she would say, "and we could name him Saultus after Dad."

"It will be a disfigured monster," you would say, "and I will name it Mandyvaughn after y'all."

"Well, I like that! That's a fine lot of gratitude for all me'n Vaughn have done for you! Who feeds you? I ask you. Who gives you a place to stay, huh? Who the hell you think is gonna pay the goddamn hospital bill and the doctor bill? Huh? You answer me that!"

And that had been the day you had run away. You had walked and walked, nearly out of the city, before Vaughn's car had caught up with you and begun to move slowly along the road beside you, for another hour or so, with her at the window, saying over and over, every mile or so, "Tired yet? Hungry yet? Shamed yet?" until you gave in.

And there had been the time you read in the newspaper about the law permitting abortions in the case of violent rape, and you had asked Mandy if she had known about that law, and, if so, why hadn't she done something about it while there was still time.

"How you gonna prove it was rape?" she'd said. "Who would believe you? If ever time you'd gone off in the bushes with a feller was rape, then, sister, you're a regular rape-catcher. Besides, you won't never tell who done it. They've got to catch the feller and make him confess, and if you won't even tell who done it, how can they? Come on, honey, for the last time I ask you, please tell me who it was."

"I'm glad to know that's the last time you're asking me," you'd said.

And Vaughn and his endless remarks:

"'Course she won't tell you who done it. She's hopin he'll come back and do it again."

"Whoever he was, he must've been a awful big and strong feller, to of broken down her notorious resistance."

"Bet he had a pecker on him so thin and tiny she didn't know she'd been raped until she found herself knocked up."

"Bet she run first thing to her dad and hollered, 'Paw, a feller just ruined me! What are you goin to do about it?' and ole Saultus he just smiles and says, 'first I got to take care of that feller who ruined you last week.'"

"Wouldn't surprise me a bit if it was a gang shay, and she has quintuplets, each one different."

"Well, maybe they'll catch the feller and put him on trial and the judge'll call on her to testify, and he'll say to her, 'Miss, this offense occurred on or about the middle of June. Has the man ever bothered you before or since?' and she'll answer, 'I'll say he has! It's just been rape, rape, rape, all summer long!'"

That small, small room—it would not have been so bad if you could have locked yourself into it, but since you had refused to leave it, they had to come into it to vent their verbal indignities upon you, and it was crowded with the three of you in that small small room which you never left except to go to the bathroom—and Mandy had taken the lock off the bathroom door after she discovered you trying to take a bath.

"Have you lost your senses completely?!" she stormed. "Don't you know you can't take a bath when you're pregnant? Don't you know you're not supposed to immerse that pore thing in water?"

"How'm I going to get *clean?*" you'd whined.

"Just use a sponge, you idiot!"

And you had used sponges, and Vaughn, sometimes, in your room, would say, "Pee Yew! I'll shore be glad when warm weather comes so we can open that window and air it out in here."

And because the lock was removed from the bathroom door, he could barge in on you, saying, "Oops!" but lingering long enough to take a good look.

"Why, I'll declare!" he had exclaimed recently, pointing. "Lookee there, sugar, yore belly-button has popped wrongside out!"

On the faded wallpaper of the small room was a calendar, March of 1922, with a large circle drawn around March 6, and heavy black X's over March 7, March 8, March 9, March 10, March 11, March 12, March 13, March 14, March 15, March 16, March 17, March 18, March 19, March 20, March 21, March 22, March 23, March 24, March 25, March 26, March 27 and March 28.

You were sitting in a chair with your feet propped up on the window sill, on March 29, counting the weeds in the vacant lot next door and then reading the script in the branches of the sycamore tree, when suddenly you felt a snap in your womb and then you flooded the chair and made a puddle around it. You went to the kitchen and looked for the mop. *Where would Mandy keep the mop?* You looked on the back porch. But you could not find the mop. So you got a towel from the bathroom. But when you returned to your room, you found that you could neither kneel nor squat to mop the floor. Using the chair as a brace, you slowly lowered yourself into a sitting position on the floor, with your legs out straight before you. You began to mop. Then the first pains started, and you had to stop mopping. You waited. The pain went away. You finished mopping. You found then you could not get yourself up off the floor. You tried to remember where Mandy had said she and Vaughn were going. You only half-listened to anything she'd said lately. Were they out playing cards with some friends? Had they gone shopping? Were they away off up in Hunton visiting Vaughn's relatives for the weekend?

If you could get up, you might go on to the hospital by yourself. *Which hospital?* you wondered. *Where is it?*

You scooted backwards across the floor to your bed, and just as another pain started you turned over and got a good grip on the bedpost and pulled yourself up and collapsed on your back in the bed.

That is where you spent the next seven hours, and when Mandy and Vaughn came home, around midnight, you were screaming.

"You get her legs," Vaughn said, "and I'll get her arms and let's see if we can carry her out and dump her in the car."

"It's too late, I think," Mandy said. "You know anyone who has a telephone?"

"Not around here."

"Then drive on out and try to get Dr. Rory and I'll stay with her and try to deliver it if you don't get back in time."

You screamed, and you screamed.

It seemed like days passed before Vaughn returned. "This is all I could find," he said. "Doc Rory's out of town."

The stranger came and looked at you and then snapped at Mandy, "What are you sitting on your ass for? Why haven't you got some water boiling on the stove and some clean towels ready?"

Mandy got up off her ass. The stranger placed his cool hand on your brow and felt your pulse. "Easy, girl," he said. "Easy." It was the closest approximation to pleasant words you had heard in quite some time. But still you screamed.

"Get out of the room!" the stranger said to Vaughn.

"Aw," said Vaughn, "it aint no different than watchin a mare foal."

"Is she your wife?" the man asked him.

"Naw, she's my sister-in-law, Doc. She aint even got a husband. Claims the guy raped her."

"That true?" he asked you.

You screamed.

"Listen," he said to you, "do you *want* this baby?"

You screamed, and thrashed your head violently from side to side.

"She does too!" Mandy hollered, coming in and clutching the man's sleeve and saying, "Look, Doc, we got to have that baby. Even if she don't want it, I do. I'll take care of it, Doc. Me and Vaughn caint have no children of our own, so I'd be more than happy to have it. Please, Doc—"

"Get out of here, both of you!" he snapped. "I'll holler for you if I need you."

Then you were alone with him, and he went to work.

"Relax, girl," he would say. "I swear, I never saw anybody so tense.

"Relax. Try to take a deep breath.

"Now. Bear down. Hard.

"Relax. Easy. Easy, girl, easy. Deep breath.

"Bear down.

"Relax.

"Bear down. You're not bearing down. Pretend you're trying to evacuate if you were constipated.

"Ease up. Jesus Christ, girl, how long have you been tying yourself in knots?

"Come on now, *press! press! press!*"

He sighed loudly. You screamed loudly.

"I don't want to have to do a Caesarean. Need you in the hospital for that.

"Let up.

"Squeeze.

"Goddamn you, mister, I told you to stay out of here! If you show your head again I'll come after you with a scalpel!

"Let up. I'm sure it's a breach. Now relax completely, I'm going to try to turn it. Easy. Relax. Relax."

He gave you chloroform. For a while it was paradise. You heard nothing. You felt nothing. Later you heard:

"Mr. Twichell, come back in here a minute! Listen, I want you to telephone for an ambulance."

"No telephone, Doc."

"Then go out and get one! No, wait, just get your wife, and the three of us will carry her out to the backseat of my car."

You were lifted, screaming, and manhandled out to the car.

The doctor knelt on the floor of the rear seat beside you. "Twichell, you drive. And I mean *drive!*"

More chloroform, blessed oblivion.

A white room. Bright lights. People all around. An old white-haired man saying to the doctor, "What the hell does a goddamn *interne* know about giving Caesareans anyway? Shit, you don't even know how to turn a baby! Here, nurse, she's rousing, let's clap that ether coat on her. That's eno—"

Another room. A woman in another bed. A nurse. Mandy. Mandy saying, "Well, sister, you can go out and get raped all you want to, now, and never worry about having any more babies."

You opened your mouth to scream again, but a calm question came out: "What do you mean?"

"Doctor tied your tubes. Caint have no more babies."

"Why'd he do that?"

"*I* told him to." Smug, self-proud.

"Now that's not strictly true, Mrs. Twichell," said the nurse, stepping forward. She carried a bundle in her arms. "The doctor simply asked for your permission. He himself considered it a wise thing to do, as future pregnancies might endanger her life."

"Well," said Mandy, "after you take a gander at this little monstrosity you produced, you'll be glad you caint have any more."

"It's a beautiful baby," the nurse protested, and brought the bundle forward and placed it in your arms. It was not a beautiful baby. It was hideous. It had a horribly misshapen head as if it had been hit with a sledgehammer in several places. It bore no resemblance to either its mother or its father. Thus you could not understand why you suddenly felt such deep, overwhelming love for it.

"Is he...is he...all right?" you asked the nurse.

"She," she corrected you. "It's a girl. And she's just fine. Weighs eight pounds, eleven ounces. Not a thing wrong with her. She'll be a beautiful girl."

"But all these bumps and creases in her skull..." you said.

"Those'll clear up. Always do. Give her time, and she'll have a lovely head on her."

Later Mandy and Vaughn came together, with the old white-haired man.

"How you feel?" the white-haired man said. "You had us pretty worried for a while there, but everything turned out just fine. That's a near-perfect baby. Have you been thinking any about names? I'd like to get these papers filled out."

"Yes I have," you said.

"Fannie Mae Twichell!" Mandy said. "After Momma."

"That's a right pretty name," Vaughn said, and tried it out: "Fannie Mae."

You had been listening to the baby crying, and there was such a sweet quality about her cries, like songs, little songs. "Sonora," you said to the doctor. *Little song.* "Sonora Bourne is her name."

"The hell with that crap!" Mandy said.

The doctor said to you, "I understand the infant has no father. Legally, that is. You don't plan to keep it, do you?"

"Why not?" you said.

"Well, don't you understand, there would be difficulties…"

"We'll keep it, Doc!" said Mandy. "Just put down Fannie Mae Twichell and we'll keep it."

"The child's name is Sonora Bourne," you said.

"Well, look," said the doctor, "this is just for the birth certificate, and you can change it later if you like. Why don't I just put it down as Sonora Twichell?"

"Oh no you don't!" said Mandy. "It's our baby and we got the right to name it, and its name is Fannie Mae Twichell, and if you don't like it you know what you can do about it!"

"Madam," the doctor said, "I'm trying to compromise. She is the mother, after all, and as such she ought to have the right to name the infant, at least for the mere purpose of this certificate."

"Doc," said Vaughn angrily, "you heard what my wife said. Now you put down Fannie Mae Twichell on that thing, goddamit, or I'm walkin out of here and washin my hands of any responsibility. I won't pay a cent."

"Sir," said the old man, "I personally don't give a shit for your cents…or your *sense*."

"Come on, Mandy," said Vaughn. "The hell with it."

"Bye bye, sister dear," said Mandy. "Hope you have fun getting yourself out of this fix."

They left.

"Shall we make it Sonora Twichell?" the doctor asked you.

"Sonora Bourne," you said.

"Very well," said the doctor, and took out his pen.

But two days later Mandy came back, just as the nurse was bringing the baby in for feeding. She hovered over the bed. When you gave your breast to Sonora, Mandy said, "Hey, don't do that!" and clutched at the baby and tried to pull her away from you. You slapped viciously at Mandy's hand. She retreated, slightly, protesting, "That's so...so backward! And it's also unhealthy! And it will ruin your figure, and also it's just not *nice*. You're way behind the times, kid. I've been studying up on it, and all the latest modem scientific—"

"Shut up!" you said.

After you had finished feeding Sonora, Mandy came and took a good look at her, and exclaimed disgustedly, "Holy cow, isn't she gosh-awful ugly, though! I'd have to be blindfolded before I'd let that creature suck on my tits. I just don't know if I can bear to keep her...."

But when the time came for your release from the hospital, there she was, and Vaughn with her. "Vaughn paid the bill, after all!" Mandy declared with a laugh. "I bet those jerks thought he couldn't do it. But just wait till you see all the things we've bought for the baby!"

Among all the things she had bought for the baby, you discovered when you were returned to the house on West Nineteenth, were a dozen glass bottles with rubber nipples.

You ignored them.

One day after finishing your bath you returned to your room and found Mandy holding the baby in her lap and trying to force a bottle on her. "Come on, Fannie Mae, sweetums, open your nasty little mouth."

You slapped her.

She dumped the baby on the bed, and slapped you back.

Then she slapped you once more, harder. "Damn you!" she shouted. "We paid hard money for them bottles, by God, and I mean to *use* them!"

"You leave my baby alone, you," you said.

"She's not your baby!" she shrieked.

You said nothing more. You said nothing more at all, not at all, for the days and weeks following. You said not a word to either of them. You did not even talk to your baby.

Nearly two weeks went by before it dawned on Mandy and Vaughn that you had not been saying anything.

"Cat got your tongue?" Mandy asked one day.

You did not reply.

"She's just being high and mighty," Vaughn explained. "Just stuck up."

"Say something, sister," Mandy urged you.

You did not.

"See if I care, then," Mandy said. "Button your lip for the rest of your life, for all I care. Who'd want to listen to you anyhow?"

But your continued silence began to fray their nerves.

"Want a nice piece of custard pie?" Mandy would ask, and wait for you to respond. You did not.

Vaughn would sneak up on you and yell "BOO!" at the top of his lungs but you would not even flinch.

"Would you like to go for a ride today, honey?" Mandy would ask, and wait, and wait.

Once when you were in the bathtub (and the lock had never been replaced on the door) Vaughn came in and sat on the edge of the tub and gazed at you. "Caint tell me to get out, can you?" he taunted you. "Caint even open you damn mouth long enough to say 'Get out,' can you?" You just glared at him. "All righty," he said, "I'll just sit right here and feast my eyes until you're finished."

It was not that you were deliberately holding yourself incommunicado, Bug. You were not consciously refusing to speak to them. It was simply (maybe not so simply) that you were unable to speak to them. Occasionally, there were times you wanted something, like a particular medicine for some distress, but you were unable to open your mouth and ask for it.

They ceased trying to get you to speak. They began to pretend you were not there, and to talk about you in your presence.

"She don't really want that baby."

"Of course she don't. She's ashamed of it, I bet."

She won't even talk to her own baby. What kind of mother is that? Pore little Fannie Mae, she needs somebody to sweet-talk her and baby-talk her."

"She's so stubborn and standoffish she won't even talk to her own baby."

"What kind of mother is that?"

"She don't really want it."

"'Course she don't."

"She'd be a lot happier without it."

"Sure she would."

"Maybe it would be happier too, if she weren't around."

"More'n likely."

But still they would occasionally stare at you and study your face and bite their lips or chew their thumbnails.

One day they took you and put you in the car and said they were going for a ride.

They drove you out to a park, and through the park to a group of large white buildings on a hill. They took you into one of these buildings. In a room was a desk with a man in a white jacket sitting behind it and they tried to get you to sit down at the desk. Wordlessly, you broke and ran. Mandy and Vaughn took your arms and brought you back. You shook your head and shook your head and shook your head.

"Please sit down," the man said, and came around from behind his desk and pushed down on your shoulder to make you sit. Then he returned to his seat behind the desk and looked at the papers in front of him. "You can talk to me," he said. "Will you tell me your name?"

You would not.

"I told you her name," Mandy said. "It's Latha Bourne."

The man frowned at her. "Will you two leave the room, please?"

When they were gone, he said, "Now, I already know your name. You can talk to me, I know. Will you tell me your age?"

You spoke. "Almost twenty-one."

"Good," he said, and wrote something on the paper. "Now, do you know why your sister and brother-in-law have brought you here?"

You shook your head.

"Now, now," he chided. "I'll bet you do. I'll bet you think it's because they're trying to get rid of you. Am I right?"

"Are they?" you asked, puzzled. "I don't know. Are they?"

"No," he said. "They are not. Why do you *think* they have brought you here?"

"I really don't know," you said.

"Oh come now, Miss Bourne. Really. Do you know what place this is?"

"A hospital?"

"Do you know what *kind* of hospital?"

You shook your head.

"Really now," he said. "If you don't know what kind of hospital it is, why did you break loose and try to run away when you were brought in?"

"I...I was frightened," you said.

"Of what, Miss Bourne? Of *what* were you frightened?"

"I...I don't...really know...."

"Was it perhaps you were frightened that we might keep you?"

You lowered your head and nodded it.

"Very good. So I'm sure you can tell me what place this is, can't you? *Try* to tell me, Miss Bourne,"

"Is it...is it an...an insane asylum?"

"There!" he exclaimed, beaming broadly. "I *knew* you could tell me. Now, I'll bet you think that there's no reason why you should be here. Am I right?"

"You are right."

"But I am told that you have not spoken a word to anybody for nearly two months. Why is that, Miss Bourne? Are you perhaps feeling angry at the world?"

"Not the world. Just *them.*"

"Why are you mad at *them,* Miss Bourne?"

"They're trying to take my baby away from me."

"*Why* would they want to do that?"

"They want her."

"Don't you think that it might be because they are concerned for the baby? Don't you think that they might feel you are not in the best mental condition for taking care of the child?"

"That's not true!"

"I understand that you don't even communicate with your child, Miss Bourne. Do you think that's good for the child?"

"I try to talk to her! I just can't talk to her when they're around. Often at night when they're asleep I talk to her."

"I understand that the child is illegitimate, Miss Bourne. Perhaps you feel some guilt for your error, and this guilt is being reflected in your conduct toward the child."

"I love her! I take very good care of her!"

"A child needs a father, Miss Bourne."

"I'll marry somebody!" you said.

The man's voice became cold. "I understand further, Miss Bourne, that when the child was still in your womb you pounded your fists upon your abdomen repeatedly, as if you were trying to kill the child."

"I didn't want it then. But I want it now. Oh, I want her so!"

The man signed his name at the bottom of a sheet of paper and said, "I am recommending, Miss Bourne, that you remain with us for observation."

"You can't do this to me!" you protested. "You have no right to do this to me! I'm as sane as you are!"

"But I should point out that, legally, you are still a minor, and your older sister has signed papers appointing her your legal guardian. In the eyes of the law, Miss Bourne, she is perfectly within her rights to have you committed."

"She's just trying to get rid of me, so she can have the baby!"

"I *knew* you would feel that way, Miss Bourne, but you are mistaken. It is the child that we are concerned for. Our job is not merely to help people with mental problems, but also to protect the rest of society from them until they can return to their responsibilities; therefore—"

You stood up and began backing away from the doctor's desk. He pressed a button on his desk. You turned and ran to the door. You twisted the knob but it would not open. Another door opened and two men in blue jackets came into the room and took you by the arms. You struggled. You yelled.

"Please go along peacefully," the man behind the desk said, "or else we might have to use force."

You continued yelling and struggling.

They used force and took you away to a cell, and locked you in it.

You tried to cry, Bug, alone in your cell you tried with all your might to cry, but you would not be able to cry for another seventeen years.

You spent three weeks in B Ward.

You were transferred to C Ward, where you spent five months.

After six months, at Christmastime, Mandy and Vaughn came for a visit, bringing candy and flowers, but without Sonora.

You fell down on your knees before them and raised your hands in supplication. "Please get me out of here!" you begged. "Please! I'll do anything for you! I'll cook for you! I'll sweep for you! I'll do everything for you! Please get me out of here!"

"See!" Mandy said to Vaughn. "I told you she was just playing possum. I told you she could really talk, if she put her mind to it."

"Please, please, please, oh *please*...." you pled.

"No," she said. "You'd be a bad influence on the baby."

You were transferred to D Ward.

FOUR: Evening

Dear Heavenly Father, we thank Thee for this food, the yield of Thy gracious bounty, and for the loving hands that hath prepared it and brought it before us. Bless those hands, Lord, and bestow Thy loving grace and kindness upon her who uses them to enrich Thy bounty for the pleasure of our mouths and the strength of our bodies. Bless also, we pray, this lovely girl, her niece; keep her near Thy heart; do not let her stray far from Thy hand. And finally, Lord, bless me Thy servant; strengthen me; grant me the power to meet what comes my way. In Jesus' Name we pray, Amen."

"Have some beans, Every."

"Thank you."

"Pickles?"

"Don't care for any, thank you."

"Sweetening for your iced tea?"

"No, thank you. I'll declare, Latha, I never thought I'd see the day I'd be drinking iced tea in Stay More. How do you do it?"

"Well, the mail truck brings ice from Jasper, and twice a month a truck from Harrison comes through with lemons and other fruit. Have some potatoes."

"Thank you. Sonora, you care for any pickles?"

"Thank you. I'll bet they're *Dill* pickles, why don't you have some yourself?"

"Ha! Now don't you go poking fun at me too, young lady. Has your m—has your Aunt Latha told you that everybody used to call me 'Pickle' when I was a kid?"

"Just because of your name? Or because you were sour?"

"Dill pickles aren't really sour, are they? I reckon I was pretty full of vinegar, though. And I was kind of pickle-faced too, wasn't I, Latha?"

"You sure weren't much to look at,"

"Maybe you're still full of vinegar," Sonora said. "How'd you get that shiner?"

"That what?" he said, and "Oh," he said and raised his fingers to his blackened eye. "You mean this? Well, I'll tell you. I was so busy tacking up my posters on trees this morning that I didn't watch where I was going, and ran plumb head-on into a big elm sapling."

"I've got a slab of beef you can lay on that eye after supper," Latha said, "and maybe it will go away. You'd look just fine preaching a revival meeting with a black eye and all those bruises."

"I tore my britches, too," he said, "and my coat-tail barely covers it. Could you lend me some needle-and-thread?"

"I'll patch them up for you myself," she offered.

"How'd you rip the back of your britches running head-on into an elm sapling?" Sonora asked.

He laughed. "Well, that *is* pretty complicated. It was like this: when I smacked into that elm sapling it kind of bent over and then sprung back and flung me right up against a barbed-wire fence. My, Latha, these sure are fine pork chops!"

"You think it's right for a preacher to tell big fibs?" Sonora asked with a grin.

"Why, no," he said. "It's sure not right, at all. But depends on what you mean by a fib. For instance, tomorrow morning I'm going to stand up there in front of those people and I'm going to say to them—" Every began to imitate his own preaching voice "—my friends, you see this here black eye? And you see these bumps and bruises? And you see this here patch on my britches? Well, my friends, as I was coming into Stay More I met the Devil blocking my way and telling me he had Stay More in the palm of his hand and he wasn't about to let me meddle with his territory. But I just said to him, 'Get thee behind me, Old Harry!' But Old Harry said to me, 'Not without a fight first, by nab!' So me and Old Harry just squared off right there in the road. Now, my friends, I'm afraid I caint tell you that I got the best of him, but he sure didn't get the best of me, or else I wouldn't be here to tell it to you!"

Sonora shook with laughter, and Latha found herself laughing too, and marveling at a certain spell-binding quality in Every's voice. He had made his point, she realized: it doesn't matter that what you say is a ridiculous fib, if you say it right.

"Well," said Sonora, "I was thinking maybe there was some connection between your black eye and Latha's red eyes."

"Now, there *is*, since you mention it. When she saw what a pitiful condition I was in, with all these bumps and bruises, she just broke down and blubbered. What's the matter with you, girl, how come you're not crying too at the sight of such a pore ole battered-up man?"

"Maybe I don't love you as much as she does," Sonora said. Every choked on a bite of pork chop and blushed deeply. "But I might," Sonora said, "if you'd stop telling fibs."

When Every regained his composure and coughed the dab of pork chop out of his windpipe, he said, "All right. That's a deal."

"Really?" Sonora said.

"No more fibs," he said. He crossed his heart.

"Okay," she said. "Who did you get into a fight with?"

"I don't know if you'd know him," he said.

"I might," she said. "If he was a tall fellow with light hair riding a big roan mare that's tied to the post out front."

"You got him," Every said.

"Okay, why did *you* get him?"

"Well, I reckon you might say we were quarreling over a certain lady."

"Is that the reason the lady has red eyes?" Sonora asked.

"No."

"Then why does she?"

"Mercy, gal, are you going to give me the third-degree all night? You're spoiling my supper." He glanced at Latha and said, "I think maybe I'd best let *her* answer that."

"All right," Latha said. "We were just talking over old times, honey. You know how it is. It makes you sad to think of old times."

"It must have been awfully, *awfully* sad to make *you* cry," Sonora said.

"It was," Every said, and his voice was severe. "Saddest damn thing you ever heard."

"Do preachers swear?" Sonora asked with surprise.

"Sometimes they just have to," he said.

"Tell me what it was that could make a preacher swear," Sonora asked.

"Latha?" he said.

"Honey," she said to Sonora, "it isn't any of your concern."

Every brought his palms together and looked up at the ceiling. "Father, forgive us all our fibs. Amen." But his voice was serious.

"There is only one thing worse than telling a fib," Latha said, "and that is breaking a promise. So there. That is that, and let's talk about the weather. Maybe it will rain tomorrow."

"I don't care," Sonora said. "I *know* anyway."

"Have some more cornbread, Every."

"Thank you. Could you pass me the butter, Sonora?"

"*Here!*"

After supper she went out to do her evening chores, leaving Every and Sonora discussing the difference between his religion and hers—or rather that of Mandy, who had joined an Episcopal church in Little Rock. "I just can't stand all that fancy ritual," Sonora was saying to him as Latha went out. While she was feeding the hogs, she realized she was not really worried that Every would tell Sonora anything; after all, he had promised her he would not. But all this business of promises was becoming rather ridiculous anyway; that girl could sit there at the table and look across the table and see her own features written all over the face of the man sitting there talking to her. What worried Latha was not that Every would give anything away, but that Sonora would back him into a corner and try to make him confess what she had already guessed on her own. *Still I will never break my promise,* she determined. As she was milking Mathilda, she realized she was working too fast, as if she were eager to finish her chores and get back to the house. *Relax, girl,* she said to herself. *Give father and daughter a chance to get acquainted.* She began to move more slowly, and to take her time.

While she was feeding her chickens, she heard a commotion coming from the front yard, and she went around the house to investigate, wondering if it had something to do with Dolph. But Dolph's horse was gone, and so was he. It was just the W.P.A. boys and the local boys having their nocturnal free-for-all, for Sonora's audience. Every came running out of the house and saw the fight and ran out into the midst of the ruckus and began separating the battlers, grabbing them by their shirt collars and pulling them off one another, and saying, "Here now, what's this all about? Here now, let's break it up a minute!"

He had trouble separating Junior Duckworth from Clarence Biggart, and when he finally succeeded, Junior grabbed him by his shirt front and said, "Who in hell are you, you ole geezer?"

Sonora, from her throne on the porch, laughed and said, "He's my father, and he can lick all of you guys put together, if you don't watch out!"

"*Sonora!*" Latha said to her.

Junior removed his grip from Every's shirt front and offered his hand. "Gee, sir, I'm sorry," he said. "I didn't know who you was."

Every said, "Sonora's just a-foolin you. I'm not her dad, but I *might* just have to lick y'all all together if you don't knock it off. Now tell me, what's all this rumpus about, anyhow?"

"It's his fault," Junior said, pointing to J.D. Pruitt. "He hit me first."

Clarence Biggart said, pointing to Junior, "Burl Coe put im up to it. He darred im to trip ole J.D. and ole J.D. couldn't do nuthin but hit im fer it."

"Well, why are all the rest of you fellers fightin?" Every asked.

"Aw, we aint fightin serious," Earl Coe put in. "It aint a real fraction. We'uns was just horseplayin, to show them damn Dubya Pee Ayers who rules the roost around here."

"No need somebody gettin hurt for that," Every said. "If all you want to do is find out who rules the roost, why don't y'all just hold a Indian wrasslin?"

"Whut's thet?" Junior asked.

"You aint never Indian-wrassled?" Every asked. "Well, come over here to the porch and I'll show you." He and Junior sat down in opposite directions on the porch steps and Every put their arms up together, elbows down on the cement step, and their hands clenched. "Now the idee," Every said, "is to see if you can force my hand down and I try to force your hand down. Winner's strongest. Not only is he strongest but he's also got the most will power and spunk. Okay. Here we go."

Every and Junior strained together, the knot of their clenched hands vibrating for a moment before Every let his hand be pushed down, saying, "There! See, you beat me. Now you take on one of the others."

There began a round of eliminations. Junior Indian-wrestled with Clarence Biggart and lost; Clarence matched Earl Coe and won, but lost to Gerald Coe. Gerald beat Merle Kimber but lost to J.D. Pruitt, who defeated both Burl Coe and Chester Duckworth, and then engaged Hank Ingledew in a match that lasted nearly four minutes before Hank forced J.D.'s hand down.

Hank then took on Eddie Churchwell, Leo Dinsmore, and Dorsey Tharp, defeating each of them.

"The winner!" Every declared, raising Hank's arm. "What's your name, son?"

"John Henry," he said, and added, "Ingledew. And now I'll take you on, sir, if you want to Indian-wrassle."

"Why, I was the first one eliminated," Every protested. "This boy here beat me in the first match."

"I saw that," Hank said. "You let him. You just let him do it. Come on and Indian-wrassle with me."

"Okay," Every said, and sat down and matched arms with Hank.

Their clenched hands strained and quivered for half a minute, then Hank smashed Every's hand down. "Oof!" Every exclaimed. "Wow, that's too much for me."

"Aw, you wasn't even tryin!" Hank protested. "Come on, god-damn ye, and *try.*"

"Swear all you want," Every said sternly. "Just don't bring the Lord's name in to help ye." And he took Hank's hand again and they matched up for only a few seconds before Every drove his arm swiftly down.

"Haw!" Hank exclaimed, "I knew you could do it! Come on, best two out of three. I took one, you took one, now let's settle it!"

Once again they matched up, and Hank closed his eyes and gritted his teeth, and all the muscles in his neck bulged out. Minute after minute went by, and each of them began to grunt with enormous effort, but their hands remained totally immobile, not even trembling.

Five or six minutes passed. Seven. "Let up!" Latha said. "Your eyeballs are going to pop right out of your heads." But the others were urging them on. "Break his arm off, Hank!" "Give it to im, Hank!" "Come on, Hank boy, you can do it, Hank boy!" The W.P.A. boys were taking sides with Every. "Kill im, mister!" "Attaboy, hold im thar, ole feller!" "Don't give an inch, Dad!"

Soon they stopped yelling and held their breaths, waiting. The clenched hands began to move, an inch this way, an inch that way.

The only sound was the insects in the grass, and the noises of toads. Latha suddenly looked at the porch swing and wondered where Donny was. Not like him to miss a night. She returned her eyes to the contest, in time to see that Every had Hank's arm tilted at a downward slant. And then with a crash it was over.

"Jesus H. Christ!" Hank complained. "You aint human, mister! That aint a human arm you got, it's a ox's! Who are ye, anyhow? Whut's yore name?"

He told him his name.

"Oh," Hank said. Then he said, "I'da knowed that, I'da tried a little harder and whupped ye."

"I'd be glad for another go-round," Every offered.

"Not me," Hank said. "My arm feels lak it was pulled plum loose off my shoulder, I caint even feel nuthin in it."

Gerald Coe said to Every, "I've heerd my dad say some fine things about ye, mister, I don't keer whut others say."

"Who's your dad?" Every asked him.

"Lawlor Coe," he said. "My name's Jerl, and them thar are my brothers, Earl and Burl."

"I'm sure pleased to meet you," Every said. "Your dad's one of the finest men I've known. Him and me were friends all the way back, and he was just about the only true-blue pardner I ever had."

Merle Kimber spat, then said, "Birds of a feather always flock together."

Gerald Coe doubled his fists at Merle and said, "You son of a bitch, I'll pluck all yore feathers!"

"Now, boys—" Every said.

Latha found herself wondering again why Donny had not come. It was so unusual for him not to be here that she felt like going up to his house to make sure he was there. Her attention was returned to the argument by something Hank Ingledew was saying.

"Wonder," Hank was saying to Every in a low, snide tone, "wonder if ole Lawlor helped ye rob thet bank."

The quiring of the tiny lives in the grass and trees was all the sound for a long little spell. She was alone with him now on the porch— Sonora and the boys had gone off somewhere—she was alone with him, but fretting more about Donny's absence than Every's anguish. She wondered if Dolph had made good his threat to "fix that durn kid." Could he be so mean? If Donny didn't show up soon, she was just going to have to force herself to go up to the Murrison place and ask about him.

Every sat brooding with his elbows on his knees and his jaw in his hands. *He's sure in a fine mess,* she reflected, and even had a notion that Every was a bringer of bad luck. Why else would she have received—on the very day he appeared—a letter ordering the post office to close and a letter ordering her to send Sonora back to Little Rock?

Every spoke. "Latha," he said, and his voice was nervous, "what if they try to have me indicted for that bank robbery?…"

"Every," she pointed out to him, "there is something called a 'statute of limitations,' I don't know exactly how it works, but it means that you can't be convicted of a crime committed long ago."

"Oh?" he said.

"But even if that didn't work for you," she said, "there's another law that would. The only way they can convict you is to get the testimony of the one person who saw you do it. And the law says that a wife cannot testify against her husband."

He thought that over for a while, figuring out what she meant, and then he laughed and said, "Are you trying to blackmail me into marrying you?"

I was sort of hoping he'd come and kiss me when I said that, she told herself, feeling disappointed. "Come into the house," she said, "and I'll mend your trousers." She led him into her bedroom and got a needle and some thread from her sewing table. She inspected the rip, lifting his coat-tail. "Goodness, that's a bad tear," she said. "Well, take them off and I'll see what I can do."

Every reddened, and began to look around him. "Uh," he said, "why don't I just step into the closet and pass them out to you?"

"Why, Every!" she said. "For shame!" And he blushed even deeper. "How can you be so modest with *me?*"

"Aw, heck, Latha," he protested. "It's not like we were already married yet."

"It's not?" she said. "Yet?" she said. "Seems to me like we've been married for eighteen years, at least."

"Aw, now, heck, shoot," he mumbled. Then he said, "Well, at least pull down the winder shades."

She pulled down the window shades, and lit a coal-oil lantern to see her work by. He unbuckled his belt, and turned his back to her and unbuttoned his fly and lowered his trousers. He was wearing polka-dot shorts, and she laughed. "Them's mighty snazzy underpants fer a preacher," she said, and he said, "Goshdarn ye, no wise cracks, now," and without turning to face her he reached back and handed her his trousers. Then he whipped the coverlet off the bed and wrapped it around his waist and sat down on the bed.

She sat down at her table and began mending the tear, but she kept an eye on him. "Tsk tsk," she clucked. "I'll bet this is the first time a woman's seen your hairy legs since you became a preacher."

"You—" he said, then he laughed and said, "Why, no, it's not, neither. Sometimes when I give a baptizing in a shallow creek I roll my britches up as far as they'll go, and I'll have you know there's many a woman has admired my hairy legs."

"Is that all they've admired?" she asked.

"How do you mean?"

"Has a woman ever admired your hairy legs except at a baptizing?"

"You trying to get me to tell if I've had a girlfriend?"

"I am."

"Well, yes. There was one I nearly married a few years back, out in California, but as far as that matter goes, she never saw my legs, nor me hers."

She asked then what she wanted to: "Why have you never taken a wife, Every?"

"You'd never believe me if told you."

"I might. Try and see."

"Naw," he said. "You don't believe I can talk with the Lord. You don't even believe in the Lord, as far as that goes. You'd just laugh and poke fun if I told you."

"Every," she said solemnly, "if you wanted me to, I would believe anything you say."

"Then believe the Lord talks to me!" he said. "Or talks *in* me, at least!"

"I believe the Lord talks in you, Every."

"All right!"

"All right, what does He have to do with your being a bachelor?"

"Well, Latha," he said, "you see, He told me one time that if I was patient enough, and good enough, He would allow me to find you again."

Her hands stopped sewing, and her blood pounded in her ears, and for a moment she almost did believe in the Lord; she wanted to believe in the Lord, she wanted the Lord to talk to her or in her too, and tell her what to do. She was too choked up for speaking, but finally she said in a small voice, "That's very flattering."

"Of the Lord?" he said. "The Lord don't flatter nobody."

"Are you happy you found me?" she asked.

"I caint tell you how much I am," he said.

"You've been rather reserved," she remarked. "You haven't exactly been acting like a man who's found his long lost love."

"Well, I didn't know how you would take it," he said. "I didn't know if you would be glad to see me, or not. I guess I was sort of waiting for you to make the first move."

"You seem to be still waiting for me to make the first move."

"I caint help it."

"Well, are you going to come over here and kiss me, or do I have to come over there and kiss you?"

He laughed happily. "Why don't we meet halfway?"

"All right," she said. "Here I come." And she put aside his trousers and stood up.

He stood up too, but when he did so the coverlet wrapped around his waist came loose and flopped to the floor. He bent down to pick it up, but she had already gone beyond the halfway line, and when he raised up she shoved hard against his shoulders and pushed him back and down on the bed and she climbed up beside him and brought her mouth down to his and kissed him for a long, tight, moist time. But he did not raise his arms to put them around her.

"There!" she said, when she broke the kiss. "I met you more than halfway."

"You sure did, didn't you?" he said. "And if you don't backtrack a little bit, there's going to be an embarrassment coming between us."

"I don't care," she said, misinterpreting him, and lowering her face to kiss him again. Still he did not put his arms around her.

He twisted his mouth loose from hers. "Latha!" he said sharply.

"What's the matter?" she asked. "Don't you like to kiss?"

"Not in this position," he said.

"You want to get on top?" she asked.

"No, Latha, this isn't right. We can't let ourselves get carried away."

"Why not?"

"We aren't really married yet," he pointed out. "In the sight of God we have no sanction."

She rose up off of him, and got off the bed. He sat up and drew the coverlet around his waist again. She felt like using some choice profanity. Instead she asked, "Do you mean we have to be legally hitched before you can even make love to me?"

Instead of answering, he asked his own question, "You never have read much of the Bible, have you?"

"No," she said. "It's never had anything to say to me."

"That's your loss, then," he said. "For if you knew your Bible you would know how important it is for you to be married to the man you give your body to."

"The father of my daughter was not married to me!" she came back at him.

"I've repented that," he said. "Can you repent?"

"*Repent being raped?*" she demanded. "Every, you *are* insane."

"I didn't mean that," he said. "I didn't mean you have to repent acts committed against you. I ask only if you can repent those sins which you have committed yourself."

"What sins, for instance?" she asked.

"Laying with Dolph Rivett, for instance," he said.

"That was no sin," she said defiantly. "That was heaven. Every, take off that silly coverlet and make love to me. We can both repent afterwards."

"I can see I've got a lot to teach you about the meaning of repentance."

"I won't be taught. Life's already given me all the lessons I can handle."

"You're wrong, Latha. If you're rejecting the Word, then you're rejecting me. I come to you with more than love; I come to you with the precious gift of the Word of God, and if you reject that present without even opening it to see what it's like, then…why then I reckon you don't want me either."

"There's another present I'd like to open first to see what it's like," she said.

"What's that?" he asked.

"Your drawers," she said.

"Don't talk dirty," he said.

"Dirty!" she said. "*Dirty!* Maybe your drawers are dirty, but that's not what I'm talking about. Every, I swear, if that precious *Word* of yours teaches you that it's dirty, then I don't want to hear a word of your Word."

He gazed sternly at her for a while, and then he said, "You've always been pretty feisty, haven't you?"

"Feisty is another word like dirty," she replied. "It doesn't mean anything to me because it means so many different things to everybody else that I don't care what it means. Anyway, I have never been 'feisty' as *you* mean it."

"All right. You asked me if I'd had any girlfriends, have you had any boyfriends?"

"Lately, you mean? Sure. Doc Swain is my boyfriend. So is Tull Ingledew. My very special true love is a five-year-old towhead named Dawny."

"But you haven't made love to them…"

"Well, last night me and Dawny—"

"Be serious, Latha."

"No, I haven't been made love to."

"Except—?"

"You want a case history, darn it?"

"I'd be obliged."

"Okay. Eighteen years ago last month I was violated by force. Since that time I've been made love to twice, which averages out to once every nine years."

"Once was with Dolph Rivett, of course. When was the other time? Do you remember?"

"I sure do."

"But—" he said, puzzled. "I thought you couldn't remember anything of that time."

"Shouldn't be too hard to remember," she said. "Let's see, how long ago was it? I'd say, roughly, about four and a half hours."

He did not say anything. A minute or two went by. Then he said, "Would you hand me my trousers, please?"

"I'm not finished with them yet," she said.

"I don't care. Just hand them over."

"I'm not finished with you either," she said.

"What more've you got to say?"

"I want to ask you a few questions."

"Ask em."

"Are you going to propose to me, or not?"

"I was. I might still. I caint right now."

"Why not?"

"What would you say if I did?"

"I would say, 'Yes, on one condition.'"

He laughed hollowly and said, "Wow! I'm making progress. Eighteen years ago it was, 'No, no, no, not if you were the last man on earth!' All right, what's your one condition?"

"That you come down off your religious high horse long enough to make love to me."

"Why is that so important to you, Latha? Eighteen years ago I had to take it from you; now you're practically begging *me* for it. Are you trying to get me to prove that I can still do it?"

"Maybe I am," she said.

"Well, then, I give you my word I can. Just as soon as I get that ring on your finger I'll prove it to you."

"How do you know you can? If you haven't done it in eighteen years."

"Not eighteen," he said. "Fourteen."

"Oh," she said. "Who was that?"

"You," he said.

SUB FOUR: *Fourteen Years Ago*

Can you remember anything of that dark time, Bug? I would be rather surprised to know that you could, for I am told that following that particular type of fugue state [*fugue* = flight] there usually is what was incorrectly known as aphasia, now properly known as a form of amnesia. You would not remember; you would remember a dank December afternoon sitting in a rocking chair at the end of a corridor, and a doctor approaching you and asking you a question; you would even remember the first part of the question he spoke, but then the next thing you would know it would be a bright morning in late March and you would find yourself in a small hotel in Nashville, Tennessee.

When you woke that morning you would not yet have been technically "sane" [whatever that means for somebody like you, Bug, and although I have had your thing explained to me over and over, under such fanciful terms as "The Control of Aggression by Dissociation and Disavowal," I am still not able to accept that you were ever actually mad], but you would have begun to record again in memory what was happening to you. Before that point you were as Sleeping Beauty [a particularly apt comparison; I think *she* must have been in a fugue state too], so I must attempt to see all of this through the eyes of the Prince. Certainly the labors of your Prince were as great as those of hers.

On the afternoon of March 23rd, he parked the stolen car in a weed-choked vacant lot on West Fourth Street bordering the grounds of Fair Park. He was wearing a blue pin-striped double-breasted suit he had obtained that morning at Pfeifer's Department Store by putting it on beneath his old work clothes in the dressing room. But his shoes, scuffed brogues, were incongruous with the splendid suit. He had wanted to buy some shoe wax and touch them up a bit, but he was impatient.

He used the Visitors' Entrance and went up to the desk.

"Ma'am," he said, "I'd like to visit with Miss Latha Bourne."

"Are you a relative?" she asked.

"Distant cousin on my mother's side," he said.

The woman consulted her list and said, "She's in E Ward."

"How do I get there?" he asked.

"You don't get there," she said.

"How's that, ma'am?"

"The only visitors permitted in E Ward are members of the immediate family."

"Oh. So you mean I can't see her?"

"I'm sorry."

"Couldn't I just maybe look at her from a distance?"

"I'm sorry."

"Well, could you just show me which window is hers so's I could just holler 'hello' to her?"

"We couldn't do that."

"Well, could you get ahold of a preacher who would marry us so then I would be a member of her immediate family and could visit her?"

The woman stared at him for a moment, then said, "Oh. You are being playful."

"No," he said. "I mean it."

"Why are you so eager to see her?"

"Aint seen her in nearly four years."

"You should try to understand, sir, that even if we permitted you to visit with her there would likely not be any communication. Most patients in E Ward are totally withdrawn."

"Oh," he said. He asked, "Can they not be cured?"

"The hopeless incurables are in F Ward. In E Ward we have a partial recovery rate of about five percent."

"How long will she have to stay here?"

"I couldn't say. If you were a member of the immediate family you could make an appointment to discuss the case with one of the doctors."

"Looks like I'm shit out of luck, don't it?" he said, "not being an immediate family."

"Sir," she said.

He left. He wandered around the grounds, looking at the

buildings. There were seven white austere blocks, each five floors in height. He thought it looked worse than Leavenworth. Some patients were sitting on benches in the spring sunshine, but they did not seem to notice that flowers were blooming and trees were leafing. He approached one bench and asked the old man sitting there, "Which one is E Ward?"

"Who knows the way out of a rose," the man replied.

He wandered on; he came to two men walking. "Is either one of you fellers sane enough to tell me where's E Ward?"

One turned to his companion and asked, "Will you tell him, Doctor, or shall I?"

The other said, "I yield to you, Doctor."

The first said, "No, Doctor, I should much prefer that *you* tell him."

"I demur," said the second. "You are saner than I."

"On the contrary," said the first, "your sanity is better equipped for answering directional questions."

"Let us examine the question, Doctor," said the second. "This gentleman is not asking us for the location of E Ward. He is asking if either of us is sane enough to tell him the location of E Ward."

"I see," said the first. "Then what is your diagnosis, Doctor?"

"Frankly, Doctor," said the second, "I am inclined to detect symptoms of chronic pathological mythomania in both ourselves; therefore neither of us is capable of giving the gentleman a truthful answer."

"I quite agree," said the first. "But if we simply said 'no' to this gentleman's question, would we be lying?"

"I think not," said the second, "but of course my opinion would be influenced by my mythomania."

"In that case," said the first, "I suggest we answer 'yes.'"

"Very well," said the second. "Yes, sir, either one of us is sane enough to tell you the location of E Ward."

"Then *tell* me, dammit!" he said.

"Why do you want to know?" asked the first.

"I'm goin to visit my dear old mother," he said.

"What's the lady's name?"

"Smith."

He turned to the other, "Do we have a Smith in E, Doctor?"

The other said, "I think not. I suspect this person is delusional."

"Perhaps he is a patient. What is your name, sir?"

"Smith."

"Do we have *any* patients named Smith, Doctor?"

"Surely we must, Doctor."

"Come along, sir, and we will find out where you belong."

They each took one of his arms, but he broke loose, saying "Now just a dadblamed minute!"

A nurse came up and shook her finger at the two men. "Now, boys," she said, "we mustn't molest the visitors." Then she asked him, "Did they disturb you, sir?"

"Naw," he said, "I was just trying to find my way to E Ward."

"Right over there," she said, pointing.

"Thanks," he said, and walked away from them. He was beginning to feel half-touched himself.

E Ward was identical with the other buildings, the most conspicuous difference being that all of the windows were barred. *Just like Leavenworth,* he thought. He walked around the building. Although the windows were barred, they were open to let in the spring air. A sound came to him, and he realized the same thing you had previously realized, Bug: that E Ward was appropriately named. The steady noise characteristic of the place was a high-pitched "*Eeeeee! Eeeeee! Eeeeeeee!*"

An old woman appeared at a third floor window and looked down at him. She began to screech, "JOHN MY SON MY SON JOHN YOU'VE COME FOR ME!"

Immediately a younger woman appeared and shoved the old lady out of the way, saying, "That aint your son, you old bat! That's my man Willy." She called down to him, "OH WILLY COME AND FUCK SOME CUNT OH WILLY COME AND SUCK SOME ASS OH WILLY COME AND FLOOR YOUR WHORE WHO'LL LICK YOUR DICK AND DRINK YOUR PISS AND GOOSE YOU WITH HER PRETTY LITTLE THUMBIE THUMB THUMB!"

"I aint Willy," he told her, and walked on.

From another window a girl was staring silently at him. She was an albino with snow white hair and pink eyes, but she seemed to be completely all there. He called up to her, "Do you know Latha Bourne?" She did not answer. He called again, "Is Latha Bourne up there?" She stuck out her tongue at him.

You who shared the cell with this albino girl heard your name twice, and began to rise from your cot. You lifted a foot; you lifted an arm; you lifted another foot, another arm; you raised up your head, your shoulders; you sat up; you put your feet on the floor; you pushed down on the edge of the cot with your hands and rose up; you stood; you turned; you began to walk toward the window; you began to run; you ran and ran and ran and finally reached the window; you looked out. There was nobody there.

He wandered through Fair Park, thinking. You should realize that up until this point he had only wanted to see you. He had only wanted to see that you were alive and well. He had hoped perhaps to see you smile. He had hoped to be able to get you to hear him and understand him when he said that he was going to wait for you to get well, however long it took.

Only his bitter disappointment, his intense frustration over not having been able to see you at all, was what now drove him with the sudden determination to get you out of there. He did not even consider that there was anything wrong with abducting you away from there; to him it was not conceivable that you could actually be insane; to him you were a lovely goddess unjustly incarcerated among foul hags. To him he would be protecting your sanity by rescuing you from that place [and this notion, as we know, was not far from the truth]. The brief experience with the old woman, the obscene woman, and the albino, had impressed him deeply. That was no place for you.

But, even given his talent for having broken out of a federal military stockade unaided, he was at a loss for means of freeing you. To break out of a place is one thing; to break into a place and get somebody else out of it is, he said to himself, an apple off another tree.

He thought of bribing one of the guards (or aides or attendants or whoever ran the place). He had sixty-five dollars to his name. Would a guard accept such a paltry bribe? Even if he would, there was too much danger in dealing with people. If the attempt failed, he did not want anybody to know even that. He did not want to be seen by anyone sane enough to give a description of him to the police.

Darkness was necessary, of course. While waiting for it, he went to a hardware store and spent fifteen of his sixty-five dollars on some tools and rope. He stashed these in the trunk of his car and went off to the carnival in Fair Park to while away the early night. He rode the Ferris wheel several times before dusk; and each time it took him to its apex he would look out across the treetops and study the roof of E Ward. After nightfall, he spent an hour at the shooting gallery, winning a great armload of prizes, which he distributed among the children. He wandered around. He bought a ticket to the Girlie Show and went in and watched it through twice. He rode the Merry-Go-Round. A girl offered herself to him for ten dollars; he thought about it, and bought the girl a soda and talked with her some; but finally turned her down. He rode the shooty-shoot. A girl offered herself to him for free; he declined. He visited the ball-pitching booth, and won a giant stuffed Panda. He placed it in the hands of the first girl who passed; her escort took umbrage and accused him of getting fresh, and picked a fight. The man was a big fellow, with much beer on his breath. They squared off. The man swung a roundhouse; he ducked under it and deflated the man's intestines with one jab, then broke his jaw with an uppercut. The girl thanked him for the Panda. He walked on. The carnival was beginning to close.

At a quarter past one he went back to his car and got his tools and rope. He crossed the grounds of the hospital, keeping to the shadows of trees. There was not a soul around, but the grounds were still illuminated. He approached E Ward from the corner nearest the trees. He stood at that corner for a moment, listening, then he looped the rope over his shoulder and stuffed the pockets of the suit with his tools, and reached out and took hold of the drainpipe, a thick galvanized tin tube running up to the roof. He began to climb. At the third-floor level he paused and studied the bars on the windows.

The ends of the bars were embedded in mortar; he did not have the tools to cut them or bend them. He had a file, but that would take too long.

He continued climbing, past the fourth floor, past the fifth. The height did not dizzy him, but he was a little nervous about the drainpipe pulling loose from the mortar. It was an old building.

He arrived at the roof and clung to its gutter; he kicked out with all his might and managed to swing one leg up and hook his heel on the rim of the gutter. Then he pulled himself up.

He stood up on the sloping roof and climbed it, climbed over a gable and down to a vent on the other side of it, a louvered triangle. He took a screwdriver out of his pocket and pried around the crevices. He discovered there were three bolts in the vent—bolted on the outside, naturally, to keep anyone inside from tampering with them. He took a wrench from his pocket and removed them. Then he inserted the wedge end of his nail puller into the crack and forced the vent out. He laid it carefully on the roof, along with his coil of rope. Then feet-first he let himself down through the vent until his feet touched solid floor.

From another pocket he took a candle and lighted it and discovered he was in a small attic. He crawled across the floor and located the hatch. It was latched—and probably locked—from below. But the hinges and screws were on this side. He removed them. The hatch dropped down and swung from the padlock on its underside. He slowly peered below. It was the end of a corridor; there was no ladder; it was a good twelve feet to the floor. He lowered himself to his full length, hanging on by his hands on the hatch, then he let go and dropped, flexing his knees to cushion his drop; even so the corridor rang out with a crash of his feet upon the wooden floor. He waited, listening, for several minutes until he was convinced that nobody was coming to investigate the noise.

He explored the corridor. Apparently all the rooms on this floor were storerooms. He went to the stairs and descended to the fourth floor. The rooms on this floor had names on them: "Hydrotherapy," "Electroshock Therapy," "X Ray." He continued on down to the third floor.

He was almost spotted by the night attendant, a big woman sitting at a desk. He retreated, back up to the fourth floor and along its length to another stairway. He went down this stairway to the third floor again, but the door at the foot of the stairway was locked. Yet once again, however, the attachments were on the side opposite that to which patients would have access. He took his screwdriver and removed the whole lock from the door. Then he found himself in a dimly lit corridor of many rooms.

Each door had a nameplate with two names on it. "Ella Mae Henderson and Mrs. Ruby Bridges." "Mrs. Marianne Templeton and Mrs. Dorothy Grace." "Agnes Colton and Huberta Read." "Mrs. Velma Lucaster and Georgene Masters." "Jessica Tolliver and Latha Bourne."

One more locked door, with a barred window set in it, and he had no tools for this one. His first impulse was to knock gently and see if you would open it from the inside, but he realized that *this* door would lock from the outside. And who would have the key? Why, that big woman down at the end of the corridor, of course.

He moved quietly along the corridor, still firm in his resolve not to have any contacts with anybody, but determined to club her over the head from behind, if necessary.

It was not necessary. The woman was asleep. He could hear her snores before he saw her. Her chin was embedded deeply into her chest as she sat in heavy slumber with her hands folded over her stomach. Under her right elbow he saw a ring of keys attached to her belt by a leather thong. He congratulated himself on having the foresight to have included a pair of shears in his purchase at the hardware store.

He stole up to her and snipped the leather thong and grabbed the keys and stole away, without causing any irregularity in her heavy snoring.

He returned to your room and tried many keys until he found the one that fit. He unlocked the door and opened it.

Now, he thought.

There were two cots, and that albino girl was asleep in one of them. You were asleep in the other. He closed the door behind him.

He moved to your cot and knelt down beside it. *Maybe,* he said to himself, *maybe I ought to just try and pick her up and carry her instead of waking her up.* But he knew he would not be able to get the dead weight of you out of there. He would need some cooperation from you.

Gently he shook your shoulder and began whispering in your ear, "Latha, honey, it's me. I've come to take you home. Wake up, sweetheart, and let's get on back home."

Instantly you were awake, and in your eyes that look he had so often seen: that big-eyed look that was not astonishment nor startlement but a kind of hesitant surprise as if you were just waiting to see what the world was going to do to you, knowing it was going to do something and even wanting it to do something, and watching big-eyed to see what it would be.

You did not speak to him. Knowing what I do about your condition, I would venture a positive guess that you immediately recognized him, even subliminally, that is, that even though you could not have spoken his name to save your soul, you *knew* him. He was the first non-stranger you had seen in a long, long time.

Did you even smile? I refuse to discount the possibility that you could have. But his eyes were so close to yours that he wouldn't have noticed what was happening to the mouth down below.

"Howdy, Latha, honey," he said. "I've come to take you home." It bothered him a little bit to be lying; he had no intention of taking you home. "Now don't you make a sound, sweetheart, because nobody knows I'm here. Now you just get your dress on and we will get out of this place and I will take you home, away from all these crazy people."

Slowly you rose up out of bed, and he impulsively turned his face away when he saw that you were naked. You stood there for a while like a statue. He had to return his eyes to you to see what you were doing, and when he saw that you were doing nothing he began to look around for a garment to put on you. He could not find one. Had they taken away all your clothes? While he was searching the room he was surprised to discover that the albino girl was awake and watching him. He put his finger to his lips and said to her, "Shhh."

There was hardly anything in the room other than the two cots—no closet, no wardrobe, nothing. He took the wool blanket off the bed and wrapped it around you, then he said to you, "Come on."

"Take me," said the albino girl.

He tried to determine whether she was asking him to rescue her too or whether she just meant she wanted him to lay with her. "I caint," he said. "No time. I'm sorry."

"Take me!" she repeated, insistently.

"I'm sure sorry," he said, and began pushing you out through the door. He closed it and re-locked it, but even the closed door would not muffle that girl's loud sobbing. He began to get jittery for the first time. "Wait right here," he said to you, and then he moved quickly down the corridor to where the night attendant's station was, and, finding that she was still asleep, he gently lay the ring of keys on her lap. Even when she woke and found the leather thong of the key ring cut, she would not dare mention the thong to the investigators, for fear it would be an admission that she had fallen asleep on duty.

He returned to you and said "Come on" again and led you up the corridor stairway, and pushed you far enough up the stairs so that he could get the door closed and then carefully replace the lock he had unscrewed. Then he led you on up to the fifth floor.

Only when he arrived below the hatch to the attic did he realize his most serious error. "Of all the boneheaded stunts!" he said. How was he going to get back *up?* The hatch was twelve feet above the floor; he should have left his rope dangling down. Feeling near the edge of panic, he began to look around for a ladder or even a box to stand on. He could find nothing; all the storerooms were locked.

At this point for the first time it occurred to him that if he were caught he would get at least twenty years, maybe more.

There was only one thing to do. He came back to you and put his hands on both your shoulders and spoke slowly and gently, "Now listen careful, Latha, here's what we've got to do. I'm going to boost you up there and you climb out and then you'll find a triangle vent-hole and right outside that vent-hole is my rope. You get that rope and bring it back to me."

Those big eyes of yours stared at him.

"Kin you understand me?" he pled. "It's our only chance. The rope, we got to have that rope. I'll boost you up to the attic, and you'll see that there vent-hole that I opened up, and right outside it on the roof is a coil of rope. Bring me that rope."

A nod from you would have eased his mind, but you did not nod. You did, however, crane your neck and stare in the direction he was pointing, upward at the hatch.

It was his only chance. He clenched his hands together and opened his palms to make a stirrup for your foot. You stared at the stirrup for a moment. "Come on, honey, you kin do it!" he urged. You put your foot in the stirrup. You raised your arms and put your palms against the wall. He began to lift. Up, up you went. When your feet were level with his chest, he unclenched the stirrup and got each of his palms under the soles of your feet and pushed upward until his hands were as high above his head as he could reach, and him on tiptoe. The blanket in which you were wrapped fell off of you and covered his head but he did not flinch. Your fingers strove upward and felt the rim of the hatch. You caught hold. You tried to pull yourself up. Your feet left his palms and he whipped the blanket off his head and looked up at you. You were straining. The hospital had never given you any exercise, and you were weak.

You fell. He caught you, breaking your fall and falling with you to the floor. He got up, sighing, and helped you to your feet. There would be bruises on your back where you had mashed against the hard tools in his pockets. He covered your nakedness again with the blanket, knotting two corners of it together around your neck.

"Let's try it once more," he said. "See if you caint get your hands on the sides of the hatch, that way you'd have more leverage."

Again he made the stirrup with his hands. Again you rose slowly up the wall until your hands reached the hatch, one hand on one side, the other hand on the other. Again your feet left the palms of his hands. Again you began to strain, every muscle in your arms and shoulders exerting itself.

You began to rise, but reached a point where you could strain no longer and were on the verge of falling again. Suddenly he leapt. He leapt upward for all he was worth, shoving his hands upward against your feet and propelling you upward beyond that crucial point. You got your chest up onto the attic and clambered up and out of sight.

You were gone for quite some time. He was exceedingly nervous. For all he knew you had fallen off the roof. Maybe you were gazing at the stars. Maybe you were just trying to find that triangular vent-opening. Maybe you had forgotten what he had asked you to get, or had never understood him in the first place. We do not know. At any rate, you caused him considerable anxiety.

But at last you re-appeared, and you had the coil of rope. Now another problem presented its ugly self to him: could he explain to you how to tie one end of the rope to something so that he could pull himself up? He did not wait long enough to formulate the explanation in his mind. "Just drop it down," he said, and you dumped the rope on him.

He quickly fashioned a lariat, and, after two or three misses, he lassoed the dangling hatch-cover, pulled the rope tight, grabbed hold and climbed hand over hand up the rope with his feet braced against the wall until he could reach the hatch. He pulled himself up through it.

Then he untied the lariat, and replaced the hatch cover, screwing the hinges back on. He was covering all his tracks.

There remained just two tracks to cover: he led you out onto the roof and after cautioning you to be careful not to fall off he replaced the louver in the vent opening and bolted it back on. Then he fashioned a small loop on one end of his rope and dropped it over an iron finial on the corner of the eave.

"Now here comes the tricky part," he said. He could not trust that drainpipe to remain attached to the mortar. Nor could he trust you to lower yourself alone down the rope.

He turned his back to you and said, "Wrap your arms around my neck." You hesitated. He reached back and took your hands and raised them and wrapped your arms around his neck and clenched your fingers together and said, "Hold on tight as you can."

Then he threw the coil of rope down off the roof and watched

it uncoil to the ground. He knelt with you straddling him at the edge
of the roof and grabbed hold of the rope and edged himself over.

As he began to lower himself hand under hand down the rope
he cursed himself for overestimating his strength. The weight of you
on his back was such that he dared never release one of his hands
from the rope; instead he had to slide his hands down the rope and
the rope was burning the heck out of his fingers and palms. Then
the clench that you had on his neck tightened as you yourself sensed
fear, and you began choking him. He could not even get his throat
unclenched enough to ask you to stop choking him.

He was near to passing out, and began to think it would be a
blessed release to let go and kill both of you. Then out of the survival
instinct's self-centeredness he began to think that if he fell you would
fall first and land on your back and cushion his fall so that even if
he killed you he might survive and escape and whoever found you
would think you'd somehow done it all on your own.

But while he was thinking these mad thoughts he was making
swift progress down the rope; his hands and his neck were in such
pain that he was oblivious to his own progress. He did not even realize that he was so near the ground. When he finally could stand his
pain no longer and said to himself *The hell with it! Let us die!* and
let go of the burning rope with both hands he was surprised to find
that he was standing on the ground.

He collapsed. You collapsed with him and let go of his neck,
and finally he got his wind back and stood up. There was just one
track to cover. He could hardly bear the touch of that rope again on
his raw hands but he grasped it once more and gave it a whip, and
the whip undulated higher and higher but did not quite reach the
top. He gave it another whip and the whip undulation rose and rose
to its end, and snapped, cracked, and the loop popped off the finial
and fluttered down to the ground. He coiled the rope and said to
you, "Okay, let's go."

It would have been insanely ironic if someone had caught
you leaving the grounds, but maybe the night watchman was over
in F Ward helping subdue a maniac. The grounds were deserted. So

were the streets beyond them. In Little Rock at three o'clock in the morning only the milkman is out on the streets.

You made it to his car. He opened the door for you and got you in, and then he opened his door and threw the rope and tools into the back seat, and got in. He started the motor and drove away.

"You're *free,* gal!" he cried. "Call me a monkey's uncle if you aint *free,* by granny!" And as he drove he began whistling loudly and happily the tune of "She'll Be Comin Round the Mountain When She Comes!"

You quietly uttered your first word: "Free."

We do know of the phenomenon whereby certain mental patients, resistant to and perhaps resentful of all efforts to make them well, have become spontaneously cured, as it were, upon being removed from formal treatment. There are on record a number of cases of patients, many of them considered incurable, who, when abandoned or sent home or left alone in some corner of the institution, seemed to become so relieved at being free from the intense attention of the doctors that they rapidly cured themselves.

We do not know at what precise point during this episode you began to heal. It might have been at the very moment he came into your room and woke you up. It might have been during those minutes when you were required to climb up through that hatch and fetch that rope. Possibly when you muttered that first word, "free," you were beginning to feel a definite sense of relief from the treatment. Any one of a number of incidents occurring in the days following could have been the trigger. We know you would not be wholly "well" for weeks to come, and we know you would not even regain use of your memory until that morning in the Nashville hotel. But you were on your way.

He did not cross the Arkansas River at Little Rock, because he did not want to drive through the downtown business area and risk being spotted by a policeman. He drove through Fair Park and emerged on the other side into a dirt country road, and he kept to backroads up through northern Pulaski County, and Perry County, heading toward the ferry that would get the car across the river and on toward Conway.

He talked a blue streak the whole time, trying to be amusing. He told jokes by the dozen. It must have been a relief for you to listen for the first time in three years to a voice that was neither screaming obscenities nor trying to get you to confess when you first masturbated.

"You remember back when the big craze was riddles," he would say, "and folks would stop strangers right on the road to try out some new riddle they heard. Well, I was riding up to Jasper one day with ole Till Cluley when the wagon got stuck bad in the mud, clear up to the hubs. Ole Till was whippin all four horses and hollerin cuss words at the top a his voice. Just then this preacher from Parthenon come along and says to Till, 'My friend, do you know the name of Him who died for sinners?' And ole Till says, 'I aint got no time for no goddamn riddles. Caint you see I'm stuck in this son-a-bitchin mud?'"

And he would slap his leg and laugh, then turn to see how you would be taking it. But if you were smiling, it was hard to tell.

And speaking of being stuck in the mud, those old backroads were in pretty soggy condition, what with the spring rains and all. Most of the time he would put the car in low gear and bull his way through, slipping and sliding wildly with the engine roaring. But a few times he got mired. I think if you tried hard enough, Bug, you might be able to remember that.

The first time the car got stuck, he turned the wheel over to you and got out and pushed, but when he pushed you free you drove on for nearly a quarter of a mile before finding the brake, and that gave him a bad thought or two. So the second time the car got stuck he made you get out and push, and pretty soon that blanket you were wrapped in was considerably splattered with mud.

Then before long the car lurched into a mud hole that seemed more like quicksand than mud, so both of you had to get out and push together. It was very laborious, and by the time you got the car back onto a semblance of dry land, you were both covered with mud from head to toe.

You stood there panting and staring at him in that fine blue pinstriped suit all covered with mud. The dawn was coming up.

Something about his muddy appearance, and an awareness of your own weird appearance in a mud-soaked blanket, suddenly got through to you. You began to laugh.

If I had my own guess, Bug, that would be the moment when you began to get well.

And when you laughed, he began laughing too, and you each pointed at each other and howled with laughter. And then you were in each other's muddy arms. And then you were not laughing.

Could anyone imagine that a muddy kiss would taste so good?

· He stopped in the small hamlet of Bigelow and prevailed upon the keeper of the General Store to leave his breakfast and open the store long enough for him to buy some fresh clothes for the two of you, and a jar of salve for his rope-blistered hands. Then he even persuaded the storekeeper's wife to sell him some boiled eggs and biscuits and pork jowl and a Mason jar full of steaming coffee. The storekeeper's wife accompanied him back to the car, and she saw you. He explained, "My wife and I got pretty badly muddied up down the road aways and my wife ruined her dress and had to wear the blanket."

"Them roads is sure awful this time a year," the woman said. Then she asked, "Whar you folks headin?"

"Conway," he said.

"Wal, I'll tell ye. Ron Lee Fowler don't start runnin the ferry till noon, but he lives not too awful fur up the road that runs north of the landin, so if you'uns was to go to his house and ast him, he might take you on across."

"Thank you, ma'am. Much obliged," he said, and drove on.

Before going on to the landing, he pulled off at a creek, and the two of you cleaned up, washing all the mud off, and donning the new clothes he'd bought. Your dress was a size too small, but it did nice things for your figure. Your shoes were two sizes too big, but they'd do, for a while. Then you sat on the grass and ate breakfast together. It was very good.

Ron Lee Fowler agreed to take the car across, for 35 cents. The roads on the other side of the river were better, and Conway was reached and left behind before any of the stores had opened.

He headed east across Faulkner County, still keeping to back-roads, avoiding highways, pointing in the general direction of Memphis. The traffic was light, a few wagons and horsemen, no automobiles. Still he began to get nervous as the day wore on and more and more houses and people were passed. By this time, word would have been sent out that a nut was on the loose from the state hospital.

Around ten A.M., east of Beebe, he turned off into an old trail that led through a grove of cypresses in and alongside a bayou. He drove as far as he could before the road got too muddy, then he stopped. It was a cool place, nearly dark, like a primeval jungle, with all the big cypresses and their beards of Spanish moss.

"Let's take a nap," he suggested, and got out of the car and found a shady patch of soft ground covered with a bed of cypress needles. You followed. You felt very sleepy, and possibly you were feeling grateful for the chance to stop and nap.

The two of you lay down, a few inches apart. He folded his arms over his chest and closed his eyes. He was dead-tired. You turned your head and smiled, and then you snuggled against him. He opened his eyes and smiled back at you and then he wrapped one arm beneath you and you fell asleep with your head on his shoulder.

You woke, in the same position, seven hours later. As soon as you raised your head from his shoulder, he woke too. The two of you rose and brushed the cypress needles off you, and resumed your journey.

He drove all night. Sometimes he sang songs, "Old Joe Clark," "Sourwood Mountain," "The Jealous Lover," and "Sally Goodin." Sometimes he just talked, telling funny stories.

"I remember that day we was going off to war, and the Jasper Women's Club come down to the staging area where the Army was fixin to pick us up, and those women said they was throwin a seein-off party for us patriotic fellers. So they served us punch and cookies, and this one lady comes up to me and says, 'Young man, would you make a speech?' And I choked on my cookie and says, 'For God's sake, what about?' And she says, 'Just anything you like, and tell em what you think about it.' So then I stood up and I says, 'Well, I like Miss Latha Bourne better than anything else, and I think she is wonderful.' And then I sat down, a-wiping the sweat off my forehead, and afterwards everybody comes up and says that is the best speech they ever heard.

"J'ever hear the one Doc Swain used to tell about one time he gave Granny Price a dose of medicine and he says to her, 'Keep a close watch, and see what passes.' Next day he came back, and she was feeling a little better. He asks her, 'Did anything out of the ordinary pass?' 'No,' says Granny, 'just a ox-team, a load of hay, and two foreigners on horseback.' Doc Swain he just looked at her. 'Well,' says he, 'it aint no wonder you're a-feelin better.'"

But you did not show much reaction to any of his stories, and he did not dare attempt to engage you in serious conversation, for fear he would find that you could not reply to the simplest question.

The Mississippi was crossed around midnight, and he drove through the back streets of Memphis and headed northeast. He stopped once at a café to pick up coffee and to consult his road maps.

At dawn he parked beside a remote barn west of Lexington, Tennessee, and you slept on the hay. Because you were in the habit of sleeping without clothing, you took off what you had on. He discovered this when he woke up six hours later. You were still asleep. He lay there and stared at your body for a while and a tremendous hard-on grew on him. Many times already he had debated with himself the question as to whether sex would have any harmful effect on your mind. Now the fact that you were asleep, combined with the intensity of his desire, broke his reserve. He gently grasped one of your ankles and spread your leg. You did not wake. He opened his fly and released his rigid phallus. He stretched himself out over you, careful not to touch you anywhere, except at the point of coupling. He nestled his crown into your folds and gently pressed forward. He pressed forward less gently, but you were dry and tight. He drew back and knelt and moistened you with his tongue. Then he stretched over you again and pressed against you again. Still you were tight, but he increased his pressure and suddenly you unclenched and enfolded him. He sighed as your warm inner furrows rippled down along the length of his sinews. Slowly he withdrew, your lining slithering off the end of his crown in a wake. Then he slowly stroked into you again, not deeply, not to your depth. He backed. He forthed. It did not take much. The combination of your helplessness, the tension of keeping himself suspended above you, and the excruciating enjoyment of your swallowing his entrances and sucking at his exits, soon finished him. Almost coolly, when he sensed his unladening near, he continued moving slowly into you, deeper, to your depth this time, to his depth, where he stopped and waited totally immobile for a few seconds until his freight exploded out of him.

You slept for another hour. Perhaps you were having a nice dream, Bug. A healing dream. When you woke, and the journey was resumed, he kept studying you, trying to detect the slightest change in you, but there was nothing.

He had not meant to stop in Nashville. He had toyed with several notions, including New York. But Nashville struck him as a pretty town, a good-sized city where a man could find work, and it was sufficiently far away from Little Rock. He registered at the cheap Dixie Hotel under the names "Mr. and Mrs. Robert Smith."

He was reluctant to leave you alone in the room, but he had to go out and find a job. The hotel demanded advance payment because you didn't have any luggage, so he had to go out and earn enough money to buy at least a cheap suitcase or two. It was Friday, and he was nearly flat broke and didn't want to do any more robberies that would have to be fled from. He had enough money left to buy some bread and meat and a few magazines which he brought to you and told you to read. "Honey, I got to look for work," he tried to explain to you. "Now you just stay here and try to be as comfy as you can, and I'll be back this evening. Don't you go out."

He was terribly relieved and happy when he came back that night and found you were still there. "All I could find," he told you, "was a job washing dishes in a cafe, but I got two free meals and a dollar for it. And look what I brought you." He had stolen from the cafe a complete dinner, which he had packed carefully in a cardboard box: big slices of roast beef, baked potato, fresh sweet peas, salad, and a big wedge of fresh strawberry pie. It was very good.

That night when you undressed for bed, he turned off the light and took off all of his clothes too. He lay beside you for a while and then in a worried voice he asked the long-delayed question: "Latha, can you say anything at all?"

"Free," you said, and he was so happy he gave you a big hug and you squeezed him tight in return, and pretty soon his male figurehead had risen up to pay a call on you. He did not care this time that you were awake and conscious. He figured that since you had stripped naked and got into the same bed with him it meant you had a pretty good idea of what might come of it. Thus he was rather surprised when you put up resistance. You squirmed and whimpered in such a way that he did not enter you. He got off of you and lay there worrying for a long time. He thought about maybe waiting until you fell asleep before doing it, but then he decided to just wait and give his erection a chance to subside. He waited and he waited, and could not feel sleepy at all. When it became obvious to him that his danged dinger was going to keep a-standing there the whole night if he didn't do something about it, he asked, "Latha, are you awake?" You did not answer or stir. He decided that this didn't mean anything. He got up and went into the bathroom and jerked off into the toilet. When he came back to bed, you rolled over and snuggled asleep in his arms.

Saturday he worked in the café again, washing dishes, and that night he brought home another dinner for you. After you had eaten it, he said, "Let's go see a moving-picture show." He walked you several blocks up the street to a theater. The film was *The Navigator,* with Buster Keaton. It was very romantic; also rather funny. It was the first motion picture you had ever seen. You were enthralled.

Back at the hotel afterwards both of you took Saturday-night baths. He spied on you when you were taking yours. He liked to watch the languid grace with which you lathered yourself. But although he was extremely aroused by this sensuous bathing of yours, he did not molest you at bedtime. All day while washing dishes he had been thinking about this matter, and he had decided that he had better leave you alone until you got better. You snuggled tightly into his arms again, still moist from your bath and smelling fragrantly of soap, and went to sleep. Again against his will, his penis distended and kept him sleepless. He wished he'd had enough money to have bought a pint of whiskey. In your sleep one of your knees came between his and your thigh rested on his, and for a moment he was mad to have you. But he was resolved not to tamper with your fragile senses. He counted 2,389 sheep leaping a fence and fell asleep.

Imagine his astonishment, therefore, when he woke soon after dawn and saw what you were doing. The covers were off the bed. Your ear was on his thigh and your lips were feasting upon his penis: alternately you were sucking rapaciously on the tip or lapping the shank with your tongue or wolfing the whole thing nearly down your throat. "Hey!" he said and reached down to pull you away. But his passion stayed his hand. He was then thoroughly discomposed by a mixture of feelings. One of his first feelings was jealousy: he wondered where you'd learned to do that and who taught you how. The only time this had been done to him before was once in Châlons-sur-Marne by a girl he'd paid for; and he had felt at the time that the act was debasing her; oddly enough he was not now feeling that it was debasing you—you were doing it with such greedy abandon that he figured you must be enjoying yourself. You were also making him nearly delirious with ecstasy at the same time he was nearly frantic with worry. You never opened your eyes and he thought you might be still asleep but he couldn't understand how you could be doing all that fancy work if you were asleep. He was forced now to close his own eyes and throw his head back on the pillow. He began to buck at the hips but you held on. You were no longer dallying with it; you were swallowing and unswallowing it as rapidly as you could bob your head and your head was bobbing so rapidly it shook your whole body. Abruptly both of his hands came down and grabbed you by the hair and tried to pull you away, but you hung on for dear life and buried your lips in his pubic hair and waited until the last spurtle had dribbled down your gullet.

Then slowly you slipped your mouth up off of it and raised your head and opened your eyes and smiled at him.

He smiled back at you but couldn't think of a blessed thing to say.

You sat up and continued smiling at him.

He felt he ought to say something, and he considered some possibilities, such as telling you how terrific that had been. At length he finally said, "Have you ever done that before?"

You shook your head, still smiling as if you were pleased with yourself. Your smile was so simple and so pleasant that he began to wonder if maybe being in that hospital had made you simple-minded. But your shaking your head made him glad to know that you could respond to questions.

"Why did you squirm and whimper when I tried to make love to you the other night?"

No answer.

"Was it because you didn't like me?"

You shook your head.

"Was it because you didn't want to?"

You shook your head.

"Latha, why can't you talk?"

No answer.

"Is something wrong with your voice?"

You shook your head.

"Have you forgot all the words?"

You shook your head.

"Are you afraid of me?"

You shook your head.

"Do you know who I am?"

You nodded your head.

"Say my name."

No answer.

"Do you feel good? Do you feel well?"

You nodded your head.

"Then why won't you talk to me?"

No answer.

"Do you want anything?"

You nodded your head.

"What?"

No answer, then you reached out and touched him on his penis.

He laughed and said, "Well, he shore don't look very useful right at this moment."

You smiled.

"However…" he said, and he reached for you and pulled you down to him and held you and gave you a kiss. He kissed you and you kissed him for a long little spell; by and by he swelled up again; he wanted into you, and you let him in.

Because he was below you it freed your movements, and you moved, free and wild.

It took a while but he kept with you all the way.

When you fainted and your head fell on his shoulder, he thought you were just resting.

After a while he said "Latha" and his hands upon your buttocks gave them a shake. He raised his hands and shook your shoulders and said "LATHA!"

He rolled out from under you and you flopped down on the bed like a rag doll.

He thought you were dead.

He was more scared than that time those two Germans had sprung into his trench.

He had the presence of mind to feel for your pulse. It was easy to feel, for it was racing wildly, 120 beats to the minute.

He soaked a towel in cold water and draped it across your forehead. He slapped your cheeks. He wanted to run out and fetch a doctor but that might be dangerous if they had to hospitalize you and find out who you were.

He was in such an agony of distress that he began looking wildly around the room, as if he could find some magic talisman to restore you. He felt so helpless that he was unconsciously searching for something outside himself, just as the drowning man looks for a board to clutch at. By some accident of destiny, his glance fell upon the Gideon Bible on the bedstand.

He picked it up, this drowning man's board, and on the

very first page he saw written, "For Help in a Time of Need, Read: James 1:6,7; Psalm 91; Ephesians VI:10–18," etc. He found every one, and read it, but it wasn't much help. He was left, however, with a strong suspicion that God had something to do with this, and the only thing that would help would be to take the case directly to Him.

He was not a religious person, to put it mildly, and James 1:6 had cautioned him, "But let him ask in faith, nothing wavering. For he that wavereth is like a wave of the sea driven with the wind and tossed." *I am certainly driven and tossed,* he realized. His parents had been slightly religious and they had urged him to pray, yet never once had he felt that Anybody was listening to his prayers.

But we know, Bug, that the same emotional states which drive some people into psychosis can drive other people into religion; old William James got this down pat long ago. So it shouldn't be hard to understand how this crisis "deranged" him in a fashion that wasn't too awfully far removed from what had happened to you. The ironic thing, Bug, the thing that nearly kills me with irony, is that he was becoming "deranged" at the same instant you were in the process of becoming "ranged."

He knelt on the floor.

"God, can you hear me?" he asked. "No, I won't ask you that, because if I did it would mean I doubted whether you could or not. I *know* you can hear me, God, so just listen careful. I've sinned a time or two, but the only really bad thing I've done lately is help this pore girl get out of that crazyhouse. Anyway, if you really wanted to punish me, why didn't you put *me* into a trance instead of her? Anyway, the problem is: what do I have to *do* for you to get her out of that trance?"

He paused, and when no answer came he continued, "Lord, if you will just let her wake up, if you will just make her well, Lord, and I mean *completely* well, why, I will just dedicate my life to you. Is that too much to ask of you? Wouldn't you rather have a big strong man dedicated to you for the rest of his life, and doing good works for you, than keep a pore innocent girl in a trance?"

When he received no reply to that question, he continued with fierce intensity, "I swear it to you, God! Now you may be thinking that on the basis of my past behavior I shouldn't be trusted, but I'm not kidding you. I put my hand on this here Bible and swear to you that if you will make this girl well, if you will even show me some token that you intend to make her well, I will get up right this minute and devote every minute of the rest of my life to your service. Is that a deal? Answer me, God! Prove to me you can do it! ANSWER ME!"

And behold, the Lord God answered him.

My son, believe on the Lord Jesus Christ and thou shalt be saved. Find thee a minister of the Gospel of the Lord Jesus Christ, repent unto him, confess, and be received into baptism. Latha Bourne shall be healed. Sin no more. Follow me all the rest of thy days.

He continued kneeling a moment more, amazed that God had spoken to him, then he sprang up and threw on his clothes and dashed out through the door. He ran down to the desk and asked the clerk, "Where can I find the nearest preacher?"

"At this time of morning?" the clerk said.

"I don't care," he said. "I got to see a preacher."

"Well, what kind did you have in mind? Baptist, Methodist, Church of Christ, Presbyterian?…"

"Any kind, so long as he preaches the Gospel of the Lord Jesus Christ."

"Well, I guess the nearest that I know of would be Brother Shirley Norvil, lives a couple of streets over, but he aint gonna be none too happy being woke up at this time of mornin."

"Just give me his address," he said.

The clerk wrote it down for him, saying, "Big white house right next to the church. You can't miss it."

He ran out, and, forgetting he had a car, ran all the way over—four blocks—to the preacher's house. He banged on the door. He waited, and banged louder. Five minutes went by before the door was opened and an old man in his nightshirt said, "Oh well, I always get up at six o'clock of a Sunday mornin anyway."

"Are you Brother Norvil?" he asked him.

"That's right."

"Can you baptize me?"

"Be glad to, son," he said. "Come to the services at 10:30 this mornin, and we'll take care of you."

"I caint wait till then. I've got to be baptized right now."

"Well, the plumbin is busted in the baptistry, and my plumber said he'd try to get around to it before 10:30."

"Couldn't you just sprinkle some tap water on me?"

The preacher looked at him in shock and said, "Son, if you aim to be saved, you've got to be totally *immersed*."

Impatiently he said, "Well, couldn't we just use your bathtub or something?"

The preacher chuckled and said, "Well, I don't see why not. There's nothing in Scripture against bathtubs." He held the door open and said, "I never seen anybody so eager to be baptized, but come right on in and we'll shore do it."

The preacher led him into the house and upstairs to the bathroom. A woman appeared and looked at them. "Go back to bed, Ma," the preacher said. "I'm just a-fixin to baptize this young feller." The woman stared at them for another moment, then went away.

The tub took a long time to fill.

He asked the preacher, "Do you want me to take off my clothes?"

"No, generally we just baptize 'em clothes and all. That's part of the ceremony."

"All right," he said, and climbed into the tub.

"Now," said the preacher, "have you repented your sins?"

"I have."

"Do you believe with all of your heart that Jesus Christ is the Son of the Living God?"

"I do."

"Now bear in mind that you've got to be completely under, every inch of you, so when I dunk you you'll have to kind of scrooch down so your knees won't stick out. Okay? Here we go. I baptize thee in the name of the Father, the Son, and the Holy Ghost!"

Under he went.

Perhaps [and wouldn't this be sweet, Bug?] at the very same instant that he received holy baptism, you were waking up from your faint—and also waking up from your fugue and regaining memory. Your first thought was that D Ward looked awfully strange this morning. Then you sat up in bed and rubbed your eyes. *Why, it didn't look like D Ward at all!* You went to the window and looked out. You were in a hotel, by golly. You looked at the rumpled bed and you saw a man's jacket hanging in the closet. You felt a mild ache in your vagina, and you clapped yourself on the brow and thought, *Oh my gosh, I've prostituted myself!* Quickly you began dressing, thinking, *I've got to get out of here, fast.*

"Well, son, stay and have a cup of coffee with me, and dry your clothes and we'll talk about problems of the spirit."

"Thank you, but I've got to go. Do I owe you anything for the baptizin?"

"'Course not. But you owe it to yourself to come to church this mornin."

"Might see you later then. Thanks. Bye." He dashed out of the house. His soaked trousers impeded his running.

You turned a corner going one way as he rounded the corner by the hotel. He missed you.

When he found the room empty he ran back to the street and got into his car and roared up and down the streets of Nashville for two hours. All he got for it was a ticket for speeding.

"It's God's punishment on me," he said. "He kept His promise and made her well, at least she couldn't have got up and gone off unless He's brought her out of that trance."

At ten thirty he went to Brother Norvil's church and devoutly prayed and worshiped.

He stayed at the hotel for another week, hoping you'd come back.

Then he enrolled himself at a good Bible College that Brother Norvil had recommended.

FIVE: Night

WRIRRRAANG! sounded the screen door, and she came out, bringing the slab of beef to put on his eye. He leaned his chair back against the storefront, and tilted his head back, and she draped the beef slab across his eye. "There," she said, and sat down in her rocker and said, "Now while your eye is healing you can tell me all about it. Start at the start, and tell me everything."

So he began at the beginning and told her as much of the story as he could remember. He seemed to be glossing over or making little of his own efforts, which she realized must have been little short of stupendous. *Great Day in the Morning!* she thought: *My hero. I've got a hero. It's like a fairy tale,*

"...So you see," he concluded, "that was my solemn covenant with the Lord. He pledged to make you well, and He did it. I pledged my life and my service to Him, and I've done it. If you and I were to break that covenant by sinning before marriage, why, don't you see, He might just put us back where we started from, He might just put you back into that trance and me back again into being a mean hellraiser."

"All right, Every," she said. "Let's get married. Soon as we can.

But I think I ought to warn you that I might get into one of those 'trances' anyway."

"How do you know?"

"It's happened," she said. "But it's not really a 'trance.' I just get so carried off when the big moment comes at the end that I just swoon clean away, as if it were too much for a body to bear."

He frowned. "That happened...with Dolph?" he asked.

"Yes. Once."

He pondered with a long face for a while before speaking. "Well," he said, "that was just God's way of telling you that He didn't approve of what you were doing."

"No, Every," she said, "It was just *my* way of telling me that I approved of it so much I couldn't stand it."

He reflected, then he lifted the slab of beef off his eye and peered at her. "You're hurting me, you know it?"

"I don't mean to," she said softly. "I'm just trying to help you understand."

He tilted his head back again and replaced the slab of beef. "Galatians Six, seventh and eighth verses," he said: "'Be not deceived; God is not mocked: for whatsoever a man soweth, that shall he also reap. For he that soweth to his flesh shall of the flesh reap corruption; but he that soweth to the Spirit shall of the Spirit reap life everlasting.'"

"I sow to the spirit!" she protested. "It's not the flesh that makes me faint, it's the spirit!"

He whipped the slab of beef off his eye and threw it on the floor. "You don't have the first notion what the Spirit means!"

She stood up. "I'm going up the road a little ways," she said. "To Dawny's house."

"Why?"

"Just to see if he's okay. I'll be right back."

She walked rapidly up the Right Prong road toward the Murrison place, wondering again if Dolph might have done something to Donny. But if that were so, the Murrisons would have told Latha about it. Or would they have?

Rosie and Frank were sitting on their front porch, taking in what little evening breeze there was, but Donny wasn't with them. Latha stopped at the foot of the porch steps and looked up at Rosie. "Hi," she said. "Where's Dawny?"

"Well, I never—!" Rosie huffed. "Wanting to take up for him all the time is one thing, but wanting to know were he's at is something else. What's it to you, where he's at?"

"I..." she said, becoming flustered, "we...just missed him this evening, he's usually always down to the store after supper, you know, and...I just wondered...just wondered why he didn't come tonight."

"Is he supposed to come ever blessit night?" Rosie asked belligerently.

"No, but this is the first night he's missed in such a long time, I thought maybe something had happened to him, and I—" she stopped, for she could hear faintly, coming from a room upstairs, a child's muffled sobbing. "Rosie, is he all right? Tell me," she said.

"He's all right," Frank said. "'cept for being black and blue all over, he's all right."

"Why, Frank!" Latha said. "What happened to him? Why's he black and blue?"

"He got his little hide overhauled," Rosie said, "for tellin a whoppin lie. Even when I caught him out on it, he wouldn't tell me the truth, so I really mopped the floor with that little devil. He still won't tell me, so maybe you better. Whut was he doin down to yore place last night? And don't gimme no fudge about no bunkin party, neither, 'cause I found out from Selena Dinsmore and Viola Duckworth that none a their kids went to no bunkin party at yore place last night."

Latha took a deep breath and said, "All I did was provide him a place to sleep, and tell him some bedtime stories."

"*Ghost* stories, I bet! Skeered him so much he wet his pants, I bet! But if that's *all* you did, he wouldn't a refused to tell me, 'cause he's tole me afore about them ghost stories a yourn. So you must a done somethin else 'sides that. You must a done somethin real *bad*."

Latha wondered what would happen if she just went into their house and went upstairs and got Donny and tried to take him away. They would stop her, of course. *I wish I'd brought Every with me.*

"Latha Bourne, 'pon my word," said Rosie, "if you don't tell me, I'll never let that little rascal come anywhere near yore place ever again!"

How are you going to keep him from it? she wanted to ask, but she knew that Rosie would tie him to the bedpost if she had to. "You are a mean woman, Rosie Murrison," she said.

"'Druther be mean than evil. Just what do you mean, anyhow, temptin a innocent boy to stay all night with you? No tellin whut you done to him, you witch. No wonder he won't tell me whut you done, it's so horrible he can't bear to speak of it."

I wish I had more nerve, she thought. *But as it is I'm a coward.* "Good night," she said, and began walking away.

"You just come back here!" Rosie hollered after her. "Latha Bourne, you just better come right back and tell me whut you done!"

She did not stop.

"All right for you!" Rosie hollered. "You won't never see him again!"

We will just see about that, she said to herself.

She returned to her house and sat beside Every again on the porch, but she did not say anything to him. She brooded. Out of helplessness she conjectured wild ideas: *Every and I will just take Sonora and Donny and go far, far away.* But she could not ever leave Stay More again.

After a while Every asked, "Was he okay?"

"No," she said.

He waited for her to elaborate, and when she did not he asked, "What's the matter?"

Should I tell him? she wondered. *Can I tell him?* She decided that there must be no secrets between them, and that if he was to have her he would have to have her as she really was. "They beat him," she said, and her tone became fierce, "They beat him up! And it's my fault! They beat him up because he refused to tell on me."

"What was it he refused to tell?" Every asked.

She had to think about it for a moment longer before persuading herself to tell him, and when she told him she did it defiantly, as if to say: *See how bad I am? Now is there any hope for me as a preacher's wife?*

"Latha, you're sure lucky Dawny refused to tell his aunt even after she beat him. Do you know what folks would do to you if this tale ever got out?"

She did not reply. She thought of saying, "I've thought about it," but she did not.

"I just don't know what to make of you," he said.

"Oh, I'm bad, *bad,* aren't I?" she said challengingly.

"You've sure got a lot to learn, is all I can say," he said.

"Then *teach* me, Every! Come on and gospel me!"

"I don't know where to start," he said.

"Start in the beginning. Start with Adam and Eve. Teach me why they started wearing clothes. I've never been able to understand."

"Shame was God's punishment on man for disobeying his commandments." Every was trying hard to keep from sounding like a Sunday-school teacher.

"All right," Latha challenged, "then if we agreed to obey all of God's commandments, would He let us run around naked again?"

Every sighed. "You know," he said, "I sure do hate to get involved in arguments about Original Sin because it's just about the trickiest thing God ever did. Especially since I caint literally believe in Adam and Eve and the Tree of Knowledge and all that. But just look at it like this: somewhere along the line, man lost his innocence. Losing his innocence made him aware that he was naked. Now our Lord Jesus Christ tells us, 'Except ye become as little children, ye can in no wise enter the kingdom of heaven.' We've got to regain that lost innocence."

"Then I'd think that your job as preacher ought to be to persuade people to take off their clothes and become innocent again."

"It's not so simple as that, Latha," he protested. "Just taking off our clothes won't make us innocent. We'd still feel shame. We have to live a life here on earth amongst sin and corruption, amongst heathens and transgressors, keeping ourselves pure through the grace of our Lord, who promises us salvation."

"We can't take off our clothes till we get to heaven?" she asked.

"I never thought of heaven as some kind of nudist colony," he said, "but you might have a point there. In heaven there'll be no such thing as nakedness, for we'll not know that word. We'll all be clothed with the light of the Lord. There'll be no light or darkness but the light of the Lord, and in that light all things will be beautiful."

"That sounds very nice," she said. "But what if I already think that nakedness is beautiful. Does that mean something's wrong with my eyes?"

"Well, I don't know about that," Every said uneasily. "In Leviticus, the Lord spoke to Moses and told him, 'None of you shall approach to any that is near of kin to him, to uncover their nakedness.'"

"Now there you go misinterpreting again," she said. "That means kinfolks, doesn't it? It means you can't go around stripping your sister or your mother or your aunt. It doesn't mean you can't strip yourself or your girlfriend or your wife, does it?"

"All right," he said, holding out his hands as if to ward off blows, "when you get right down to it, there's nothing I know of in the Bible against being naked, except that a naked woman would cause a man to feel lust, and Jesus Christ has said to us, 'He that lusteth after a woman has already committed adultery with her in his own heart.'"

"He's talking about married women, isn't He?" she asked, and answered her question, "Sure He is. If a man couldn't lust after a maid, he'd have no desire to wed her, and where would the world be then? You still haven't proved there's anything wrong with you and me being naked to each other."

"It doesn't need proving," he said. "Nakedness would tempt us into fornication, which the Lord clearly forbids, and no dispute about it."

"Every," she said earnestly, "I don't think the Lord would consider you and me fornicators. He'd think of us as having been in a sort of common-law wedlock ever since we were about twelve years old."

Every smiled. "I like you saying that," he said. "That's sure pretty. But the Lord wouldn't consider you as bone of my bones and flesh of my flesh."

"Why don't you ask Him?" she challenged. "You claim you can talk to Him, why don't you just ask Him what he thinks of you and me?"

"He wouldn't give me permission to lay with you, if that's what you want."

"How do you know? You haven't even asked Him. Go on, right now, and ask Him."

"I would need privacy and meditation to get in touch with Him."

"Use my bedroom," she offered. "Use my outhouse."

"Don't jolly me," he said.

"Well?" she said. "Don't just sit there. Get in touch with the Lord."

"I don't think it would work in such circumstances," he protested.

"You won't even try," she accused.

"I just might," he declared. "But you better agree to accept whatever He tells me."

"All right," she said. "I can do that."

He stood up. "I think I'll just take a stroll down by the creek. I always liked that creek." He walked down off the porch.

She called after him, "Watch you don't step on my cantaloupes." Then she was alone, alone with herself for the first time in several hours, and glad of it; aloneness was her natural element, she was comfortable with it; there was a great effort to talking so much all of a sudden. Those bugs and frogs out there in the grass and trees were as talkative as all get out. But the lightning bugs never made a sound; just light; and mightn't it be the light that Every said the Lord would clothe us with in that Gloryland he talked of? The lightning bugs didn't talk; they were just *there*. "I'm here, Lord," she heard herself saying, and wondered why. Then she heard herself asking, "Are you there, Lord?" She even waited, and tried to *feel*, if not hear, any answer. There was none, no wonder. But still she felt as close to prayer as she had ever come. It was as if, having been talking so much, she had to continue, had to keep talking although there was nobody to listen, save the Lord, if He could, if He *was*, if He did, and she doubted it. "Listen," she said, "I don't believe he can really hear You, but if he can, tell him a thing or two, will You? Remind him he married me, oh, twenty-eight years ago, wasn't it? Were You in on that one? Then straighten him out. Tell him we've got just as much right as any of Your other creatures. Tell him he doesn't need to be such a Bible fanatic. You don't really think it would be fornication for us, do You? He says You preach love and mercy. Get it across to him that he misunderstood something important about that time in that Nashville hotel room. You didn't fix me up because of that 'covenant' with him, did You? Then open his eyes. I can stick with him forever if all he wants to do is preach Your love and mercy. But if he wants to stuff us with all this 'sin-and-salvation' clamjamfry, why, then I'd have to turn him away once again, and then where would I be? Where would *he* be? If You actually want him to devote himself entirely to you, then that's that, and I hope You can use him more than I could. But I just wish You'd give him to me. Now, do I have to say 'Amen,' or will You just accept—"

Hush! she said to herself, and hushed, thinking, *There's nobody listening. Nobody listens to those bugs and frogs except their mates. No reason to talk to anybody except somebody you want.* She began to rock slowly in her rocking chair, and let Time fall back into its timelessness.

Sometime later a figure riding a mule came trotting by, and turned down the main road into the village, spurring the mule for all it was worth.

As the mule and rider disappeared into the darkness down the main road, Every reappeared.

"Who was that?" he asked, jerking his thumb in the direction the mule and rider disappeared.

"I think that was Sarah Chism," she said. "Yes, it looked like Sarah Chism."

"Hmmm," he said. "A woman riding a mule. I wonder what

that signifies?" He came and sat back down in the chair he had vacated some time ago.

"Sarah Chism riding her mule signifies Sarah Chism riding her mule," she said. "Though I've never seen her out at night before."

"Hmmm," he said. "Is that a fact? Then it *must* signify something."

"Maybe the mule needs exercise," she said. "The way she was running it, she really looked to be giving it a work-out."

"Hmmm," he said again, and seemed to be in deep thought.

After a while, she asked, "Well, did you reach the Lord?"

"I did," he affirmed. "But He sure didn't have much to say to me."

"Who can blame Him?" she said. "The poor Fellow's trying to get some rest in preparation for His big day tomorrow of listening to billions of church services."

"Now you just might be right," he said. "Leastways He didn't seem much inclined to give me any of His time."

"What did He say?"

"Strangest thing," he said. "I presented the case to Him just like you suggested. But He just said one thing. All He said was, and I quote, 'Straightway will I show thee thy true vocation.' That's all. Now what do you make of that?"

"Oh, come on, Every," she said. "You're just making that up."

"No, now," he said. "I swear. I heard it in me as clearly as I've ever heard Him in me. And that's what He said, word for word. *Straightway will I show thee thy true vocation.* As if I hadn't already found my true vocation a long time ago. What do you reckon that could mean? That He was going to give me some kind of sign right away? Then what kind of sign is Sarah Chism riding a mule?"

"Maybe He wants you to be a muleteer, maybe, or a mule trader," she said, thinking, *I'd lots rather be married to a mule trader than to a preacher.*

"Why would he want that?" Every said, in an obvious turmoil of perplexity. "What does He mean by 'true vocation,' anyhow? I've *got* a true vocation, darn it, and why doesn't He know it? Unless…maybe now…yes!…maybe He knows I've got a true vocation, and he's going to prove it to me by putting temptations in my path to see if I can withstand them. Yes now, that's it, I bet! He's going to have you tempt me and try me to see if I can stick to my true vocation."

"Now I know you're just making that up," she said. "You just made that up so you could get yourself excused from having to make love to me."

"I tell you, I *swear*, just as sure as I was born, that He said those exact words to me. 'Straightway will I show thee thy—'" Every suddenly sprang up out of his chair. "Land o' Goshen!" he cried, pointing. "Yonder she comes again!"

Sarah Chism on the mule came back up the main road, riding not as fast as she had headed into the village.

Latha said to him, "Maybe the Lord wants you to be a veterinarian."

Sarah caught sight of them silhouetted against the light of the windows and turned her mule toward them and rode up to the porch.

Sarah squinted at him and asked, "Is that you, Every? Is it shore-enough a fact what they say, that you've become a preacher?"

Every seemed reluctant to answer, as if to do so would bring down upon him that awful sign he anticipated. Finally he mumbled, "Yeah, Sarah, that's right."

"Then pray fer us all!" Sarah wailed. "My man Luther's done went and shot a revenuer! I've went to git Doc Swain, and he's a comin to try and fix him. He aint kilt dead, but he's all full a buckshot. Pray fer im, preacher! Pray fer us all!"

She jabbed her heels into the mule's belly, and rode away.

"Tarnation!" Every exclaimed.

"That's it, Every!" Latha said to him. "That's your sign. That's what the Lord wants you to be."

"What, a revenuer?" he asked.

"No, a moonshiner," she said.

"Aw, heck, Latha," he said. "You can't read signs. Don't you know what this signifies? Sarah asked me to pray, didn't she? That means the Lord is telling me that my true vocation is praying for folks! That means he wants me to pray for that poor revenuer, to strengthen my true vocation as a preacher."

And Every knelt immediately on the porch and said, "Dear Heavenly Father, I thank Thee for this sign. With earnest heart I ask Thee to look after that afflicted revenuer and preserve his life. Grant, O Lord, swiftness and skill to Doc Swain. Show Luther Chism the error of his ways, but protect and deliver him from any trouble with the government. In Jesus' Name, Amen."

The closing words of his prayer were nearly drowned beneath the sound of Doc Swain's car roaring up the road. The engine roared, then coughed, then roared again, spluttered, belched, roared, coughed: the car came into view, jerking and bucking. It came abreast of the post office, roaring, then spluttered and died. Doc Swain tried to start it again. It would not start.

Doc Swain jumped out of his car and kicked it viciously with his foot. "Goddamn scandalous hunk of cruddy tinfoil!" he yelled and kicked it again. "Sonabitchin worthless gas-eatin ash can!" Then he turned wildly about, yelling, "A horse! A horse! My kingdom for a horse!"

"Here's your true sign, Every," Latha said to him. "The Lord wants you to be a doctor."

"Naw," he said, "I'm afraid it's something else."

"A horse?"

"Get me a lantern, quick," he said.

She went into the house and brought out a lantern. He took it and ran out to Doc Swain's car. He gave the lantern to Doc Swain, saying, "Hold this." Then he opened the hood of the car and bent over into the car's innards. A minute passed. He said to Doc Swain, "Just set the lantern down on the fender and get in and try to start it." Doc Swain did so.

The car started right up, and the motor ran evenly. "Hey!" Doc Swain hollered. "Thanks a load, Every! What'd you do to it?"

"Distributor cap had worked loose," Every said.

"Well, lucky you were here!" Doc Swain said. "I got to get out to Luther Chism's. He's shot a revenuer, the damn fool." Doc Swain let out the clutch and roared away.

Latha and Every returned to the porch and sat down again. Every was in a morose mood. She let several minutes pass before saying, "So *that's* it. The Lord wants you to be an auto repairman."

Every said, "Maybe," and nothing else.

"Well," she observed, "I guess it ought to be a good-paying line of work."

"Oh, it's good-payin enough, all right," he said.

"You've done it before?" she asked.

"Worked my way through Bible College working nights in a garage in Nashville," he said. "And I've had to do a stretch of car work hither and yon from time to time, just to make ends meet. Preaching don't pay enough to be called a job of work, 'less you settle down in a good-sized city with a big congregation, and I wouldn't care for that." He was silent again for a while, then he threw his head back and raised his voice so loudly she jumped. "Lord, what're You tryin to tell me, Lord?" he demanded. "Don't You want me, Lord? Don't you need me anymore? Have I not been living up to Your expectations? Do You honestly want me to be nothing but a grease monkey?"

He was staring so fixedly up at the sky that she let her own gaze follow his, as if she might find Somebody appearing up there. The sky was mulberry purple, and star-splattered. A star fell. Or a piece of one, a flaming fragment, leaving a trail. A falling star always means that somebody is dying. Maybe that poor revenuer. No, maybe it was—

"What's that mean?" Every asked her. "You remember all those old-time signs and portents, Latha. What do folks think a shooting star means?"

"Falling, not shooting," she corrected him. "Means somebody just died."

"That revenuer," Every said. "Why, if he's dead, then it means that me fixing Doc Swain's car didn't do any good anyhow, so that wasn't the real sign the Lord meant to give me. Maybe there's going to be another sign, the real one. I just caint believe the Lord would want me to fix cars the rest of my life."

"Maybe not the revenuer," she said. "Maybe the one who just died was Preacher Every Dill. The preacher's dead in you, Every."

"Don't say that!" he protested. "That gives me the creeps."

"Do you still *feel* like a preacher right now?" she asked.

"I don't feel like anything," he said. "I'm numb. Plumb numb."

"Let's go into the house, and I'll un-numb you," she offered.

He did not say anything, nor move.

"Where are you going to stay tonight?" she asked.

"Same place as last night," he said.

"On a pile of old dirty straw in the old home?" she said. "Why don't you just stay here?"

"I didn't know you had any spare room, what with Sonora," he said.

"My bed is wide," she said.

"No," he said.

"Okay," she said, "we'll put a board down the middle and you can tie me up beforehand."

"No."

"I'll even wear a nightdress for a change."

"No."

"Every," she said in exasperation, "if you won't sleep with me first I won't marry you."

"And I tell you again," he said, "that I will not sleep with you until I've married you."

"Well," she said, "that's that, I guess. Nice to've seen you again, Every. Come back again some time."

But he did not leave. Nor did he say anything. They just sat and sulked, both of them, for many minutes.

Eventually he was the first to break it. He remarked, in a low voice, "I feel just plain miserable."

"Me too," she said.

They lapsed into silence again.

By and by Doc Swain returned, and stopped his car in the yard and got out. He came up and sat with them on the porch.

"Every," he said, "the United States government ought to pin some kind of medal on you. Providing, of course, that that poor bastard ever gets back to tell them about it. Pardon my language,

Reverend. Well, I declare, if you have learned to save souls the way you've learned to fix automobiles, I reckon it's true enough that you've honestly been transformed and revamped."

"Is he all right?" Every asked.

"Well, he won't be sittin down for a right smart spell, but he can just lay on his belly. I dug about twenty 12-gauge shot out a his ass-end—pardon me, Latha—his backside is shore peppered up, but, all considering, he'll live—though for what I don't know, 'cause Luther still aint figgered out what to do with him."

"Why did Luther shoot him?" Latha asked. "That was plain stupid."

"Haw!" Doc Swain exclaimed. "Lost his temper momentarily, I imagine. Seems what happened was he caught that revenuer right in the old act of carnal congress with his gal Lucy. Caught him really with his britches down, and let fire with his shotgun before thinkin about it. Even nicked Lucy on the thigh too."

"I thought the revenuer was tied up," Every said. "How could he have seduced Lucy if he was tied up?"

"By dang if he aint still tied!" Doc Swain laughed. "He aint never been *un*tied! Reckon Lucy had to unbutton his britches for him. But Luther claims the revenuer must've talked her into it, and that's just the same as seducing her. I don't doubt it, for that revenuer is shore a talkin fool; he could talk the hind leg off a donkey. No trouble talkin his own britches off. He come mighty near to talkin me into sendin him to a hospital, so he could get loose from Luther."

"Why didn't you?"

"And betray my own people?" Doc Swain demanded. "What do you think I am?"

"Well, Luther can't keep him forever, can he?"

"Noo, but he aint about to let him loose before studying on the problem. Luther's brains is kind of slow, you know." Doc Swain stood up. "Well, I'm out way past my bedtime. Sure obliged to you, Every, for that quick repair job."

"Doc," Every asked, "are you still the justice of the peace for Swains Creek township?"

"I fergit," Doc Swain said. "Seems like I am, but I aint jay-peed in so long I fergit whether my license is still up to date. But yes, come to think on it, I reckon it is. Why?"

"Can you issue a marriage license?" Every asked.

"Sure," Doc Swain said. "Who for?"

"Us," Every said.

"Who's 'us'?"

"Me and her."

"By jabbers, it's about time!"

SUB FIVE: *Now*

I am lost, O Bug.

Even if I wanted to go back, and I do not, I could not find my way. I must be a mile up Ledbetter Mountain, beyond your orchard. A moment ago an owl hooted at me, and I peed in my pants. I have taken them off to dry. I am not running any more; if the gowrows and jimplicutes don't get me, I will turn into a snawfus at midnight, then I will go back and bite Aunt Rosie's head off, and see how she likes that. You know what she did to me. I can hardly sit down. But I promised you I would never tell on you, and I will never.

Will you marry Every Dill? Then can I never be yours? When I become a snawfus, after I finish with Aunt Rosie, I would bite his head off too, but you wouldn't love me for it, for he is dear to you. So I will just haunt these woods forevermore, protecting you, beheading with my teeth all your enemies. I shall immortalize you; you shall live forever, and when Every Dill must needs one day go to meet his Lord in heaven, you shall be mine.

I shiver, though the night is hot. My fingers feel the goose bumps on my thighs, and not because they're bare. Bear? Are there bears in these woods, if not gowrows and jimplicutes? *Real* things? I fear no boogers; I believe Tull Ingledew and trust him; there are no boogers; but *real* things? Bears and panthers and wolves and foxes and snakes and spiders. Which way did I come? *That* way, or *that* way? I put on my pants and run. I trip over a rotted log and fall. I cry. I cry unto you, O my beloved, come to me.

You are abed, and hear me not. You are abed, alone abed, for all your blandishments and your cajolery and your admonition have failed to get him abed with you. He sleeps in the store, the next room, upon a pile of your bags of feed. He not alone sleeps but snores. *Oh for crying out loud!* you say to yourself, listening to his snores. This, then, you now enumerate as the third reason why you will not marry him, the other two being that he is so all-fired religious and that you have come to enjoy your independence—if you take him to husband, mightn't he interfere with your operation of your business, for instance ordering Hershey bars in hot weather? At the moment, listening to his snores, Bug, the only good reason you can think for marrying him would be that it would increase the population of Stay More by one, and maybe one enough to dissuade the government from closing the post office.

I have stopped crying. I have cried so much tonight there's no water left in my tear ducts. I snuggle into a pile of old leaves and think I'm in hiding. I notice there aren't any lightning bugs, up this high. They must prefer the bottom lands, low meadows, yards, the creek. It will soon be midnight, and I will change into a snawfus. It's your fault you told me about snawfusses. And gowrows and jimplicutes. I feel very drowsy. We stayed awake so late last night, you and I, I'm not caught up on my sleep.

Nor are you, and you awoke this morning long before I. But you sleep not, neither do you drowse. You attempt to listen to the night-noises of bugs and frog to blot out his infernal snoring. You would like to get up and go gag him. He gagged you once. *Now we're even,* you could say to him.

What you should have done, you are thinking, was to have taken recourse to a special old Ozark folk potion: a drop of your menstrual fluid in his drink, perchance his iced tea. Guaranteed to give an erection even to an octogenarian. You laugh aloud, thinking of it, and say to yourself: *I'll put a drop in his coffee at breakfast, and then he can't give his sermon because of the bulge in his britches.* But you don't menstruate. Maybe Sonora does. But then he would fall in love with her. That's the way it works. A funny thought further amuses you in your insomnia: what if he had fallen in love with her without knowing she was his daughter, and have married her?

Thinking thus of Sonora, you are rather surprised to hear her own voice, outside your door, saying, "Mother?" You don't reply. Then she says, a little louder, "Latha, are you awake?"

You get up and light your lantern. You don your houserobe and open the door. "Something wrong, honey?" you say.

She glances beyond you at the bed, and says, "No. I heard you laughing. And there's somebody inside the store snoring something awful."

"That's Every," you explain. "And it *is* awful."

Sonora says, "Why didn't you just tell him to sleep with you?"

You smile and confess, "I did, but he wouldn't."

"Gee," she says. "That's too bad. Maybe he can't. Maybe he's too old."

"Or just too holy," you observe.

"Me and Hank have busted up," she declares.

"Come on in," you say, moving out of the door. "You want to talk about it?"

She sits on your bed. "We had a spat on account of *him*, on account of Every."

"Oh?" you wonder.

"Uh-huh," she says, hanging her head. "I told him that Every is really my father, and he said if that's true then he can't love me any more, and I said why not? and he said because all the Ingledews are sworn enemies of Every Dill, and Hank's dad and uncle would hate him if he married a girl who was kin to Every, let alone his daughter."

"You shouldn't have told him Every was your father," you admonish, "that wasn't right."

"Maybe it wasn't right, but it's true," she says. "Isn't it?"

You don't reply.

"Okay," she says. "I 'spose they forced you to vow you'd never tell me. So I won't try to make you. But I just want to say I'm glad.

I *want* him to be my father. I like him a whole lot. Compared with him, Daddy is—Vaughn is a…a klunk…a jerk, a boob. Are you going to marry him?"

You answer, "I don't think so. Probably not."

"You don't really love him?" she asks.

"Well—" you hesitate, "I'm not so sure. I haven't had time yet to tell. Today's the first I've seen of him in years."

"Mother, was he really the one who robbed the bank?"

"I wish you'd not call me Mother."

She hangs her head and mutters, "I caint call you anything else any more."

You feel near tears again, but you bite your lip and hold back. You place a hand on her shoulder, and speak gently, "All right, honey, call me anything you like. But just don't ask me if he robbed the bank. Nobody knows except the one who did it, and he didn't look like anyone I'd ever seen before, because he was disguised."

"Hank says his dad is going to make Every confess. But what if he offered to pay it back?…How much was it?"

"Around eight thousand dollars."

She whistles. "My gosh, he'd never be able to raise that much, unless he robbed another bank. But you and me could help. When I finish high school next year I'll get a job, and—"

"Sonora," you say, "let's not cross that bridge till we get to it. Let's just wait and see what happens. Maybe Every will go away for good."

"Oh, don't let him do that!" she cries. "Please marry him." She adds: "For me."

You sigh. "We'll see," you promise. "Maybe soon."

Abruptly she kisses you, then says, "Sweet dreams, Mother," and leaves the room.

You return to bed, but you do not sleep. You meditate: *Three good reasons for not marrying him, and now one great reason for marrying him. For her.* But what could come of it? Mandy and Vaughn would never let her go. She could never be their daughter. Even if Sonora insisted on it, even if she told Mandy and Vaughn she wouldn't live with them any more, she was a legal minor—*Just like I was, when I had her*—and couldn't do anything about it until she was twenty-one. And even if it did work out, Sonora might be in for a rude surprise when she discovers what a strict father Every would be.

Oh, it was all so hopeless! Everything was so messed up it could never be untangled!

The utter complication of the situation, plus your exhaustion, is what finally drives you to sleep.

But your dreams are sweet, O Bug. Just as Sonora had bade you, your dreams are sweet.

Here I give you as a gift, my beloved, the sweetest of your dreams:

You wander in the wind in your orchard on Ledbetter Mountain, in the early eventide of a fine summer's day, before gloaming. The wind holds your dark tresses aloft, suspending them in fluttering slow-motion. Your thighs tingle from the brushes of grass and flower-tops. You have reached yourself a peach from one of your trees, and the way it lusciously receives the bites of your teeth surpasses all sensuality. You can feel your stomach making love to it; your juices mate with its juices, and become one; that one imbues you, suffuses you with all its passion; you are sweeter than all peaches; your sweet passion leaves you convulsed with longing. You leap in the wind. You could open your thighs to anything that walks.

You say, *I will snatch the first creature I see.*

He comes now into view, walking down into the orchard from the mountain. He seems in no hurry to get anywhere, as if He were just out for a stroll. He catches sight of you, and approaches. He looks a lot like Every, you think. Yes, an awful lot—though His hair comes to His shoulders, and He is clothed in a white sheet, and barefoot.

"Howdy, Stranger," you say to Him, and offer Him a peach.

"Howdy, ma'am," He replies, and takes the peach and bites into it. "My," He declares, "this sure is a mighty fine one. Elberta?"

"That's right," you tell Him.

"Mighty fine," He says again, and quickly eats the entire peach.

"Where're you from, Stranger?" you ask Him, although you know.

"Galilee," He answers.

"Which part of Newton County is that in?" you ask, pretending ignorance.

"No part of it," He says, "Haven't you ever heard of Galilee?"

"Oh, you mean the one in the Bible," you say.

"The same," He says.

"You know, you remind me an awful lot of a certain fellow."

"Who's that?" He asks.

"Fellow named Every Dill," you answer.

"Oh," He says. "*Him.*"

"You know him?" you ask.

"*Know him?*" He says. "Why, the day never goes by that he doesn't yak at me. He badgers me without let-up."

You ask: "Was it you who told him that you would show him his true vocation?"

"That's right. I figured I'd never be able to get him off my ear otherwise."

"But which sign did you mean? What is it you want him to be?"

"Why, you were there, weren't you? Didn't you see the way I fouled up Doc Swain's car so Every would have to fix it?"

"Then you really want him to be just an auto mechanic?"

"What's wrong with being an auto mechanic? Some of my best friends were nothing but poor fishermen. Me, I'm just a carpenter by trade myself. Besides, in this day and age a good experienced auto mechanic stands to earn a really decent living. *More* than decent, really. Downright *in*decent, if he starts doctoring the service bills."

"Why don't you want him to be a preacher any more?"

"I never wanted anybody to be a preacher. It's a crying shame the way the world is filling up with preachers, and every blessed one of them has his own half-cracked idea of what I said…or what I meant to say, anyhow. If all these preachers can't start agreeing, I might just have to Come Again, and soon."

"But Every claims you told him in that Nashville hotel room that you would make me well on the condition he became a preacher."

"Did he say that?" He demanded. "Well, there's just another good example for you of how I never can get anybody to even *remember*, let alone *understand*, what I say to them. I didn't say a word to him about becoming a preacher. I just told him to follow me. I just told him to believe in me and follow me for the rest of his life. That's all I've been telling anybody. You don't have to call yourself a preacher just to follow me."

"But did you really make me well because of that?"

"You look pretty good, I'd say. How you been feeling lately?"

"Pretty good, thank you. And you?"

"Tolerable," He says.

"But if you were really in charge of all that situation, why did you rig it up so that he and I wouldn't even see one another again for more than fourteen long years?"

"Don't question my ways, girl. Let's just say I've got a pretty good reason for everything I do. Some of it may not make any sense at all, but I never do anything just to be contrary or crotchety."

"Well, tell me," you ask, "did you really make me faint on account of he and I making love?"

"Yes," He declares.

"You don't approve of fornication?"

He shudders. "Oh, that *word!* What I was talking about—and my followers who recorded my words sure didn't use any of that Latin gobbledygook—was unchastity and immorality without love or even affection. Marriage is in the heart anyway. I could name you several billion married couples who are committing fornication with each other as far as I'm concerned."

"Then why did you punish me by making me faint?"

"Did you think I was punishing you, child? Did I say anything about *punishing* you?"

"But you just said—"

"You asked me if I made you faint *on account of* you and Every making love, and I said 'Yes.' Yes you fainted because you were making love, but I didn't think of it as punishment. Correct me if I'm wrong, but I think it must be kind of a big thrill to pass out afterwards, isn't it?"

"Oh," you say. Then you offer, "Help yourself to another peach."

"Thank you. Don't mind if I do." He reaches up and plucks one off the tree.

"Is it all right with you if Every and I make love?" you ask.

"Don't ask *me*. That's not for me to say. My Dad gave you folks free will in the first place, to decide for yourselves what you want to do."

"But Every tells me that you've spoken out against fornication."

"That *word* again! Look, let's say I've spoken out against betrayal, I've spoken out against abusing and *using* others, I'm on record as opposed to uncleanness and dissipation, and I've taken a rather strong stand against cuckoldry, because in a triangle somebody's liable to get hurt. But I thought I've made it pretty clear that my supreme commandment is 'You better love your neighbor the same way you love yourself.' And that means *all* neighbors, male and female."

"But you don't mean *sexual* love, do you?"

"I sure do. 'Sexual' is just another one of those fancy Latin words, and sometimes I wish I had never allowed the Romans to gaum up the language the way they have. But *all* love is sexual love."

"Now wait just a minute," you protest. "If you tell me to love my neighbor as I love myself, and you say all love is sexual, then you're insinuating that I masturbate."

"Ooo!" He cries, smiting Himself on the brow, "now *that* is absolutely the godawfulest ugly word that ever got squeezed out of Latin. Please don't use that one around me."

"Well, whatever you want to call it then. Is it implied in what you mean by loving myself?"

"I don't know," He says. "Is it? Some people do, and some people don't. Loving yourself takes all sorts of forms and fashions. You love yourself when you eat one of these here peaches. Far's I'm concerned, there's not much difference between eating a peach *to yourself* and making love *to yourself*."

"Then you don't condemn it?"

"I condemn it if it's not matched by your love for your neighbor."

"Can I get into bed with all my neighbors? Do you want me to love all my neighbors sexually?"

"Now you're beginning to sound like Every when he's pestering me with questions. You're asking me a big question I'm not going to answer because I've already answered it."

"Is that why you refuse to give Every permission to make love to me?"

"My goodness, girl, don't you realize I'm not in the business of granting permissions? If I had nothing better to do than grant permissions, all my time would be taken up in a more or less bureaucratic desk job, and that's certainly not what Dad had in mind for me when He made me His only begotten son."

"But what can I do?" you plead. "You know Every won't make love to me unless I marry him, and you know I won't marry him unless he makes love to me. So one of us has got to yield, right? Why can't it be *him*, if you don't disapprove of forn—of us making love?"

"Child," He says tenderly, "my heart really bleeds for you, but there's nothing I can do. I thought I'd done enough, by showing him that sign, by telling him to stop being a preacher. That's all I can do."

"Couldn't you simply say to him, 'It's all right to make love to Latha?'"

"I'm sorry."

You sigh. "Well," you say. After a while you offer, "Care for another peach? The market's low this year, and there's plenty."

"In that case—" He says, and helps Himself to another. You also have one. The two of you munch your peaches in silence.

"You know," you remark reflectively, "there is something rather sexual about eating peaches, don't you think?"

"You can say that again," He agrees. "I think Dad wanted it that way, when he made them. But if you stopped to think about it, there's something sexual about nearly everything."

Straightway you ask, "Are *you* sexual?"

"Why not?" he says.

"Well—" you search for words "—after all, you're somebody rather special, you know, and pure and holy…"

"I'm a man," he protests. "Matter of fact, I'm not simply a man, but the *Son of Man.*"

"Have you ever had any girlfriends?"

"Have I!" he exclaims. "Why, there's never been a man in history who's had more than I."

"But have you ever slept with one?"

"You can't imagine the number I've slept with."

"But I mean have you ever actually…you know, actually *entered* them?"

He smiles. He just smiles.

You say to him, "Look, you said all love is sexual, right? Well, maybe I don't know what you mean by sexual, but didn't you also say something one time about loving the Lord?"

"With all of your heart, and with all of your soul, and with all of your mind."

"But not with all of your body?"

"That can't be done," He points out.

"Then how can you say all love is sexual?"

"Is sex only in the body?" he asks. "Isn't it also in the heart and soul and mind?"

"All right," you agree. "So let's suppose I feel a great love, which is sexual, in my heart and soul and mind, for you, and you're here in person, so why can't you just make love to me?"

He smiles. He commands you, "Close your eyes." You close them and become all excited, wondering what is about to happen. But nothing happens. He is playing a trick on you. He is mocking you. But you keep your eyes closed, until He says, "Okay, now open them."

You open your eyes. But He is gone. You are alone. "Where are you?" you call out.

"Yes, that's the question," He says. "Where am I?"

"Oh, dear heavens!" you suddenly cry out.

"Where am I?" He asks again. "Am I in your heart or your soul or your mind or your body?"

"Oh, goodness gracious!" you exclaim, suddenly lying down in the orchard grass.

"Yes, that's it," He says. "Goodness Gracious. Gracious Goodness. How does it feel?"

"I…I can't even begin to describe it…" you say.

"That's right," He says. "Not even those smart Romans could come up with a language that could express it properly. So you see the trouble I've had trying to get my message across? You see how you folks can't even express feelings, let alone understand what I've been trying to say about love? There's just not any way of—"

"Oh, don't talk," you plead. "Just—"

You are there, O Bug, not I; how am even *I* to describe it?

"Nobody will believe me," you declare. "When I tell them—"

"That's true enough," He agrees. "So why bother to tell them? Nobody would believe me either."

You moan, "I'm going to faint clean out of my skin."

You hear Him chuckle. "Now *that*," He says, "is the closest to a good description I've ever heard yet."

"Hush," you whisper, and you whisper faintly, "Could you…oh, could you make it work just a little faster?"

"Sure," He obliges.

You faint clean out of your skin.

And awake.

It is still night; the room floats with the charged light of a stormy night sky; you find the sheet upon which you are lying is twisted into a landscape of wrinkles. Your breath comes in heaves.

You marvel, *That was so real!*

You declare, *Oh, I can't wait to tell Every about it!*

You realize, *Oh no, if I told him Who that was, he would really wash his hands of me.*

You sigh.

You stare up at the ceiling for a long while, unable to fall back into sleep. At length you speak aloud, "I love you, Lord Jesus."

It begins to rain. It is the first rain in five weeks. Like any summer rain in Stay More, it is a downpour. My wetness awakens me. I whimper, and crawl out of the leaves and in under a cedar tree. But even the thick boughs of the cedar tree can't keep all the rain off me. Oh, I'm as wet as a dog.

The dog is Gumper. But when he comes sniffing and nuzzling up to me, I scream and thrash about, thinking he's a wild beast. Then, just before I could panic right out of my mind, I recognize him by his smell. There is on earth only one thing that smells worse than Gumper, and that is Gumper soaking wet. I hold my nose and yell "Git!" and kick at him.

Then an idea occurs to me: if I told him to get for home, and he got for home, I could follow and find my way out of here.

"Git home!" I yell and wave my arms and kick.

I cannot see him in the dark. Has he gone for home? But I still smell him, unless it's what he left behind.

Then a flash of lightning illuminates him. He is under the cedar tree, on the opposite side from me, sound asleep.

The only thing worse than a wet smelly dog is a wet smelly dog who's stubborn and stupid.

A peal of thunder lifts me off the ground.

Lightning, Lightning Bug, of an infinitely brighter sort than yours.

You wish you could sleep again, could dream again, could talk with Him again, but the rainstorm keeps you awake. Not even your pillow over your head will muffle it.

It reminds you of the night you slept with Every; the rain poured down hard that night; you were eleven years old; he was twelve. You think to go remind him of it again.

You arise. Again you put on your houserobe. You have left the door from your bedroom to the store unlocked, thus you do not need to search for the key. You open it.

He is sleeping deeply, sprawled out on his back upon the gingham bags of Nutreena and Purina feed. He no longer snores. Not even the crash and boom of the lightning storm seems to disturb his heavy slumber. You sit down upon a nail keg beside him, and in the intermittent flashes of lightning you study him. You remember he said he got no sleep the night before. *He is making up for it*, you reflect. Deep, deep his sleep, and deep your longing. You study and admire his face; in sleep his hair is tousled. Your gaze wanders down the length of him and back, and settles upon his groin. You detect there a tight bulge. *What is he dreaming?* you wonder. You cannot resist reaching out and touching it. Then you are taken with an urge to lay it bare. Slowly your fingers undo the buttons. As the last button is opened, the bulge rises. The polka dot shorts come into view, overlapped upon the bulge. Gently your fingers spread open the flap, and of a sudden the thing stands.

You regard it lovingly and a little wonderingly, thinking, *It's sure changed since he was twelve.*

You dub it, with a smile: *His Every-thing. My Every-thing.*

You ask yourself: *Do I dare?*

If you did dare, it would surely waken him, and then what would he do? Would he hate you for tricking him? You do not know of the time on the road in Tennessee when he took you in your sleep, for he had censored that from his narrative. Had you known, you could have said surely, if he woke, "See, now we are *really* even." But not knowing this, you are reluctant, and afraid. *I do not dare*, you think.

So you merely bestow a fleeting kiss upon it, and return to your room and your bed.

But you did not replace it. As you fall asleep again finally, you are amusedly wondering, *What's he going to think when he wakes up and finds it hanging out? Oh, won't he wonder and wonder!*

"Please, Gumper," I plead. "Please get up and show me how to get out of here." But he just lies there. Exhausted I lay my head down on the wet earth.

Ending

From the woods, night, forever, Stay More, Ark.

IT WILL END:

we sleep. They will sleep.

In the morning, early, they will go out looking for him, all of them, first his aunt who will discover him missing and then will discover, while hunting for him at Latha's place, Brother Every Banning Dill, who will be asleep in the store on a pile of feed bags with, to her profound shock and offense, his male member hanging from an open fly. Rosie will not be able to resist telling this to her husband Frank, and Frank in turn will not be able to resist mentioning it, during the height of the search, jokingly to Every himself, who forthwith will quit the search, and quit the town as well.

She will run after him. When Sonora will inform her that she saw him walking rapidly off up the Parthenon road with his suitcase in his hand, Latha will run after him, walking for a while, then running again.

She will go all the way past Jesse Witter's place before she will spot him up the road ahead. Then she will slow to a rapid walk again. She will be panting hard, and sweating. "Every!" she will call after him, but he will neither stop nor turn his head. He will increase the pace of his walking.

She will run again, and she will catch up with him and grab his arm. He will shake her off and keep walking, his face grim. She will throw herself in front of him.

"Get out of my way!" he will snarl.

"Every, please!" she will say. "What are you doing?"

He will not stop walking. "I'm putting distance between Stay More and me," he will say severely.

"You're leaving me?" she will cry. "Can you leave *me*?"

"Easily," he will say.

She will not be able to keep trotting alongside him. She will stop, and as he goes on past she will wail, "BUT WHY?"

He will stop, at last, and turn to her. "Because you've mortified me, that's why! I caint ever show my face in that town again!"

"Just because Rosie saw you through the store window?"

"Oh, so you know about it too!" he will say fiercely. "Well, I wish you'd told me! If you'd told me, you'd've spared me the embarrassment I've done been put through!"

"What happened?" she will ask. "Did Frank bawl you out for it?"

"Naw, he laughed *at* me! He laughed and got downright sarcastic and told me I was sure gettin my revival off to a *big* start! Haw! As if I would even dare hold a revival after the word got around! I don't even dare appear anywhere in this whole county again! Or this whole state, for that matter!"

"I thought the Lord had already told you to stop preaching," she will say.

He will not say anything to that. He will turn and resume walking.

She will catch up with him again. "Is that more important than me?" she will ask. "If you really love me, or even care for me at all, can you just walk out on me like this?"

"If you cared for me at all," he will answer, "you would never have done that to me!"

"I never dreamed you'd be seen," she will say. "How was I to know that Rosie would be prowling around at six o'clock in the morning?"

"What if anybody had seen me?" he will say. "What if Sonora had seen me? What if the mail truck came, and everybody came to get their darn mail and saw me?"

"The mail doesn't come on Sundays," she will point out.

"It was just downright shameful of you!" he will say. "Your conduct has been astonishing me from the first moment I came back, and it got worse and worse until that was just the last straw! You might think it's a big joke, but it don't strike me as the least bit funny!"

"You'll get over it," she will say.

"Naw, I could never live it down!" he will maintain.

"Maybe Frank and Rosie won't spread it."

"Likely chance! It'll be all over town before noon!"

"Well," she will say, "so what if it is? Folks will just think that you and I were fooling around, and I don't mind them thinking that."

"That's your whole trouble, you don't give a thought to what folks think of your conduct. I just don't care for that kind of wife."

She will sigh. "Well," she will say, "I don't suppose we could ever have got married anyway, because you wouldn't make love to me before marrying me, and I wouldn't marry you before making love with you. So you're going to walk right on out of my life, just after walking right on into it again for the first time in years." She will sigh again. "I guess I'll marry Dolph Rivett."

"He's your type," he will retort.

"And you're not?" she will ask, sadly. "Weren't you ever?"

"Latha," he will say gently, "come with me if you want to, but I'm not ever going back to Stay More."

"And I'm never leaving it," she will declare.

"Well, then, I guess it's goodbye," he will say.

She will say, "I think you're being a dirty bastard to run off like this when Dawny's lost."

"The whole town's out looking for him. One less won't matter."

"Then good riddance," she will say. "I'm wasting my time arguing with you when I ought to be out looking for him."

"Well, so long, then," he will say.

"Goodbye," she will say.

But neither of them will move.

"Get on back and look for him," he will say.

"Get on up the road," she will say.

"I am," he will say.

"I don't see you doing it," she will say.

"I don't see you doing anything either," he will say.

"I'm waiting to watch you walk out of sight," she will say.

"Why do you have to do that?" he will ask.

"It means," she will say, "if you watch somebody walk out of sight, it means they will die."

"You want me to die?" he will ask.

"You're as good as dead to me if you leave Stay More."

"Well, I'm not superstitious like you," he will say. "I don't believe it will work."

"Go on, then," she will say.

"All right then, I will," he will say.

But he will not move.

"Well?" she will say.

"Latha, you don't really have to do that, do you?"

"Do what?"

"Watch me walk out of sight."

"Why not?" she will say. "What's the matter, are you scared? I thought you didn't believe in superstitions."

"But it's not going to be easy for me to walk out of sight, knowing that."

"It's not going to be easy for me, either."

"Then don't do it. Go on and get back to town."

"You come with me," she will say.

"No."

"Then get on up the road."

"Okay, but don't watch me."

"Why not, if you're not superstitious?"

"It'll just seem kind of spooky and make me nervous."

"Then you are *superstitious," she will say.*

"No, I'm not, neither."
"Then go. I dare you."
"All right" he will say. "I'm going. Goodbye, Latha."
"Farewell," she will say.

He will turn and begin walking away, walking slowly, swinging his suitcase by its handle in his hand. I *will* watch him, *she will tell herself,* all *of the way out of sight. She will not think that is cruel of her. It is cruel of him to leave. It is cruel, and childish, and thoughtless, and sanctimonious, high and mighty, and downright mean. Let him die.*

There will be a turning in the road ahead, and he will be near it. In a moment he will have been gone. Steadfastly she will watch him, her eyes burning holes into his back. Oh, how could he do that!

He will arrive at the turning. In an instant the trees will have hidden him from sight. He will seem to sense that he will have been immediately hidden from sight, for he will stop. He will stop and turn and look back at her. He will stand there for a moment, looking back at her.

Come back, Every! Oh, come back or you'll die!

He will come back, walking slowly, hanging his head.

When he reaches her, he will lift his head and smile sort of sheepishly and say, "You know, maybe if I was just out in the woods looking for Dawny I wouldn't have to show my face to a soul anyhow."

So then, yes. He will stay. He would never, he will never, leave her again. So that is settled, done. He will rejoin the search, and, good as he is at searching, having searched for her three times and found her three times and lost her only twice, he will be the most apt to find Dawny. It will become like a kind of competition: Tull Ingledew, who can fling a flintrock straight up and tell by the direction it falls which way the lost boy is, Doc Swain who not only can organize and direct the other 112 people in their search operation but can also use his car to patrol every road and byroad in town and be ready with his gladstone bag to treat the boy in case he has suffered from exposure or any injury, Dolph Rivett who can go all the way home to Spunkwater to fetch a bloodhound [not realizing, however, that the heavy rain of the night before would have washed any scent away], *and Every Dill who will throw his heart and his wits into the search because the lost boy is dear to her who is dear to him, and will be the most apt to find the boy, if anybody does, because he is most experienced at searching and finding and also because he as a lad of five-going-on-six was the spitting image of Dawny and had a mind just like his, and will even be able to guess where the boy might be hiding or lost, and who, in search of him, maybe is the one who most needs to find him.*

[My intelligent friend from Andover, Mass., who was last heard from in the prelude with his view that the proper name for lightning bug is firefly, has now interrupted with the comment that "The allusion to Pirandello is too obvious." Well, yes, my friend, maybe if you've read Pirandello. But I never did. And I doubt that Latha ever did. Or Every.]

Every will interrupt the search, just once briefly, during the late afternoon, at the request of Luther Chism, to perform what will be his next-to-last act as a minister of gospel: to officiate the quick nuptials of Lucy Chism and an agent of the U.S. Revenue Department, who has agreed, on condition that he be untied, freed and then hitched to Lucy for life, that he will never divulge the location of Luther's still, or of Luther, to his employers.

Luther, losing Lucy, will gain permanent amnesty or immunity or at least franchise, to pursue his trade to the end of his days. "Great Gawd!" he will never tire of exclaiming to all his friends, "Thet thar was the best swop I ever made."

Dolph Rivett will not fare so well. He will return with his blood-hound, to the admiring comments of other searchers—"Lookit the nose on thet dawg!" "He ort to do the trick." "Thet's a right fine snoop-dawg ye got, mister"—and will self-importantly begin to put the hound on Dawny's trail, using for the scent a snotrag (hand-kerchief) thought to belong to Dawny, but which, as it will turn out, did not belong to Dawny but to his uncle Frank. After a spirited chase, Dolph's bloodhound will lead Dolph and a dozen odd others to the Stay More schoolhouse, where Frank Murrison will be found in a compromising position atop Miss Estalee Jerram, schoolmistress. Frank, oblivious to the grins and leers and smirks around him as he hastily buttons his pants, will declare, "me and Esty figgered maybe Dawny was over here to the schoolhouse maybe." "He aint," somebody will observe.

Frank will be heard at various other times of that day remarking, to no one in particular, "Well, heck, aint none of us perfect."

[And Frank will have said it. None of us are. Nor is it likely that the pot will be so inclined to remark upon the color of the kettle, that is, I doubt that Frank will be spreading any gossip about Every.]

As for Dolph, at just about the same instant he discovers the uselessness of the bloodhound, he will discover, with mingled anger and fear, a young man sitting upon a horse and pointing a shotgun at him.

"You, Purdy," Dolph will say. "What you pointin that arn at me fer? Whut you doin here anyhow?"

The youth will reply, "I follered ye over, Paw, when I seen ye come and git ole Gloomy. Whut ye doin with old Gloomy, Paw?"

"Sheeut far," Dolph will grumble, spreading his hands apologetically, "I jest taken him for to help find a pore tyke what's lost from these good people. You aint aimin to use him today, nohow."

"How you know I aint?" the one called Purdy will challenge. "You never ast me. You been comin and goin' thout ary word to me or Duke or Mom even. I done stood for all I aim to stand. Now you jest fetch yore hoss, Paw, and let's us jest git on back home."

"Don't ye be a-bossin me, Purdy Rivett!" Dolph will say. "You stop pointin that there arn at me, too! I'll take ye to the woodshed! I'll whale the tar outen ye! I'll whop the soup outen ye!"

"Naw, Paw," Purdy will say, noisily cocking the hammer of his shooting iron, "I don't reckon I'd stand for that neither. I'd as soon shoot ye, you dawg-stealer."

"I never stole no dawg, dammit," Dolph will protest. "He's a fambly dawg. Old Gloomy don't belong to you, he sort of belongs to the whole fambly."

"Lak hell," Purdy will say, and will spit. "The whole fambly never paid fer im, nor fed im nor trained im neither."

"Well sheeut," Dolph will protest. "I never stole im nohow. I was just a-borryin him to help these good folks find that there boy lost. That's a good cause, aint it? Besides, ole Gloomy aint been no good anyhow. You aint trained him right, maybe."

"I aint?" the youth will challenge, and then he will turn to the dog and will make a noise, "Fftt!" and then will command the dog,

"*Sic im, Old Gloom!*" *and will point at Dolph, and the dog will leap at Dolph, striking him a blow with his forepaws that will topple Dolph backwards into the dust, and then the dog will aim his fangs at Dolph's face and will have bitten off his nose if Purdy will not have snapped* "*Hold!*" *in the nick of time, and then* "*Back!*" *and then* "*Sit!*" *and then to his father* "*See?*"

"*Yeah, yeah, okay, yeah,*" *Dolph will say, getting up amidst the howling laughter of the spectators.* "*But, boy, you jest wait till I git you alone by yorse'f. I'll settle your hash! I'll mop up the hills with ye!*"

"*You aint never gonna git me alone, Paw,*" *Purdy will return.* "*I aint gonna let ole Gloomy out a my sight again. You wouldn't a got him offen me this mornin if I wudn't out a doin your work fer ye. Me'n Duke are plum tard a doin yore work fer ye, Paw. So's Maw. Now git on yore goddamn hoss, afore I sic ole Gloomy on ye again!*"

"*You son, now you jest lissen a me...*"

"*I'll lissen on the way home, Paw. Git yore hoss, and git her now!*"

Dolph will mutter a string of profanities under his breath, then turn and look at the folks gathered around, and will say to them, "*I don't aim to 'low this kid the upper hand fer long. So any of you folks happen to see Latha Bourne, you jest tell her Dolph Rivett will be back again jest as soon as he straightens out his brash young uns.*"

Purdy will comment on that, "*You aint never comin back over here to fool around any more, Paw. Not as long as me'n Duke are still alive.*"

And Purdy will be right. By whatever coercion or debate or plea that he and his brother and his mother will employ, Dolph Rivett will stay home and be a semblance at least of a dutiful father and husband, and will resume, at whatever great effort, the life he had led before Latha reminded him what a man is. He will never find the lost boy.

[We should not miss him. We should feel as Latha will feel when somebody will happen to mention to her the circumstances of his forcible removal from Stay More by his own son—that he was, after all, for all his rampant virility, rather coarse, less than couth; Latha could never have married him, even if Every had never come.]

So those two, the revenuer and Dolph, will be eliminated. Who else? Well, although they were never here at Stay More to begin with, Mandy and Vaughn Twichell will be eliminated, when they come. They will come, later in the week, and find that Sonora refuses to go. They will create a scene; they will attempt force, as Purdy Rivett had in removing his father, but they will not be armed, except with words, angry words, and these words will be successfully countered by Sonora, and Latha, and Every too, who will give them pure hell. They will make threats, which, however, will never be carried out.

Sonora will not be eliminated. Upon graduation from Jasper High School, she will give her hand to John Henry Ingledew, although Every will not accede to her request that he momentarily re-enter the ministry long enough, just long enough to perform the ceremony. "No, honey," he will say. "I guess if I was to do it, it wouldn't somehow be official."

"But you did it for your own self and Mother," she will point out. "Do you call that official?"

"Back then," he will explain, "I still had just enough of the preacher left in me; he hadn't all got out; there was enough left over and I used up the last of it doing it. I spent the last and there wasn't any more. But anyhow, I want to walk you down the aisle and give you away."

John Henry and his bride will have a large family, interrupted by the war, in which he will serve with distinction and come home a captain.

After the war, they, like so many others, will move to California, and live for several years on John Henry's high earnings as an electronics technician, but they, unlike so many others, will get homesick and come back, and John Henry will build a house on the side of Ingledew Mountain, and commute to Jasper, where he will service radios and will install the first television set in Newton County, and, eventually, all of the television sets in Newton County.

But these will be eliminated: Gerald Coe, who will die a hero with the Marines at Iwo Jima in 1945, and have a bronze plaque in his memory in a hallway at Jasper High School; his brother Earl, who will die, some will say, of grief; and the survivor of the triplets, Burl, who will never come back from California.

These also will never come back from California: Junior Duck-

worth and his brother Chester, Merle Kimber and the other W.P.A. boys who built the bridge (year by year the floods of Banty Creek will wash logs against the sides of that cement bridge, and to break the jam the cement crenellation of the sides of the bridge will be sledge-hammered away, so that eventually, when Stay More will become nearly a ghost town, only the roadway of the bridge will remain with one pier of the crenellation with its cement stamped like a tombstone forever: "Built by W.P.A. 1939"). Forty-seven other Stay More residents will make a kind of Stay-More-in-exile colony in Fullerton and Anaheim, California, and never come back.

Many people will simply grow old and die, without issue, or with their issue scattered. Doc Swain and Doc Plowright will die; Luther Chism will die; all of the brothers Ingledew will die, first E.H., then Odell, then Bevis, then Stanfield, and finally Tull will die—but he will live the longest, spending out the days of his seventies loafing at Every's garage and chatting with Every while Every repairs cars and trucks, but the day the "Dill's Gas and Service" sign is taken down for lack of business and because Every is working then for the Ford agency in Jasper, Tull will silently expire, sitting upright in an abandoned Ford pick-up behind Every's shop, with, in his pocket, the very last installment of his share of the bank's money that Every had finally managed to repay.

The "Dill's Gas and Service" sign will be the last to go; before, sometimes long before, these signs will go: "U.S. Post Office," "Stay More Public School," "Ingledew's General Store," "Duckworth & Sons, Tomato Processing," "Lawlor Coe, Blacksmith." Every will train Lawlor to fix car engines, but will have to lay him off when business drops, and Lawlor will move to the city of Harrison.

There will be no signs in Stay More.

A traveler passing through will never know a town was there.

If they will have found me, they will have made a day-long project out of it, for with the coming of sunrise I will have risen up off the ground and sought to find my way home, only to have been lost deeper and deeper into the woods. Of course, the daylong search will have kept Every from beginning his revival meeting, even if he will have wanted to, after Latha had so shaken his faith, not in God nor Christ but in his calling as a preacher. So there will have been no services. The whole town will have gone out to look for me.

Sonora will have prepared and served a mass breakfast, serving it to the searchers from the front porch of Latha's store, and later have acted as dispatcher at what Doc Swain will have referred to as "our rondy-voo point." Doc Swain will have directed most of the search, although Oren Duckworth will have felt that *he* should have had this privilege.

The searching will have consisted mostly of small parties of two, three or half a dozen, who will have wandered more or less aimlessly around the Stay More countryside, beating the brush and calling out periodically "Dawny!" and "Oh, Dawny!" If the aggregate of these individual parties will have totaled over a hundred people, or the entire able-to-walk population of the town, then it will have been likely that every inch of the terrain will have been checked during the course of the day.

But still, because I shall have stumbled off into the remote reaches of Ledbetter Mountain, I shall have unwittingly managed to avoid being found.

If I should have known that so much fuss and bother will have been taken over me, I shall probably have been tickled in a way, secretly pleased, but more likely I will have been scared, knowing that when I will have been found at last I will have really gotten a thrashing from Aunt Rosie and Uncle Frank both for having put all those folks to such trouble. So I reckon it will have been just as well that I will never have been found.

Except that, if I will never have been found, what will have become of me? Will I have perished in the woods? If that is so, then how will I have come to have written this? Or will this ever come to have been written? Or shall I, will I, ever have been?

But the point is, my beloved Bug, that you shall have been searching for me, still, still searching, you and Every, who will have been the most likely to have found me.

Maybe, late in the afternoon, almost near on to lightning-bug time, it will have been Every who will have remembered that on the few times he had seen me I had been followed by a dog, and he will have inquired the name of this dog from Latha, and then he will have followed his "hunch" and will have climbed Ledbetter Mountain and probed deep into the woods, not calling out "Dawny" as the others will have been doing, but instead he will have begun to call out the name of the dog, Gumper, and maybe, just maybe, the dog will have come to him and he will have said, "Gumper, lead me to Dawny," and maybe, just maybe, the dog will have led him to me. And I will have been found. And Latha will have hugged me to her warm breasts.

But then, when all of the people will have congratulated Every and then will have all gone back home, and I will have been alone again with Aunt Rosie and Uncle Frank, Aunt Rosie will have said, "Jest whut do you mean, anyhow, you rapscallion, puttin all them folks to such bother? I never been so mortified in all my born days!" And then she will have clobbered me all over again. And Frank too, with his razor strop.

So yes, it will have been just as well, it will have been nearly perfectly all right, that I shall never have been found. After a year or so, I will have been forgotten. Latha will have remembered me sometimes, with a sigh, or maybe even a tear, and she will have reflected, perhaps, that all of this would not have happened if she had not allowed me to have slept with her that night.

She will not ever have been able to forget me, completely.

There will be no honeymoon, nor even the traditional "shivaree"; in fact, it will be the first wedding anybody can remember that was not followed by that traditional ritual whose name comes from the French charivari *and which consists of a riotous teasing and harassment of the couple on their wedding night. It will be felt that both the honeymoon and the shivaree are unbecoming in a time of bereavement. So Latha and Every will enter into married life without any fanfare, almost as if they had already been married since childhood, and in a way they had. And in a way this will console her, that she can remember that Every at the age of five-going-on-six was just exactly like lost Donny, and she will even be able to pretend that Every is Donny, grown-up. But still the early days of their marriage will be sad.*

Sitting on the porch together one waning day in the waning of summer, Every will remark, "Maybe the poor kid just sort of gave up and walked clean on out of the country. Maybe he's trying to find his way on back home to his real folks."

"Maybe," Latha will say, without much conviction, knowing he would not willingly desert her *like that.*

"Maybe his folks'll send a letter saying he showed up there, all right. Or maybe somebody else will spot him and wonder what a six-year-old kid is doing on the loose. Or maybe—"

"Hush, Every," she will say.

But she, later, will bend down a mullein stalk up in the orchard meadow, and wait to see if it straightens up, grows back up again. If it straightens, the boy is not gone for good. She will visit that meadow several times and look at that mullein stalk. She will even talk to that bent-down mullein stalk, plead with it.

Every will never cure her of her superstitions; rather he will absorb them himself. But it will be like a kind of trade: she will make him superstitious, he will make her religious, [for although he will give up being a preacher, he will never give up believing in the Lord].

The very last thing that Lola Ingledew will sell out of the big old Ingledew general store before closing it for good will be Latha's wedding band, to Every, but Latha, being superstitious, will protest that they ought to just wait and order one from Sears Roebuck, because a store-bough-ten wedding ring might have been tried on by somebody else and have absorbed bad luck from her—but Every will poo-poo this, not knowing that the ring had in fact been tried on before, by Lola herself, who never married, who lost in the sawmill the arm of the hand of the finger on which she put the ring.

But Latha will never lose an arm. Superstitions don't always work.

The mullein stalk will grow up again.

IT WILL END WITH THIS MOOD:

[Hell, what is the mood of an end, of an ending? Are all endings sad, because they are endings? Can there truly be a happy ending? If not, then better no ending at all, for your story is a happy one, Bug, and I would not for anything spoil it by my loss. So then it does not end. But anyway:] *the porch again, and cowbells clapping faintly in the* distance. They will have to sound like French horns, though, echoing up and down the valley. They will have to sound like French horns because only the French horn is capable of that particular poignant, mournful, wistful sound.

But the other instruments, the katydids and crickets and tree frogs and bull frogs, will have to play in adagio un poco mosso too, with an almost holy slowness. They cant do this, but they will have to. It will be necessary, to match the intervals of flashings by the lightning bugs.

The air will have to be thick enough, dew-laden enough, to hold aloft the drifting lightning bugs. The air will have to be all blue. All the air will have to be blue. And the blue air will have to be full of green things, strange wildflowers and magic weeds, creek-water, a trace of distant cow manure, a trace even of Gumper sleeping on the porch floor, a trace of the boy's milk-and-honey-and-grasshoppers-and-skinny-skin-skin, and of the woman's spicy creek-water-with-fish-in-it, and of the man's musky sweat, and of the dew, especially of the dew, which is all the green and wild things essenced together.

The air will have to yield its fragrances in slow time, in pace with the music and the flashes.

Gumper, sleeping, will have to strike the porch floor with his tail in adagio un poco mosso. This sound will not lead to his eviction; it will blend with the other sounds; he will be left to lie.

The cats will not mind him; they will festoon the porch rail and the porch and the shrubbery, and will move, stretch, writhe, in tune to the music and the flashes and the air.

The man and the woman will be talking; they will have to keep their voices from being understood; their voices will have to be heard but not understood; their voices will have to be pure sounds playing also in adagio un poco mosso. If the boy will actually be sitting in the swing near them, they will not want him to hear what they are saying. If the boy will only be thinking that he is sitting in the swing near them, he will not want to hear what they are saying. He will want instead to listen to the theme of the music and the flashes and the air.

The theme will be of loss. Of loss and search, of losing and finding, of wanting. The cow wears the cowbell so she can be found; the distant dull thing-thang of the cowbell must now sound like a French horn, which *sounds of loss and yearning and the always possible finding. The cow can be found. The cricket chirps, the tree frog peeps, the bullfrog croaks, to find, to search, to be found. In the finding-time, which is evening, night.*

The lightning bug flashes to find, and finds by flashes and is found by flashes. But is lost until found. The flashing is of loss, and yearning.

The smells of the things in the air of the night are the calls of the lives wanting to be found. Why else are fragrances fragrant?

We see to find, we hear to find, we smell to find and be found. Until we find or be found, we are lost, and wanting.

The theme of the mood of an ending is of a loss or finding.

IT WILL END WITH THESE PEOPLE:

the man sitting on the porch, in the straight-backed chair, sweating because the night is hot and because he will have been spending the whole day tramping the hills, searching. It will have been his last search, he who has searched so, and lost, and found, and lost again. He will be thinking that he will not have to be a searcher any more, he will be saying to himself, "It's over. I've done come home to roost. I reckon I've got what I want," and he will be thinking Now if only I can figure out some way to get married to her proper without sinning beforehand. *Which will be his biggest problem, bigger even than the problem of how he is going to pay back all the money he stole a long time ago. But this problem, this problem of marrying her before making love to her, he will solve, ingeniously, in just a few more minutes. His name will be Every. The way these folks will say it, it could be "Avery," but it will happen to be Every. If this story will have a hero, it will be him. He will be the one male whose name will endure longest in the mind of the creator of this story. He will be the one male whom the creator of the story will identify with, will even confuse himself with, and will remember the longest, will even be so unable to forget that whenever he, the creator, happens to verge upon mindlessness, or helplessness, or intolerable loss or wanting, the very thought of those two words, "Every Dill," like a magic incantation, will bring him back from the brink, will find him, will find him.*

the woman sitting on the porch in the rocker, rocking some, who in just a couple of minutes will join her life forever with that man's. She will have been the Bug who gave her name to the story, who gave her life to the man, and who gave her love to the boy who will become her lover and creator. Her name will be Latha, and she will come to look, in the eye of his mind, like Vanessa Redgrave, and she will come to be, in the heart of his soul, all womankind, and in the pit of his gut, all desire. She will converge all his wanting, all his searching, but she will never be found, not by him; his loss of her will keep him going. But for all these lofty sentiments, for all this love and lust and longing, the only thing that will be on her mind at this moment is how she can get that man into bed before marrying him. But she too will solve this problem in just about the same instant that the solution will hit him, in just another minute. She will think, "If there's any of the preacher still left in him, he can use it to marry us at the same instant we marry ourselves with ourselves." *She will smile at this thought, and think,* "And when he says, 'I now pronounce us man and wife.' I will faint," *and possibly she will even laugh, lightly, aloud, and he will look at her, and she will look at him and know that he knows what she is thinking. Then she will glance at the door which leads off the porch into her room.*

the boy who will think that he is sitting in the porch swing, watching the man and woman yet listening not to them but to the theme of loss and search and finding being played in the grass and the air and the night, who will be lost. He will be called "Dawny," but then he will not be called that, any more. He will think that he is sitting in that porch swing and brooding because the man will be going to take her away from him. He will think that he is listening to all of that adagio un poco mosso *out there, and reflecting,* Maybe they don't want me around. Maybe I ought to whistle up old Gumper and head for home. She loves *him* now. She don't even know I'm here. She and him are going to get up and go inside and do what she and that other feller were doing yesterday afternoon, that makes her smell like creekwater afterwards. She won't wait till I grow up and do it with me. But that's okay, I guess. When I get growed up, I'll just marry somebody that looks just exactly like her. But it won't be the same thing. Darn it, it won't never be the same thing. *He will think he is sitting there thinking these little-boy thoughts, but he will not be, for he will not be there, ever again.*

IT WILL END WITH THIS SOUND:

the screen door pulled outward in a slow swing, the spring on the screen door stretching vibrantly, one sprung tone and fading overtone high-pitched even against the bug-noises and frog-noises, a plangent twang, WRIRRAAANG, which, more than any other sound, more than those other sounds, evokes the heart of summer, of summer evenings, of summer evenings there *in that place, and ends the music, ends the song, on a last quavering tone of loss and search and finding, of an opened door about to close. WRENCH. WRUNG. WRINGING.*

About the Author

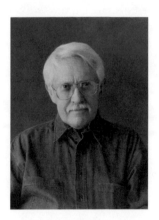

Donald Harington

Although he was born and raised in Little Rock, Donald Harington spent nearly all of his early summers in the Ozark mountain hamlet of Drakes Creek, his mother's hometown, where his grandparents operated the general store and post office. There, before he lost his hearing to meningitis at the age of twelve, he listened carefully to the vanishing Ozark folk language and the old tales told by storytellers.

His academic career is in art and art history and he has taught art history at a variety of colleges, including his alma mater, the University of Arkansas, Fayetteville, where he has been lecturing for fifteen years. He lives in Fayetteville with his wife Kim, although his in-habit resides forever at Stay More.

His first novel, The Cherry Pit, was published by Random House in 1965, and since then he has published eleven other novels, most of them set in the Ozark hamlet of his own creation, Stay More, based loosely upon Drakes Creek. He has also written books about artists.

He won the Robert Penn Warren Award in 2003, the Porter

Prize in 1987, the Heasley Prize at Lyon College in 1998, was inducted into the Arkansas Writers' Hall of Fame in 1999 and that same year won the Arkansas Fiction Award of the Arkansas Library Association. He has been called "an undiscovered continent" (Fred Chappell) and "America's Greatest Unknown Novelist" (Entertainment Weekly).

The fonts used in this book are from the Garamond family